PURE MAGIC
WITCHES OF WINDSOR
BOOK THREE

A.S. FENICHEL

Edited by Penny Barber

Proofreading by OopsieDaisyEdits.com

Cover by LoveTheCover.com

Images from Depositphotos, Design Cuts

First Electronic Book Publication March 2023

SARA BETH

At nineteen, I replaced my mother as the high priestess of the Windsor coven. Duty bound to protect my coven and the king, and for almost ten years, I have worked to transform the coven from the rigid system of Mother's rule to a warmer community of witches. News of men being admitted to the Windsor coven has spread, requiring me to consider more of their petitions. Legend says that male witches destroy and kill, often turning to dark magic. This was the reason for the ban. Will my removal of the old prejudice bring us all to ruin?

ADAM

For over eight years, I've been running from my home in the Scottish Highlands, always staying a step ahead of my siblings. Each new town where I work my illusions and make a name for myself as a showman gives them the chance to catch up with me. I hope the Windsor coven will accept a man living in the light of magic. All I want is family within a coven.

I am not received with enthusiasm, as the high priestess is as wary as she is beautiful. If not for the ancient great mother's intervention, Sara Beth would have sent me away immediately. Instead, I'll be tested for light and dark magic. It's unpleasant, but I'd do almost anything to stay by Sara Beth's side, and finally find a home.

All is going well until Ariana and Kaden arrive. My sister Ariana is pure evil, and Kaden, my twin, follows in her darkness. Ariana's plans will destroy more than just our world if we don't stop her. To obtain her evil goals, she needs me. More than my coven acceptance and my attraction to Sara Beth are at stake when I join the Witches of Windsor.

ACKNOWLEDGMENTS

When you're a writer, people often tell you to write one thing and stick with it. They may be right, but where is the joy in that? When my muse takes me down a path, I have to follow her. That's what happened with these lovely Witches of Windsor.

I have some wonderful friends who support and encourage me. For always having my back, a big shout out to Gemma Brocato and Juliette Cross who were with me when this project began.

Karla Doyle, thank you for daily words of encouragement and humor. I don't know where I'd be without you.

For Dave, you are my heart.

CHAPTER
ONE

SARA BETH

I've been making a market list for twenty minutes. Generations of Windsor witches have gathered at this long table for celebration and somber occasions. Today, I have the coven house to myself, a rare instance of solitude.

Great Mother Prudence left a month ago to spend some time in the country, and the resident witches went with her. Usually, noise would come from the kitchen behind me or activities downstairs in the gathering hall. The only sounds are my own sighs against the white-washed wooden walls. After ten years of running this coven, I feel twice my nine and twenty years. My closest friend, Minerva, has moved with her new husband to a small farm outside of town. I'm happy for her, but I miss her living in the coven house with me.

I'm being selfish and maudlin. I see her most days. She and Jonah run the apothecary shop, and she brings their baby to the coven house often. It's just that things are changing, and I've never been very good at accepting change.

"What has put such a scowl on your face, Sara Beth?" Sylvia has a rasp to her voice, and there's no need to look up to know the question came from her.

Surprised that my musings have a witness, I force my expression to soften. "I thought you were helping at Esme's shop today."

With a wave, she sashays to the bench across from me, sits, and props her chin on her fists. "I was just there helping with some spells. I thought you might like some company, so I came here before heading home."

It was kind of her to think of me, and if I'm honest, I don't like the coven house being empty. I love the bustle of witches at work and play. "Thank you."

"So, what has you looking like the world weighs heavy on your brow?" Sylvia has no sense of easing into a topic. Whatever she wants to know or whatever she thinks, she is always at liberty to say.

"Just thinking about change." The things I've allowed that my mother would have forbidden roll through my mind: witches marrying and men joining the Windsor coven. "Perhaps I have gone too far away from the old ways."

"Nonsense!" She slaps the table. "All the new members, both male and female, have added great power and value to our lives. I think a bit of trousers in the mix is a good thing." She winks.

I can't help laughing. "You would."

"The great mother returns today?" There's a happy note to her tone.

"Yes. I was just making a list for the market. I plan to cook." It's rare that I get a chance to work in the kitchen, and I always love to fix a good meal.

"Oh, a treat. I'll be staying for one of your meals. Shall I join you at the market?" Sylvia cranes her neck to look at my list of chicken, flour, and potatoes.

"I've been struggling to think of what to cook." I cap the ink and rise to put it and the quill in the chest in my room.

Sylvia waits by the stairs, toying with the end of her thick, dark-blond braid.

I touch my tightly bound bun and think of how my mother rarely let her hair free of the same style. "Sylvia, why did you move out of the coven house?"

Shrugging, she gives me a rather sad smile. "I have a futile hope of finding love and having a child. It seemed more possible if I were out of the hen house full of younger, prettier chickens."

My laugh is full of understanding. "I hope you find someone who sees you for the witch and woman you are, my friend. A man who chooses his chicken solely based on her youth is not the kind we want anyway."

Threading her arm through mine, she takes the basket by the door, and we head into the street. "Perhaps not, but I'd like to find a man, and the young witches like Trina and June are harder to ignore in favor of a witch of five and thirty."

"We witches live a long time. You have sixty or more years to find a mate and have a child." I pat her hand. "I have faith in Goddess that if this is what you want, it will happen."

She grins. "I hope not to wait until my centennial for the occasion."

"There is one man who we both know favors you." I'm only half teasing.

She lets out a humph. "Henry Dove is not a witch."

I shrug but let the subject drop.

The market square, a long wide street filled with colorful tents and vendors selling their wares. Flags wave in the mild winter breeze, and people crowd the way.

Someone bumps my arm, and I stumble.

Mr. Markham, the cobbler, steadies me. He's a few inches shorter than me, but sturdy and strong. "I'm terribly sorry, Miss Ware. Forgive my clumsiness."

"Where are you going in such a hurry?"

His attention is still diverted by whatever had him rushing away. Others are hurrying in the same direction.

Mr. Markham points to the east end of the square. "A mesmerizer is performing at the other end of the square. I'm told he can make a dove appear out of thin air."

The hair on the back of my neck stands up. "Is that so?"

Nodding, he adds, "That may seem a small feat to you ladies, but it's all in good fun."

Putting on my best warm smile, I say, "Carry on, sir. We'll follow behind and have a look with you."

Rather than rush off, Mr. Markham accompanies us to the small platform where announcements are often made and the occasional performance is given. Since Mr. Markham has been making shoes for witches for over two decades, as did his father before him, he's well aware of what we are. In fact, most of our close neighbors know and respect what we do to protect them and our king.

Still, no one speaks of magic.

It's an amicable arrangement, and the neighborhood is warm to witches making life easier.

"Oh, my Goddess." Sylvia clutches her chest as the man onstage comes into view. "How entirely delicious he is."

I can't argue with her. The man is stunning with red-tinged brown hair, bright blue eyes, and a lean, tall figure. Magic tingles along my skull. I lean toward Sylvia's ear. "He's a witch."

She moves her hips seductively. "Clearly, but what a witch." Her voice is full of sensuality.

"Have you no interest in his character before you fall for his pretty face?" Despite my schoolmarm tone, my body heats.

Sylvia shrugs. "Perhaps if I wanted to keep him, that would be important. At the moment, I'm only shopping, not buying."

Laughing despite my concerns about what brings this witch to Windsor, I give Sylvia's arm a warm squeeze.

The man scans the audience with a smile that will melt the hearts of women, young and old. He's far too handsome with his warmly tanned skin and broad shoulders. "Thank you for the warm welcome to this fine town of Windsor," he says with a thick Scottish brogue.

The crowd applauds.

It should be more of a warning, but his deep accented voice sends a bolt of need between my legs. Is that his magic? Does he seduce with his voice?

Not willing to risk it, I cast a blocking spell around Sylvia and me. I'll not be made a fool of.

Sylvia shifts and looks at me. "You think he's bespelled us?"

I shrug. "I don't know." The spell has little effect on my growing attraction for this stranger. "Perhaps he's just handsome, and I've been alone too long." I wink.

As the gathering quiets, he continues. "I have a few tricks up my sleeve today. I hope you'll enjoy my amusements." With that, he pulls two doves from his sleeve. The show continues for twenty minutes with an array of animals, flowers, and love letters seeming to appear out of nowhere.

I observe and extend my powers to feel if his magic is dark or light. He uses no magic for his performance, only sleight of hand and tricks to distract the eye. He's very good but does nothing to warrant my interference.

"One last conjuring," he announces. "I'm calling on the angels to shower the most beautiful woman in Windsor with my attention."

Magic tingles in the air. My muscles stiffen, and I hold my magic ready for whatever he might be up to.

Pale yellow rose petals flutter from the sky like the feathers of those angels he spoke about. They brush the skin of my cheeks, neck, and arms and land on my shoulders and skirt, contrasting with my navy-blue dress.

I look toward the stage, and the witch stares back with a warm smile. He bows to me as the crowd erupts in applause and cheers. They toss coins into a small basket at the edge of the stage.

Sylvia and I walk to the butcher's shop. "Do you think he knows who I am?"

"I think it's likely, but maybe he just found you lovely. You are quite attractive, Sara Beth. Perhaps both." Sylvia steps inside the shop and calls out a friendly greeting to the butcher.

I don't like being the center of attention. It seems strange, since I run a coven and am often the center of that, but this was different. The entire neighborhood was staring at me because he chose me as the most beautiful woman in Windsor. Of course, that's not true, which is more proof that he knows who I am and wants something from me. Perhaps he wants to distract me to accomplish his goals, whatever they may be.

Sylvia says my name as if she's said it a few times without a response.

"What?"

"Are two chickens going to be enough for dinner tonight?"

It takes a few seconds for me to focus on the food, not that witch. "Yes. That will be fine. Perhaps we'll roast them with some nice potatoes and vegetables. I can make gravy and bake some bread."

When we return to the coven house, our basket is full of lovely things. I'm ready to get into the kitchen and forget about the mesmerizer and his tricks.

The cart's wheels at the back of the house alert us to Prudence's arrival. I place our wares on the table in the still room and run out to greet the great mother.

I don't know exactly how old the great mother is, but it's somewhere in the neighborhood of two hundred. Witches, if they don't get sick or meet with an accident, can live a very long time. Even so, Prudence Bishop is ancient even for a witch. She's also the kindest and most generous person I've ever known. She shares her knowledge and wisdom without any attempt to usurp my position as high priestess. I love her like a mother.

She climbs from the fine carriage on loan from Sir William and Esme Meriwether. As a gentleman and a witch, Sir William straddles the line between societies. He's always gracious in offering his vehicles when needed.

Prudence gives me a warm smile and opens her arms for my embrace.

I rush forward and hug her gently. "I missed you, Great Mother. Did you enjoy your time in the country?"

Pulling back, she pats my cheek. "It was nice to spend some time there without demons lurking inside witches."

Her reference to Trina's possession and the subsequent battles with the demon Forrester, my old lover Orin, makes my gut twist.

Trina alights from the carriage. "It was nice to see the place through my own eyes as well." She flips her brown hair over her shoulder and grins before hugging me. "We had a lovely visit with the townspeople and a relaxing summer."

The other witches, June and Winnie climb down and greet me.

As I take Prudence's arm to go inside, another carriage rolls down the alley. Minerva and Jonah Allen rush to see Prudence.

Once we're all in the gathering room upstairs, I say, "I'm going to cook if you have no other need of me, Great Mother."

She waves me off. "I'm well attended. Oh, I invited someone to join us for dinner."

I stop at the kitchen door. "Who?"

"I've been corresponding with a young man from Scotland. He's come on hard times. Actually, he's had a long struggle, not of his own doing. He should be in town by now, and I'm sure he will join us tonight." She blinks at me as if daring me to challenge her invitation to a stranger.

Of course, I know better. He will sit at this table if the great mother deems him worthy. "Scottish, you say?" The hair on the back of my neck stands up.

Sylvia laughs. "He wouldn't pass himself off as a traveling mesmerizer and trickster, would he?"

"I cannot say." Prudence smiles, and her gray eyes light with amusement.

It will be an interesting night.

Two hours later, I'm deep into my cooking. Other witches rarely enter the kitchen when I'm preparing a meal. I prefer to work alone. When the door opens, I call out, "I'm not in need of assistance."

"I only came with an apology and to introduce myself. I shall note your lack of need, though." His voice is deep and full of amusement.

My body might burst into flames from his rich tone and woodsy scent. Steeling my expression, I turn. "You might have introduced yourself in the market square today."

Goddess! He's even more handsome, dressed in simple white shirt and trousers with a black coat. His cravat is perfectly tied in a simple knot, and those green eyes are warm as they study me. "I apologize. I admit I knew who you were. I'd made a few inquiries when I arrived this morning. The local people gave me a very intriguing description."

"I can only imagine." I try not to care, but my eyes roll just the same. "Go ahead. What did they say? Did they call me harsh and overbearing? Did they say I've cursed all the men to impotency?" That one is my favorite.

His laugh is round and does inappropriate things to my female parts. Not that I'm a prude or a virgin, but I don't even know this witch.

One step brings him inches from me. He takes my hand and bows over it. "I should have made my presence known immediately. I'm Adam MacNab. The great mother has been a friend to me for a year and invited me to Windsor, for which I am grateful. I didn't come to you this morning because I wanted to make a few coins to pay for a room with a bath and have my clothes properly laundered before we met. I apologize, but I only wished to make a good impression."

Smooth words are always a warning flag to me. I jerk my hand out of his. "Why?"

"Why?" He takes one step back. His russet brows dip to hood his eyes. "Why did I want to impress you?"

"Yes, Mr. MacNab, why do you want to impress me? What is it you want? I'm not a woman to be charmed and taken in by a pretty face and smooth words. I don't generally wait to ask questions in my coven house for a more polite time. I just ask. Don't think me rude." I shrug. "Or do. It's of no consequence. My purpose is to protect this coven, its witches, and the king of England. I have little time for niceties. What do you want?"

He looks at his feet, and his cheeks pale a little. "I had hoped to meet you and then find a quite time to discuss my past and my needs." His shoulders rise and fall with a sigh.

Suddenly I feel the shrew. "Sylvia!" I call through the door.

She pops her honey-blond head in. "High priestess?"

"Can you watch my stove while Mr. MacNab and I have a talk in private?" I ignore her grin and wink, and without waiting for her response, turn my attention back to Adam. "Please, follow me, sir."

The winter is mild, but still has brought a chill to the night. When we reach the hearth at the center of the large empty hall below stairs, I light the wood with a flick of my wrist. We are alone as all the other witches are in the gathering room doting on Prudence. I pull a chair from near the wall.

Adam takes it from me and gets another as well. He waits for my instruction and then places them a few feet away from the warm fire. Once I sit, he does as well.

"I was harsh, and for no good reason other than I'm wary of charming men. That wariness is not your fault, and if Prudence Bishop invited you, you deserve a chance and some politeness at the very least." I fold my hands in my lap and clutch my fingers together because he makes me nervous for no good reason. I'll not be turned into a ninny by a pretty face. I practically scream that in my head.

"Thank you."

When he says no more, I prod. "You have my attention, and we are alone, Mr. MacNab. What is it that brings you to Windsor?"

Those green eyes of his meet mine, and it's impossible to look away. I sense no magic. He's just so damned beautiful, and there's so much emotion behind his gaze. "My name is Adam, and you have brought me here, Miss Ware."

CHAPTER
TWO

ADAM

I thought I'd have a few days to work out how best to talk to the Windsor high priestess. I thought I could make her like me, at least. I see now that she is not an average woman or witch.

It's probably wrong that I wish she were not so lovely. Even though her dark hair is pulled tightly back from her heart-shaped face, I can imagine it flowing around her shoulders.

To keep my thoughts on my need of a coven and not this woman, I stare at the floor, which has clearly been recently patched. In fact, it looks as if much of the coven house was recently repaired.

Laughter from the room above filters down the steps. The sunlight is waning, and other than the hearth fire, the room grows dark around us. The long, large room is much like casting rooms in other coven houses. Buckets of water and sand as well as chairs line the walls. The shades are open to the neighborhood, so these witches and what they do is accepted by those around them without magic. That's unusual and says a lot about Sara Beth Ware's leadership.

My breath shakes a little, and I try to shut out my nerves. "I came looking for a coven to accept me. I came hoping for a family."

Pursing her full lips, she studies me with fierce dark eyes. "Have you no clan in Scotland? No coven?"

"My parents are dead." There is so much more to tell, but when she knows of my family and all that happened, she'll send me away. I have to prove myself before she can know everything.

The hem of her dark-blue day dress skims over my leg. "Mr. MacNab…"

"Adam, please." I don't like my begging tone. I hate needing more from people than quick applause and a few coins.

She lowers her gaze to her hands clutched in her lap. It's the only outward sign that she's the least bit frazzled. She looks up. "Adam, I need to know that you are a witch in the light of Goddess before I would ever even consider allowing you to stay in Windsor. You've won the favor of our much beloved great mother, and that is why you are still under this roof. If you want more from me, you will have to do better than the fact that your parents are dead. Please, try to remember that I'm a witch and a high priestess. I can feel that you have more to tell."

I can't divulge everything, but I can still be honest. "I have a brother who falters from the light on occasion. He caused my family to be banished from our clan and coven. My parents died because of him, though not by his hand. You're right. There is a great deal more to tell, but I fear if I tell you all, before you know my character, you will send me away out of hand."

Her deep breath forces her breasts to the edge of her low-cut dress. I'm not capable of keeping my attention from the sight, though I immediately return my gaze to her face. She raises a brow. "What is so important about being part of a coven? You travel from town to town and make your amazements for the coin of nonmagical folk. You get the girls to smile at you and bat their lashes. I'm sure you do quite well with both money and feminine favors. Why do you need a coven, and why Windsor?"

"Have you always been part of this coven, Sara Beth?" It's forward to use her given name without permission, but I can't help myself. Why does she have to be so pretty?

Her eyes widen, and she shakes her head in the way my mother used to when I let my mouth get ahead of my brain. "I was born into this coven, and my mother was high priestess before me."

"She must have died very young. I'm sorry." It's a silly diversionary tactic, but I'm used to skirting the truth.

"She did. I'll not be distracted, Adam." She pushes a stray hair back into her tight bun.

It's probably wrong, but I love the sound of my name on her lips. I love her lips. Brushing those baser thoughts away, I nod. "You have never known the loneliness of being a solitary witch."

Warning flashes in her dark eyes like daggers. "You have your brother."

Pain slices into my gut. "My brother and I have gone our separate ways. I thought, foolishly, that I could guide him back to the light. Maybe a better witch could have, but I failed. I have to live with that. Still, I miss family. I miss a coven and having a purpose in life. You're right, I could make my way through life with money at every town and perhaps even a woman willing to spread her legs for me. It's half a life, a torrid and empty existence."

Sarah Beth stares at me silently for a long minute. The skin on my neck and chest tingles. "At some point, I'm going to need the full story, Adam. For now, you may stay in Windsor. When I know your character better, I may allow you to live in the coven house, but for now, not being expelled from this town is the best I can offer."

I let out my breath. "You are very kind."

"I am not. But I am curious. You do not feel dark. I saw a foolish man on stage today, yet you come here with apologies and sincerity even if it's not total honesty. Two faces on the same man. What I am, is curious." She stands. "If my curiosity turns to fear for my witches, I'll have a price to pay."

Standing with her, I bow. "I will not betray you, Sara Beth. I swear it to Goddess."

The air around us tingles with fire and light. Magic sifts through like a warning before settling with warmth and love. I touch my cheek and find it warm with my flush of nerves.

Cheeks pink, Sara Beth chuckles. "You had better keep that promise. I fear breaking it would anger Goddess."

"Is that what that was? Did Hecate hear me?" I follow her to the steps.

Standing on the first brings her almost to eye level with me. She presses her hand to my chest. "Goddess always hears us. When something important is afoot, she responds. I take it as a good sign that she favored us with notice this night." Her gaze flits to my lips and then back to my eyes.

I've never wanted to kiss anyone more. Where had that come from? Keep your wits MacNab. You need Miss Ware on your side.

I think she's going to take the decision out of my hand and lean forward until our lips touch, but she jerks back. "Dinner should be ready. Join us and get to know more about the coven."

"Thank you, that would be a treat." She can't know how much a family dinner will mean to me. It's silly, but these are the little things that hurt the most.

We're halfway up the steps when the door below opens, and a tall gentleman, well-dressed with a hat clutched under his arm and a lovely green-eyed woman walk in. The woman is wearing a fine wine-colored dress with a white cloak. "Are we late?"

"Not at all." Sara Beth grins down at them. "Come up and meet our guest. I'm just about to carve the chickens."

Esme and William Meriwether introduce themselves to me. Williams' magic feels different from any I've ever noticed before. Perhaps he'll tell me about it when we know each other better. For now, it's none of my business.

The gathering is loud and full of laughter.

I follow Sara Beth to the kitchen. "Can I help you with the chicken? I'm quite good with a knife."

She cocks her head to study me. "You're a guest. You should go and drink wine with the ladies."

I'd rather serve food with her. "You prefer to work alone in the kitchen. I understand. Perhaps you'll let me cook a meal one evening to prove my skills."

As if Goddess sent a miracle, Sara Beth smiles. It's only for an instant, but my heart soars at the sight. Her expression returns to serious. She turns away, her skirts swirling around the swell of her hips. "Perhaps another night, Adam. Go meet the men and women of Windsor coven."

Reluctantly, I leave her to her kitchen and join a group of ladies chatting with Prudence Bishop. The great mother's gray hair is pulled up in a bun. Her eyes are bright blue and full of kindness. She takes my hand and draws me to the bench beside her. "She didn't toss you into the street, our Sara Beth. You must have impressed her."

I give her hand a little squeeze, as gently as possible. Stooped and ancient, she's frailer than I expected from her strong handwriting and kind letters. "Thank you for the invitation, Great Mother. I pray it will work out for all."

She pats my cheek. "That is my prayer as well, child. Now, Sylvia, pour this man some wine and tell him all about your virtues."

The blond witch in question is curvaceous and a fine flirt. If I had never seen Sara Beth Ware, Sylvia would be very attractive to me, with her full bosom pressing for freedom from an earthy green dress.

Cocking one shoulder down until her dress slides to show a bit more skin, Sylvia grabs a glass and fills it with dark red wine. "My pleasure. Mr. MacNab, where is it you come from in Scotland?"

Thickening my brogue for effect, I say, "Lass, I go by Adam and hale from Inverness, where we fight the loch's monster daily and drink ale for breakfast."

Laughter fills the room as Sara Beth carries out a large platter of chicken, vegetables, and potatoes. Everyone rushes to sit, and I remain at the great mother's left.

Sara Beth sits across from me and avoids my attention.

Admittedly, I can't keep my eyes from her stunning face. Her dark eyes are full of worry and tenderness. Not to say that the other witches aren't lovely. June is a young witch with pale hair and gray eyes. She's almost otherworldly. There are some very pretty young witches whose names I can't recall yet. But it is Sara Beth whose attention I seek. It's foolish, so I push it aside and enjoy the wonderful food and family atmosphere.

Jonah is sitting to my left with his wife, Minerva, between us. He's a giant of a man with much to say, and by midmeal,

I've learned his passion is for herbs and fixatives. He and his wife are the town's apothecary. "Adam, what kind of witch are you?"

Minerva elbows him then fusses with a bit of blond hair that's escaped her braid. "That's not polite."

"Why not?" Jonah asks. "I'm an earth witch. My magic didn't come to light until a year ago. Until then, I thought I was without any power. Now I know my powers lie in my medicinal mixtures. I can also detect dark magic from light."

I hold my breath. If I were dark, would he know? Would he say, *"You are not dark?"* I wonder. My brother's voice answers, *"But you could be."*

The table has gone quiet, and everyone is staring at me.

"I'm a fire witch," Minerva says, as if she feels required to divulge the information.

"You are not required to answer." Sara Beth's stare is so penetrating, I wish we were alone.

Ripping my attention from her, I look around the curious eyes at the table. When I reach Jonah, I say, "I'm an elemental witch."

"Wow." Sylvia shakes her head with a grin.

"I'm not familiar with that." William finishes the last of his potatoes and places his fork and knife carefully at the edge of his plate.

Afraid of what I might find, I force my attention back to Sara Beth. "Shall I explain, or would you like to, High Priestess?"

She says, "An elemental witch is very rare. A witch who can command all four elements with equal success. I've never actually met one...until today."

"Are you very powerful?" This is from a young witch in a simple brown dress who won't meet my gaze.

"Trina!" Sara Beth admonishes.

Trina immediately lowers her gaze and fusses with the end of her long brown plait.

"It's all right." I hold up a hand to stop any further discipline. "The subject has been opened. I imagine everyone is curious. Trina, I would say that I am strong enough to be useful or dangerous. I hope to be useful."

William laughs. "Well said, Adam. I could say the same about myself."

Many witches nod and discuss others in the coven who they might say the same about.

Esme gives me a sympathetic look, and grinning, I shrug. I want to claim I'm in the light, but my own brother turned, so I have my doubts. Appetite lost, I poke at my food and avoid Sara Beth's gaze. I feel her watching me, but I flirt with Sylvia, talk to Prudence, and joke with William and Jonah rather than see her scrutiny.

When the plates are cleared, more wine is brought out. I decline. "I appreciate the hospitality. More than I could have hoped for from an English coven to extend to a Scot. Thank you for the meal and the good company." I bow, and I head down the stairs.

In the street, the prickle of magic warns me I'm not alone. Holding very still, I scan the street.

Sara Beth steps out of the shadows of the coven house. She must have floated down from a window, but I have no way of knowing. Still, she's here, and I can't help wishing I'd met her the way a normal man meets a woman. "High priestess, have I offended you?"

"Not yet." Half a smile lights her eyes in the moonlight. "Why didn't you tell me you were an elemental witch?"

"You didn't ask, and it can sometimes put people on edge." I close the distance between us. "I want you to like me."

She shakes her head and clutches her elbows. "Oddly, I

want to like you, Adam. I think you've had a hard life and that most of that is not your fault. However, I don't trust you."

Longing to touch her cheek, her neck, and the swell of her breasts, I make fists and keep them at my sides. "How can you? We've only just met. Trust must be earned."

"I'm glad we agree. So, earn my trust." She narrows her eyes and crosses her arms, which pushes her plump breasts up and out and makes my mouth water.

Refocusing on her face and avoiding looking at those stunning and kissable lips, I ask, "What would you have me do?"

"Is the company of a coven as you had tonight what you crave?" She looks up at the candlelit room filled with laughter.

"More than anything." I actually thought it was the only thing I yearned for until I saw Sara Beth in the market this morning.

"Go with me to our sacred circle tomorrow. Show me your magic. Let me feel the light and dark inside of you. Open yourself to me as your high priestess. Then we will see." She waits, as if she asked for a token of my affection rather than a baring of my soul.

Fear and excitement rocket through me, and it's impossible to decipher which is winning. "You ask a lot. I hardly know you either, Sara Beth. What you ask is very intimate."

"I do. I feel the conflict in you, and I need to know where it comes from." She's so matter of fact it might put a man at ease or send him running for the hills.

Laughter and conversation are still filtering down from the upper window. I long for a sense of belonging. "I don't know if I can do as you ask, not because I don't wish to," I add quickly. "Others have tried to open my magic and failed. I will go with you and comply with whatever you ask that is within my capabilities."

She rises on her toes and leans in until her nose is an inch from mine. "If you lie to me, I will know. Goddess will decide the rest."

When she turns, I touch her arm. I don't want to part. I want to see her smile, and I have no idea how or why that's important to me. "Would it be too much to ask to take a walk together and become acquainted before you drag me off to be judged?"

Studying me, she purses her lips. "If you have plans to kidnap me or do me harm, it would be foolish of me to walk with you alone. You should know that harming me will not disrupt this coven from its duty to the crown. There are plans in place to carry on without me."

My gut is in knots. This is what she thinks of me. How do I overcome such censure? "I am not evil, Sara Beth." It's not easy to keep my voice soft and even. My anger and disappointment struggle to the surface. "I withdraw my request. I will be here in the morning and travel to your sacred circle. Thank you for a fine meal and good company." I turn and walk toward my hotel.

Quick steps follow me, but I don't turn until I'm several blocks away from the coven house. I need to gather my emotions. Finally, I stop. When she reaches my side, I say, "You know, I'm generally an enjoyable companion. People like me when they meet me. I make them laugh and do a few tricks. I'm probably described as affable and pleasant. You make me feel like a troll."

"It wasn't my intention," she says in her staid monotone.

"Wasn't it?" I continue down the street. "Why are you following me, Sara Beth? I said I would return in the morning, and I will keep my word."

"Tell me about your childhood, Adam." She touches my elbow.

The heat of her touch through my coat and shirt is like a

bolt of lightning. What is it about this witch? "What if I tell you about Inverness? My childhood is a longer conversation than the street to my hotel."

"As you wish." She tucks her arm through mine. "What is Inverness like?"

Visions of the Highlands roll through my memory. Sunlight glistening on the loch. Old men talking of monsters beneath the surface. "My home is like a warm embrace. Witches are accepted much as they are here in Windsor. I've traveled quite a lot and learned this is seldom the case. They may not burn us at the stake anymore, but I've been run out of more than a few villages. Still, I don't regret my travel. I learned a lot." I draw a breath and love the way the side of her breast grazes my arm. "I've gone astray. Inverness is busy with people and life. Not so big as here, and far wilder. Mountains and the loch of course. My parents had a small farm where they raised cattle. I ran in the fields and climbed mountains. Ruined castles were our playgrounds. It was a fine way to grow up with nearly fifty witches to keep an eye on us and keep us from harm."

"Fifty! Dear Goddess." She laughs.

I would give a limb to hear that sound every day. I shake my head to banish the thought. It doesn't work, but it reminds me of whom I'm with. "It is a thriving witch community."

We arrive at my hotel, and I turn toward her. "As a gentleman, I feel I should walk you back."

That laugh again, and my heart is tight with emotions I didn't even know existed inside me. She drops my arm. "I'm safe in Windsor, and more powerful than you give me credit for."

"I have no doubt. Thank you for walking with me." I bow.

With a nod and a flick of her wrist, she shifts out of sight and leaves me standing on the street alone. I've never wanted anyone back more.

CHAPTER
THREE

SARA BETH

We take the cart to the stone circle. Today, rather than the thoughtful and staid man I met last night, Adam is animated and amusing. His auburn hair catches the sun like fire. When he glances my way, his eyes are full of joy. I liked the thoughtful man I met last night, but this version is charming.

He is sitting next to me on the bench of the small cart, and his leg leans against mine. His heat seeps through our clothes despite my heavy skirt and his working-man's trousers. The cooler weather is a stark contrast to his warmth.

"In Sussex, I stayed with a family of air witches. They have a twelve-year-old daughter who hasn't learned control of her magic yet. Each morning, the entire family and I would find ourselves floating like clouds above the floor." He uses his hand to demonstrate the lofty feel of floating.

I laugh. Actually, I've laughed more on this ride than I have in years. "I think you've made that up."

He clutches his chest and pouts. "I'm wounded. I swear it's the truth. On the first night, I thought I'd died and gone to Goddess. To be honest, I was relieved I had been accepted into her arms."

My skin prickles. "Have you done something to make you believe she would send you elsewhere?"

"No." His quick response is followed by the first silence of the ride.

"But," I prompt.

"But my family has. I hope to not be guilty by association. Though I have not always followed the path of righteousness, I have always lived by Goddess's laws. I have done no harm, yet I failed to save my parents." All the joy and fun have gone out of his tone.

I should push him to tell me more about his parents and how they died, but I want the light banter back. "How long did you stay in Sussex with the floating family?"

No man should be as good looking as Adam MacNab. His green eyes spark with joy and mischief, and my heart does a flip it has no business doing. "Two weeks. I spent my days moving from town to town performing tricks as you saw in Windsor, and my nights floating."

Just because I want to ask him about women doesn't mean it's any of my business. Witches don't adhere to the strict rules of conduct and propriety that nonmagical society does. Still, the thought of him jumping from bed to bed stirs a new emotion within me. Is it jealousy? Surely not. I have no right to feel such a stupid thing. "It must be exciting to travel and meet new people."

He leans lazily against the backrest. "I was just thinking

that it must be nice to have a reliable home where everyone knows and respects you."

"I suppose it's normal to be curious about what we don't have." The stones are only about a mile away. The horse, Daisy, has made the journey many times and speeds her steps as we roll closer.

Feeling his stare, I turn and meet it. "What?"

"You're very lovely, Sara Beth." He says it softly, as if it were a revelation.

I hate that my cheeks heat. "Telling me you think so is not going to sway any decisions I might make."

Laughter fills the air. He reels his amusement in. "No. I've known you less than a day and could have guessed that."

"Then why mention it?" Slowing Daisy, I direct her left as we make our way through the grassy field.

"Do you have a lover?"

I jerk the cart to a stop.

Knowing I'm delaying her grain, Daisy whinnies.

Still, I pull the brake and turn toward him. My heart races, and I know my cheeks are bright red. "That, and anything else of a personal nature, is none of your business, Mr. MacNab."

Dropping his gaze, he nods. "No. I know."

His immediate contrition softens my anger and embarrassment. "Why would you ask such a thing?"

When he looks up, those green eyes of his are magnetic. "Because it's been on my mind since I first saw you. Maybe even before. The great mother spoke of you often in her letters. Even in her handwriting, you intrigued me."

Releasing the brake, I snap the reins and we move forward. "Why should my having a lover make any difference? You and I could both have multiple lovers, and no one in our circle would give pause."

Hidden behind a row of trees, a narrow road leads us into

the sacred ground of the standing stones. I stop the cart, jump down, and grab the feed bag from the back.

Adam helps me unhook the cart and leads the horse to a tree, where he ties her, and I attached the feed bag.

We stand there while she eats for a few moments.

"May I be completely honest, Sara Beth?" He runs his knuckles along my arm from shoulder to elbow.

A shiver runs up my spine that is not at all unpleasant. Part of me wishes he wouldn't say my name so often, and another part loves the sound of it from his full lips. I'm silent on the subject. "Honesty is always welcome."

Stepping around Daisy's munching form, he stands inches from me and meets my gaze. "I want you." He rushes to add, "It's far too soon. Despite the lack of acceptance of multiple lovers within our communities, I would not wish to share you. If you honored me with your body and your time, my selfish heart would claim you entirely."

Shocked doesn't begin to describe how I feel. I know my mouth is open, and I force it closed. Still, I don't know what to say to a declaration like that after knowing a man for less than a day. "Those are very pretty words. You clearly are a man who knows how to woo a woman. I admit I'm not unaffected by what you claim. However, we are strangers to each other. While the great mother's letters may have made you feel as if you know me, I never heard of you until yesterday. Forgive me if I don't fall all over you with kisses."

He smiles, looking undaunted. "I would be disappointed if you did. You are not that kind of woman. I really can't explain how my feelings have assaulted me so quickly. I just thought it important to tell you that I do intend to woo you."

"I'm the high priestess. I don't have the time to be courted. Let this go, Adam. If you wish in earnest to become a witch of Windsor, I will decide without bias. Don't cloud the issue at hand." I'm pleased that I sound sure of myself while my heart is beating out of my chest.

Stepping back, he bows. "I respect your position and you as a woman. It changes nothing. The desires of my heart are as much a surprise to me as they seem to be to you."

Needing some space and time, I stomp toward the stones. Inwardly, my heart pounds, my stomach churns, and a very stupid part of me thrills at the idea of being wanted so intensely. Striding to the stones, I pray the heat in my cheeks has dissipated by the time he joins me. "Why would I want a man who travels his country and mine, hopping from town to town and probably bed to bed? What could you have to offer me even if I was interested, which I'm not?"

"A fine point. I have nothing to offer. I'm not even close to worthy of you. I shall endeavor to change that." He sounds full of regret.

That takes the fire out of me. He stands just outside the circle with his hands in his trouser pockets, staring at me as if I were the moon. No amount of training or experience as a high priestess or as a grown woman prepared me for a man who looks like Adam laying his heart open so fully.

Shaking my head to try to clear away all the silly romantic notions, I move to the middle of the circle. "Come." I offer my hand. "Let's see what your magic is made of."

With slow, tentative strides, Adam steps inside the border. He lets out a long breath. "Goddess didn't strike me down. I count that as a good sign." A hint of a smile tugs at his lips, but his eyes are full of earnestness.

When he reaches me, he takes my hand. Energy and magic thrill up my arm. I suppress any show of surprise. Maybe he didn't feel it. Meeting his gaze, I see surprise in those green depths. Still, I say nothing about the sensation of touching him, and thankfully, neither does he.

"Now what?" he asks.

"Gentle your thoughts, Adam." I press my hand to the center of his broad chest. "Breathe."

He lets out a huff.

It takes some strength to keep from laughing. "If Goddess wills, I seek the nature of her magic within. Let seen the element of water which flows through me."

Blue light slides like a thread from Adam's heart and winds its soft touch around my wrist. His magic shines bright and speaks to my magic, soft and sweet.

I want to stay and admire the merging of magic, but more must be discovered. "Let seen the element of air, which opposes yet lives within the water."

A silver strand flows from him, just as strong as the blue. It is more tentative, but after a moment, weaves itself with the water wrapped around my wrist and arm. They creep higher to my elbow.

Energy flows through me as air looks for its like within me.

"Let seen the element of earth that feeds us all and loves both air and water."

As a green thread spills from his chest, he stares into my eyes, clearly moved by the merging of our magics.

Heart pounding, I have to steady my breath as the green forms a braid with water and air and travels farther up my arm.

Desire rockets through me, and I have to remind myself that magic can be arousing. Perhaps I should have brought Prudence with us. The great mother might have done this ritual, and I wouldn't be so exposed.

Light surrounds him and flows through me, finding its way to my head, heart, palms, feet, and between my legs. I long to drown in the sensation and be wrapped in Adam's arms.

"Are you all right, Sara Beth?" His voice is rough and strained.

I nod. "Let seen the element of fire that brings warmth and sustenance while also offering protection."

Like a cunning serpent, red light shoots from him and winds its way up my arm, weaving in and out of its sister elements. All four grow as one, and soon I'm encompassed in his magic. He's full of light, with only the hint of darkness that can be found in anyone.

Adam takes my hand from his chest, steps forward, and wraps me in his arms. "Is this always so intimate?" His shaft presses thick and hard between us.

Desire rushes through me. It takes me a moment to find my voice. I grip his shoulders. "Not quite this intimate." Unable to resist the impulse, I press my cheek to his chest and revel in the warmth of his skin and the pleasure of his magic.

"I'm glad to hear that." He kisses the top of my head. "Did I pass this test, Sara Beth?"

Goddess, why must my name sound so good from his lips? Indulging in one last moment with his arms and magic surrounding me, I draw a deep breath then step back. "You are in the light. I sense no more darkness in you than I would in any witch."

There is no mistaking the state of his erection. "Did you test the other two men in the coven?"

"To some degree." My cheeks are on fire.

His jaw ticks, and he crosses his arms. The threads of his magic seem almost reluctant to unwind from me as they slip back into his heaving chest. "And were the results similar?"

This is the most awkward conversation I've ever had. If this were anyone else, I would state facts and feel little embarrassment. Why is he so different? I swallow hard. "If you are asking if they or I became aroused by magical tests, the answer is no.

Perhaps your earlier declarations have something to do with it."

Even with two feet of space between us, heat emanates from us. "My arousal may be more prominent from the spell, but I can assure you, I have been in some state similar since first seeing you in your kitchen."

As high priestess, I want him to stop saying such things. As a woman, I want to let him take me here on the ground of the sacred circle. Pulling my shoulders back, I look him in the eyes. "I have responsibilities."

He crosses his arms over his broad chest, making the ties of his shirt open enough to show his throat. Today he wears no cravat. "I understand."

How can he? Yet, he makes no move forward to touch me or convince me that sex would ease this thing burning between us. Maybe he does know my struggles. A glimpse of skin below his collar shouldn't be erotic. "The balance of elemental magic inside you is something I've never seen before. You are blessed by the Goddess."

Thrusting his hands into his pockets, he stares out at the shadows of the woods. "As with all gifts, there is a cost. Elemental witches are said to have shortened lives. It's said the magic drains life."

It shouldn't matter to me. Why would I care if he dies in twenty or thirty years instead of living to two hundred or more? It shouldn't. Unable to think about his death, I change the subject. "Do you need to rest, or should we continue with another test?"

"May I sit for a few minutes before we continue?" His skin is paler than when we arrived, and some of the spark has dimmed in his eyes.

"Of course." Knowing he'll be hesitant to sit while I stand, I go to the smaller rocks in the center, where a fire would burn, and sit.

He cradles his head in his hands. "I feared my fire magic would put you off."

"No element is evil. Minerva is a fire witch. She hid her nature for many years, though we are very close, and I knew. She feared others would shun her based on the nature of her magic." It's hard for me to admit to my own prejudices, but by the slump in his shoulders, I see his worries are not eased. "I used to believe as my mother before me, that men were likely to turn to darkness. I have learned no witch is immune to the lure of power with dark origins."

Sitting straighter, he takes my hand. His is warm and has calluses of a man who works. "It was hearing that the Windsor coven was open-minded that first urged me to write to the great mother. I looked for a new home in Scotland, but some covens sent me away for being a man, some for being elemental, and some only wanted my seed to breed more witches. I'm not a horse to be put out to stud." Anger rings in his tight voice.

I long to know how he comes by his rough, strong hands. "Many men would be happy to provide such a service."

His head snaps up, and his eyes are fierce until he sees I'm teasing. He squeezes my hand before lifting it to his mouth and kissing the back. "I'm looking for a family. If I fathered one child or a dozen, I wouldn't be going anywhere. Preferably, my children would be borne of a woman who cares for me and wishes my company."

Pulling my hand away causes me to immediately miss his touch. "I'm sure you could easily find a woman to warm your bed and give you children, Adam. She need not be a witch."

"Perhaps." He grins. "I may have set my standards too high."

"How so?" It's hard to look at him without desire flooding me.

Leaning on his elbows, he stretches his long legs out and crosses his ankles. He looks like the perfect man of leisure, without a care in the world. "I want more than a woman to warm my bed. I want a partner in life, and I want to love and be loved."

A sharp laugh pushes from my mouth before I can stop it. "You have set your goals very high, Mr. MacNab. I wish you luck on your quest." I stand and return to the center of the circle.

He follows. "I liked Adam better."

"When you speak of love and lifetimes, I feel it better to return to formality." I have no idea how I will clear my mind and focus on the test when my mind is full of Adam's life with some random village woman who dotes on him and fills his home with children. *Don't be an ass, Sara Beth.* I shake off the vision.

Something fierce flashes in his eyes, but he says nothing. "What would you have me do, high priestess?"

Closing my eyes causes the visions to intensify. Adam with a blonde laughing on a porch while sipping wine. Adam working in a back garden with a brunette. Adam toiling in a still room with a red-haired beauty. One by one, these images flash in my mind like poison.

Goddess, help me.

Warmth flows over and around me, and I know Goddess is here.

CHAPTER
FOUR

ADAM

Sara Beth shifts from foot to foot, clenches and softens her fingers. The skin around her luscious mouth pinches then relaxes as she breathes deeply. Calm magic settles over the circle of stones.

I've never felt anything like the warmth of this magic, and I want to know what's happening inside the woman. In my travels, I've met hundreds of witches and never longed to have the gift of mind reading. Sara Beth is different. I see calm flow through her, feel her magic tingle, and long to know what she thinks.

"Do you?" A soft, alluring voice fills my mind.

Startled, as the voice was not Sara Beth's, I step back. "Who said that?"

Still calm and with soft features, Sara Beth opens her eyes. "I didn't say anything. What did you hear?"

Had it been my imagination? I'm not given to hearing voices. "My mistake. It must just be nerves."

She cocks her head, and again I wish I know what she is thinking. Probably that I'm a madman.

Inside me, the unknown woman replies, *"She thinks a great many things and has a great many burdens placed upon her, but your sanity is not in question."*

I shake my head. "What is this?"

Sara Beth cups my cheeks. "What is it you're hearing, Adam?"

Her skin touching mine is calming, like a warm bath. I don't want her to stop touching me. "I heard a woman's voice in my head." Certainly, she'll think I'm mad.

While her brows rise, she doesn't look doubtful. "What kind of voice was it?"

I place my hands over hers. I want to be a part of the touching, and I don't want it to end. "What do you mean?"

"Was it a voice from your past, like a memory?"

"No." Despite my best efforts, being this close to Sara Beth stirs arousal within me. "I've never heard the voice before."

"Did the voice threaten or frighten you?" Slipping free of my hands, she caresses my temples.

"That feels good." I close my eyes and revel in her touch while my hands go naturally to her waist. "I wasn't scared. Surprised, but the voice had a calming effect, and she seemed to know what I was thinking."

Gently, she traces a path from my temples to my neck and soothes the tight muscles there. "What were you thinking?"

"That I wished I knew your thoughts." I'm caught in the soothing strokes of her touch on my shoulders, and I relax.

"Did she tell you?" Her voice has an edge that wasn't there a moment earlier.

Opening my eyes, I meet her gaze. "She said you carry a great burden, but no. She didn't tell me what you're thinking."

Lowering her hands, she steps back. "Has Goddess never spoken to you before?"

"Goddess? You think Goddess is here with us and spoke to me?" I look around stupidly as if Hecate, Goddess of Witches, would care to appear before the likes of me.

"Goddess is most definitely here, Adam."

The most musical laugh rumbles the air around us.

My heart pounds faster. "Was that her?"

Sara Beth nods, lowers her head in reverence, and steps back.

Terror rocks me off my feet, and I drop to my knees as the air shimmers with light, and the most stunning woman materializes into view. Her white gown flows around her as if blown by a light breeze, and her eyes are the lightest, most intense blue I've ever seen. "I am with you, child."

Lowering my head, I have to catch my breath. "I'm not worthy of such an honor, Goddess."

When I find the courage to look at her again, Hecate smiles. "That is for me to decide."

"Forgive me." I'm asking for more than my current statement. I long to be forgiven for a lifetime of sins.

Hecate places her less-than-solid hand on my head. "You have no control over the acts of others. Know you that your sires are safe in my arms. All things must occur in their order. Live in the light, as you have, and let go of that which is not your doing."

"I don't know how to do that." My gaze flits to Sara Beth, who watches without a hint of emotion. I can't tell if she's awed by Goddess or curious about my sins.

Floating back so that she can look at Sara Beth and me at once, Goddess smiles. "It has been a long road to come to this place, children. Trouble is coming, as it always does. Darkness will always beat at light's door. It is the nature of the world and the nature of magic. Find strength in each other. You will not find peace apart."

It's on the tip of my tongue to demand some clarity, but I'm too stunned to voice anything. Goddess magic covers me like a blanket before Hecate shimmers and is gone from the sacred circle.

Sara Beth looks at me as if she's seeing me for the first time. "You may stay in Windsor, as clearly, it is the wish of Goddess that your path has led you here."

Too shocked to respond, I sit back on my heels. The calm of Hecate's magic flows through me, and while it remains, my chaotic magic works its way to the forefront. After a moment, I ask, "Does that mean my testing is over?"

As Sara Beth moves to the center, her chest rises and falls more quickly, and it's the first indication that seeing Goddess had any effect on her. When she reaches me, she kneels, facing me. "I have many questions about your magic. While I want to see you use it, we can return to Windsor if you are tired or overwhelmed."

I take her hands and stand, pulling her with me. "I am both, but I'll deny you nothing. What would you like me to show you?"

"Let's sit for a while." She walks to the stones and sits. "Will you start the fire?"

Slightly off center of the ring, wood is piled. I draw in my fire magic and send it from my hand to the wood. It can be used as a projectile to harm, but I release it gently, and the wood sparks before the flames catch. Realizing a moment later that she could have lit the fire herself, I'm impressed by her clever way of testing without making me feel under scrutiny. "Did I pass?"

She pats the stone next to her and smiles. "You wield fire

with more flair than I would have expected. No great explosions or drama, just enough to accomplish the task."

"That sounded like a compliment." Besides the clear fact that I'm attracted to her, I've never wanted to impress a woman more. I sit and watch the fire.

"It is only recently that I've grown to understand the magic of male witches." The admission is hesitant, and a long pause follows where she looks from me to the fire. "My mother's beliefs prejudiced me against men. Changing something so ingrained has not come easily to me."

"I wouldn't expect it to." I draw a breath and force myself not to defend male witches. "I have traveled for three years and have met witches, both male and female, who are of light and dark. Your mother wasn't completely wrong. Many men dabble in the gaining of power and will use it for ill in the attempt to gain more. It appears the more they get, the more they crave."

"But there are women who fall prey to this as well." She draws a shaky breath.

"Yes. Some witches are dark, and their sex is irrelevant. Your mother might have worried that a male witch within the coven may have tried to usurp her place, like a king who outranks the queen."

Sara Beth's shoulders stiffen, and her eyes narrow. "We have no such hierarchy in a coven. If my sister and brother witches find me unfit or find another better suited to the job, they will ask me to step down."

"And would you leave the post without argument?" It would take moving my hand only an inch to take hers and feel her warmth. Resisting is not an easy task, but I don't touch her.

Her shoulders relax. "I respect my coven family. I was a girl when I took over for my mother. It might be nice to be led rather than lead." As sad smile pulls at her lips. "How would you extinguish the fire?"

The testing continues. "I would remove the air from the fire ring."

"Why not douse it with water or earth?" She studies me with her hands placed demurely in her lap like a schoolmarm.

I love this staid version as much as the soft caring side and the fiery protector. "At this moment, the wood is still a viable resource. If I douse it with earth or water, it creates more work should I need to start it again."

Her smile lights her dark eyes. "Show me."

Drawing the air within me, I raise my hand and pull breath away from the fire pit.

The fire gutters and gasps, then blinks out, leaving only a whiff of smoke behind.

"Impressive."

I feel like a man on top of the world. "Thank you."

"Can you conjure or call?" She looks me in the eyes.

Mesmerized by the gold and red flecks in her brown eyes, I again long to know what she's thinking and how it differs from what she says. "I cannot create from nothing or change the nature of a thing. I can work a glamor that makes a thing look other than what it is. I can turn rain into snow. And I can make rain or snow if there is water nearby. I can call animals, but only if they're willing."

I've told her more than I've shared with another witch since I was a boy. If she wished to use it to destroy me, I would let her. Perhaps that's the most frightening part.

Her head cocks. "I've vowed to do no harm."

Had I spoken out loud? "Did you read my thoughts?"

It's adorable when her cheeks pink. A line forms between her brows. Shoulders stiff, she says, "I hear them, but I hadn't tried to listen. I wouldn't do that without permission."

Panic is brewing inside her, and I want to soothe her, even though it's not my place. I take her hand. "There is no harm, Sara Beth." Did I hear her thoughts too? I drop her hand. "What is happening?"

She draws a shuddered breath. "Perhaps Goddess granted your misguided desire."

"Is she manipulating us?" Anger flashes through me.

When she takes my hand, my fury fades away. "I don't know. Goddess does what she wills, and it's been my experience, she does so for good reason."

I close my mind. "Forgive me if I'm not ready to share all my thoughts with you just yet."

With a nod, I sense the door closing on her mind as well. "I agree. We don't even know each other."

It sounds false when she says it, yet I can't disagree. "I know enough to know I want to know more."

"Are you flirting with me?" She smiles, and somehow the clouds above seem not to matter, as the sun is brighter.

"It's my nature. You said so yourself." I'm teasing, but I don't want to let go of this first light moment between us.

She pulls her hand away and stands. "Your attentions would be more welcomed by Sylvia or one of the young witches. I know some are hoping to have children and even find love. I'm not inclined toward romance. My mother wasn't either. My father was cast out of Windsor the moment Mother conceived. It is a family tradition."

My chest aches at the idea of her sending me away while she carries my baby within her. Stepping behind her so my chest grazes her back, I press my lips just behind her ear. "I would refuse to go, Sara Beth. You would have to kill me or wipe away my memories for me to leave you and our child. Had your father been stronger, he would have found a way. He missed watching you grow into a magnificent woman. I'll not be cheated thus."

On a shaky breath, she turns. "We should return to Windsor."

Wishing I could convince her to stay at the sacred stones to talk and flirt won't make it possible. It's obvious that she's not willing to let her guard down with me just yet. As I've closed my mind off to her, I can't blame her for her standoffish behavior.

Cart and horse ready, we climb up, and she hands me the reins.

Perhaps she's showing trust, or perhaps she wants to make sure I'm too busy to touch her while we drive back. Either way, I'm happy to take on the job.

"Do you miss Scotland?" she asks as we ease onto the road.

I love the way her warmth seeps into me where our clothes touch. "I miss the air in the highlands. It's crisp and seems to fill my lungs with greater ease. I'm sure it's my imagination, but I miss it nonetheless. The coven where I was raised was a happy place for me, with many friends, whom I miss. I've thought of writing to one or two, but I'm afraid they'd not respond, or respond unfavorably."

"You'll never know if you don't reach out. They likely don't know how to reach you. If you decide to remain in Windsor, you'd have a stable place for letters to reach you." She stares straight ahead, but her cheeks pink.

She's so lovely I want to touch those cheeks and see if they're as warm as they appear. "I came to Windsor to find a family. Unless you bid me leave, I hope to be accepted into the coven."

"We'll see. I've already said you can remain in town. When I know the nature of your character as a man and a witch, your coven status will be decided." She crosses her arms, and her breasts push to the edge of her dress.

Swallowing down desire, it takes me a few minutes to regain my senses. "I'll never betray you, the king, or the coven. I know the higher purpose of this coven, Sara Beth. I'd not have come here if I didn't intend to follow that edict."

"I sense no ill will in you, Adam. Still, I've been fooled before, and evil can often hide itself."

Unable to argue with her, I nod. "Shall I come to the coven house daily and prove myself?"

She's silent, and the temptation to open my mind and hope she does the same nudges at me relentlessly. I long to know what goes on in that magnificent mind of hers. What does she think of me? How will she respond to more flirting? I want to woo her more than I want to breathe, yet I hardly know her. It could be all Goddess's manipulations, and none of my attractions are real.

Rolling down the road in silence makes me think of my family and the trips we'd take to the lowlands to visit cousins. Mother loved to travel and visit.

"You're thinking of your mother," Sara Beth says. "I heard it despite your mind being closed. You were thinking very loud. She liked to visit with family." She shakes her head as if to dispel my thoughts from her head.

I should be angry or annoyed, but I can't conjure any ill emotions. "Mother loved to go and see people. Father didn't, but he indulged her once a year." Longing tightens my chest even though the memories are happy ones.

Sara Beth places her hand over mine on the reins. "It's very hard to lose our parents. I still miss my mother very much, and she was not an easy woman."

"She made you, so in my mind, she was magnificent." I

have no idea why I say this. Maybe because she'd have heard it without the words.

Pulling her hand back, she says, "You can gather your things from the rooming house and move them into the coven house. We have several rooms vacant at this time."

My heart stops for an instant before it pounds fast and hard. "Thank you, high priestess. You are too kind."

"Maybe I just want to be able to keep an eye on you." She tries to look stern, but a hint of a smile ruins the attempt.

"Look all you like, Sara Beth." I wink, and she frowns, which makes me laugh.

CHAPTER
FIVE

SARA BETH

Rather than make him drop me off, and then go to his rooms, we go directly to the rooming house. Seeing the dingy house and rough woman running the establishment, I'm glad I asked him to come to the coven house. It's a depressing place, and I've only been here a moment.

Livy Walters looks me up and down and sneers. "Found yourself a woman so fast, sir?"

"A friend, Mrs. Walters. I'll be leaving your generosity today and would like to settle my bill." He smiles tightly.

She scoffs and spits in the street. Her gray dress might have been blue once, and it's seen more days than it had in the cloth. Frayed and threadbare, it does little to keep out the cool air. One shoulder bare, and her breasts close to making an appearance, she looks at me as if I'm a streetwalker. "It's a halfpenny for the two days. I'll not cheat you as some might." Pushing her stringy, mousy hair back from her face, she stares at me.

Adam hands her the coin. "I'll get my things."

"You know she's a witch, don't you?" she asks far too loudly, using the word witch like the worst curse.

I keep my voice low. "Livy Walters, you needn't be cross. My kind has long protected you and yours. Your father called on my mother when illness took you as a child. Scarlett fever that injured your small heart. Betty Ware healed your heart and saved your parents from losing their only child."

Sorrow crosses Livy's brown eyes, but she shifts quickly back to anger and pushes graying hair back from her leathery cheek. "And what did she save me for? This life? It's a misery. You can tell yourself that your mother did a good thing, and I suppose she did as she was asked, but my death as an infant would have saved me from a lifetime of despair."

I wish I had all the words to put forth how each person has their role in Goddess's plan, but Livy Walters would not listen or understand. "I'm sorry you feel that way, madam. How can I help?"

Livy's laugh is derisive as she says, "Send one of these big men to paint my house, witch." She stomps into the house.

After a moment of staring at the empty doorway, I shift my attention to Adam, who watched the entire scene.

Passersby stopped to listen and now move on with their day.

Adam says, "I didn't realize your family had a history with this house."

I shrug. "How could you? It was long ago, and I only know because I've read my mother's journals."

"What will you do?" He studies me as if he may already know what I'm about to say. Perhaps he does.

"Wisdom says to leave it alone and forget the altercation." I never could follow such edicts. "I'll send someone to paint her house and fix whatever needs attention."

Grinning wide, Adam touches my cheek before he rushes inside to gather his things.

When we arrive at the coven house, Sylvia is working in the still room to the right of the front door. She peeks her head out. "Do you need me, Sara Beth?"

"No. I'm going to get Mr. MacNab settled in Minerva's old room."

"I see. Glad to have you in Windsor, Mr. MacNab." Sylvia lowers a shoulder, but when she looks at me, she stands up straight again. After a short pause, she grins. "I'll be in here if you need me. Trina and June have taken the great mother to Esme's shop."

Esme, a healer, runs a small shop with curatives. Prudence surely wanted to see Esme and William's baby more than she wished to investigate restoratives and creams.

With only one bag, Adam walks around the gathering room. Afternoon sun floods through the windows, highlighting the repaired floor. He studies the new wood where it meets the old. "What happened here?"

It's hard to tell the tale without reliving the horrors of that night. "A demon infiltrated the Kent coven through a man I once knew. He came here last year with them in thrall and attacked. The demon had plans to alter history through access to the king. We stopped him, but there were costs, both in life and property."

"I'm sorry." He steps close, and his worry flushes over me.

No one ever worries for me. I'm the high priestess, and it's my job to care for others. Unable to bear the sympathy, I call out, "Sylvia?"

She steps from the still room.

"Do you know the boarding house owned by Livy Walters?"

"I know it. Not the nicest place to stay or the nicest woman to rent from." Sylvia wrinkles her nose and crosses her arms.

"No. I know. Can you arrange for the house to get a fresh coat of paint and find out what repairs need making? I'd like to extend our friendship to her. I feel we have neglected her and hold some responsibility for her life." It's more explanation than is necessary, but I refuse to be like my mother and make commands as if I'm running an army.

"Of course, high priestess. I'll allocate funds and hire help for the tasks best done without magic. I'll handle the rest personally." Sylvia cocks her head but doesn't ask for more information.

Adam says, "I would be glad to help, Miss Pelham."

"It's Sylvia, and I'd welcome the help if that is agreeable with the high priestess." Sylvia keeps her expression neutral and her flirtatious nature tucked away.

Still, a wave of jealousy forces itself into my chest, and I have to push back. "I think Livy can use all the help she can get, and has an unpleasant opinion of this house that needs fixing as much as her establishment. Adam and any other witches are authorized to help."

Sylvia steps back inside the still room. I've known her most of my life. She's brimming with questions and may ask them at some point, but she'll not question me in front of another witch. I'm grateful for that. She's an excellent witch and a good friend.

With a nod, I lead Adam up the stairs to the far right of the gathering room. At the top of the stairs, we enter the dining hall. Two doors are to the left. One is a closet, and the other is Trina's room. Straight ahead is the door to the kitchen, which runs at the back of the house. To the right, one door leads to a hallway with six bedrooms. Currently, Prudence and I occupy two rooms. The other coven witches live elsewhere. Often, when witches come of age, they stay for a short time, and then move out for privacy or marriage, like Minerva. June lives with Minerva and Jonah on their farm, though she comes to the coven house to learn magic almost daily.

I show Adam to the room that used to be Minerva's. The wallpaper is cream with painted romantic scenes like a picnic and a game of pall-mall between lords and ladies. A horse race and tea make up another scene. "Feel free to redecorate as you please if you stay long."

Looking around, he places his bag on the bottom of the wood-framed bed. A small desk stands near the door with quill and ink at the ready. Everything is neat and orderly, just as Minerva left it. As he walks back to me, the floor creaks under his weight. "This is a very nice room. I'm not offended by the painted walls. I'll stay as long as you'll have me, Sara Beth."

My cheeks heat, and I curse myself for caring if he stays or goes. Pulling my shoulders back, I lift my chin and bury my emotions and desires. "The only reason I would ask you to leave, Adam, is if you lie or betray the light."

He bows his head.

"I already know you withhold part of your story. We hardly know each other, and it is my hope trust will alter that." I step back to the door. My instinct says run away, but I step slowly into the hall and close the door. Once I'm locked inside my own room, I sit with my head in my hands.

"Mother, I know you mistrusted men, but you were wrong about so many things. Goddess approves him being here, and I cannot help my desire to have him here." The air shimmers, sending a tingle up my spine. My mother hears me and does not approve. She's never spoken to me from the grave. I've tried on All Hallows, when the veil is thin, to speak to her. She hears me. I know she does, and I feel her constant disappointment. Even in death, she's too stubborn to give me what I want.

A soft knock draws me out of my torment. I stand, unlock the door and open it.

Prudence smiles and walks into my room.

My bed is in the corner and is larger than the other beds in the house. It has four thick posts and is draped with heavy indigo. To the left I have a desk, and in the center of the room, a small seating area with four overstuffed chairs for private meetings.

Prudence sits. "I see our new friend passed your tests well enough to gain a room in the house."

Sitting next to her, I shrug. "Goddess approved him, and I saw no significant dark or ill will within him. His past is still a bit foggy and worrisome. Time will tell, but who am I to go against Goddess? She says he has a purpose here."

A soft smile pulls at the corners of Prudence's lips. Her heavily wrinkled face hardly tells the tale of a life spanning almost two hundred years. She rarely displays magic, though I feel strong power within her. Her wisdom is vast and always gently given. In a world of chaos, she is stability. "You like him."

"It is difficult to not like Adam MacNab. He is charming." I shrug in my attempt to show a lack of interest.

"I felt Betty's spirit when I came down the hall." It's half pity, half scolding.

"Knowing I should follow my own path without seeking her approval and living that are vastly different things. She doesn't like a man living under this roof." I never lie to Prudence.

Small and hunched, Prudence is still a force fully alive and vibrant. She leans forward and takes my hand firmly. "Your mother was a fine woman, witch, and good leader of this coven. She was my good friend, but it was her arrogance that took her life too soon. I'm so very proud of how you see all sides of a situation and not only the narrow path of your mother."

"My way has put this coven at risk." My breath comes out as shaky as my resolve.

"You lead by doing what is right and having the respect of your coven, while she led by fear. I think your way is far better." She squeezes my hand but keeps it firmly in hers. "What did Goddess say?"

"That we should find strength in each other, and that trouble is coming. She said he shouldn't take the blame for things he didn't do." I spread my arms. "She was cryptic, as she always is. Deciphering Goddess is the job of a lifetime, not a few hours."

Prudence chuckles. "That is for certain. Yet she said enough to cause you to let him stay in Windsor and invite him to reside here."

"He intrigues me," I admit. "I loved Orin with all my heart when I was a girl. I mourned him when he left and again when he died after the demon left him. In the thirteen years between my romance with Orin and now, I've not met a single man who..." I don't know how to complete the sentence.

"You wanted?" Prudence's eyes fill with sympathy.

I laugh. "I'm not a saint. I've not been celibate for my entire adult life, Great Mother. I have taken lovers to fulfill my needs. I barely know Adam, yet I know I would never use him in such a way. Though, perhaps if I did, this longing would diminish."

Eyes full of light and joy, Prudence listens intently. "As you said, you don't know him. Perhaps that is the first step in this journey. If trouble is coming, and Goddess is never wrong, you will need as many friends as you can gather. We all will."

She's right of course. There's nothing to do but get to know the witch I just invited to live at the coven house. My mother's spirit sizzles around me, but I shake it off. She had her time here to rule as she saw fit. This is my time, and I choose a different path.

For the next hour, Prudence and I talk of Esme's baby and shop. She tells me she plans to visit Minerva and Jonah in their apothecary shop in a day or two, depending on how tired she is. We see them all often, but I suspect part of the visiting is to teach June and Trina something, though I don't know what.

On the new moon, I hook a basket over my arm and go to Livy Walter's house to check on progress. It's been ten days since Adam moved out. He returns daily to work with the carpenter I've hired. Not sure what to expect, I approach with caution.

Livy is standing on her front step looking up at a man on a ladder, who's painting the faded wood a fresh white. When she sees me, she turns bright red and meets me in the street. "I never expected this, Miss Ware. You do too much."

I hand her the basket, and the scent of fresh bread and butter makes her stomach grumble. I smile. "It's a small gesture. You made a fine point when last we met. My mother is gone over ten years, and I have not taken care as I ought."

"I don't know how I'll ever repay you." She opens the basket and breathes deeply the warm, yeasty scents.

The painter waves, and I wave back. "When these small

changes bring you more clientele for rooming, and you are doing well, perhaps then we can speak of it. Perhaps you know the recipe for your mother's jam and will favor me with a jar from time to time."

A wide grin spreads across her face, and she's almost pretty despite the effects of a hard life. "I've not made that recipe for many years. I don't know why I stopped, since those things give me pleasure."

"Perhaps the why is no longer important, Miss Walters. We all deserve a little joy, don't you think?" I feel Adam before he steps from the front door.

"Indeed, we do, Miss Ware. I shall tell everyone that you are as good as your word." With a small skip, Livy rushes up the steps and inside with her basket of treats.

Joining me to watch the painter, Adam grins. He's far too handsome for anyone's good. We have made it a habit of sitting after the evening meal to talk at the table. I've learned much about his childhood in Scotland but more about visiting cousins in the lowlands for less harsh winters. "You've turned an enemy into a friend, I see."

"She was never an enemy, just disillusioned with life and looking for someone to blame." The scent of hard work and sawdust mixed with Adam is almost too much to endure.

"I'm done here for today. I wonder if you'd favor me with a walk in the park?" He offers his arm.

"Are you courting me, Adam?" It sounds like I'm scolding, but inside I'm not immune to the thrill of a handsome man asking for a walk.

"I warned you that I would." He lifts a brow as if to challenge me.

No one should be so charming. Men like Adam MacNab are dangerous, my mother would say. "A walk, but I'll not take your arm."

We stroll down the street away from Livy's house and head east toward the park. Adam clasps his hands behind him and makes no attempt to touch me or woo me into touching him. "It's strange this gift Goddess gave. I cannot hear most of what you think, but from time to time I feel an emotion or thought that's not my own, and there's comfort within it. Even now, I felt how little you trust me, yet your wariness didn't distress me. I like having this small bit of you with me."

"I can't understand why she gave such a gift, as you call it." It's frustrating that my blocks are not fully successful. Though, I don't disagree with his description of comfort even when the thought is not of a pleasant nature.

"I sometimes see your dreams, Sara Beth," he admits softly.

"I know." I saw him there last night. While I dreamed of a hot bath in a bubbling brook, he stood in the wooded shadows.

At the entrance to the park, he pulls me off the path, and we stand behind the gate's stone pillar. "What would you have done if I'd joined you in your imaginary spring?" He leans down, and his lips are an inch from mine.

"It was a dream, Adam." I back as far as the pillar will let me. "There is no truth or reason to it."

Though he makes no move to close the distance, I feel him all around me. "You were so perfectly beautiful in that dream. I woke quite aroused."

My own need was painfully acute when I startled awake. The fact that he was only a wall away made it difficult to keep from resolving my desire, and even harder to keep from asking him to do so. However, I held back and stayed in my own bed while the floor creaked in the room next door. "You should stay out of my dreams."

He lowers his head until our breath mingles. "It makes me wonder if it wasn't my dream you entered. Perhaps we dream as one, dear one."

"Don't call me that." I mean for it to sound harsh, but it's breathy and full of desire.

Closing his eyes, he takes a long breath, and steps back before turning back to the path.

It takes me a beat or two to gather my wits and move beside him. The path meanders through wide grassy spaces where people sit and take lunch or flirt. A stream runs through the woods. When we reach the little wilderness, the evergreens are lush around us.

As soon as we are away from the prying eyes of Windsor and in the shadows of the trees, Adam takes my hand and threads his fingers through mine. "I know you said you don't wish me to touch you, but I sense your words do not convey the truth."

I sigh out my frustration. "It might be better if we consummated this madness. Then, perhaps, then we might get over it."

Adam stills and his grip on my hand tightens.

CHAPTER
SIX

ADAM

My shaft is at full attention. Even if her comment was meant to tease or make light of the desire roiling between us, my body thinks it is a grand idea. "I wonder why you say such things when they only torture me."

She pulls my hand and steps to a large oak. Putting her back against the bark, she narrows her gaze. "Is this not what you want? You might just take me against this tree and be over it. Then you'd feel no sense of not being able to have something you want. You could move on to the next woman whom you fancy."

Anger rolls off her in waves and sears my soul. Someone else chuckles. I shake my head to rid myself of the laughter. "What is that?"

Cupping my cheeks, she looks into my eyes. "You hear her?"

It starts again and gets louder. I hold my ears, but it's a

cackle now and only gets worse. "Sara Beth, what's happening?"

"I'm sorry." Stepping back, Sara Beth raises her hands and casts.

My world turns black. The woman's laughter eases but doesn't go away. I'm floating in a dark abyss. I call out, but no one responds, and my voice is hollow and will not carry. I scream, and the laughter begins again before something muffles the sound.

I may have died, and this is where I wait for Goddess to decide my fate. Yes. This lack of anything must be death.

"Adam?" Sara Beth's soft voice penetrates the emptiness.

Searching the darkness, I long to find her. "I'm here."

And then, so is she. In a white dress that flows around her, Sara Beth stands before me. "It's time to come back now."

"Back? Where are we?" I reach out and touch her soft cheek.

Pain lances across her eyes. "I had to put you in a trance. My mother... It's complicated, but Prudence has blocked her power in our world. She's trying to protect me, but it is wrong, and I'm more sorry than I can say."

"The cackling was your mother?" I'm trying to put it all together. "You put me in a trance in the park?"

"I had to get you away from her. Then I had to call for help to bring you home. Now we can't wake you, Adam. Come back." Desperation rings in her voice.

"How?"

She holds her hand out with her palm up. "Just choose."

"What is the other choice?" I can't deny there is peace in this void.

"You could stay here until you die and go to Goddess. In my world, you will wither away despite our efforts to keep you alive." Her eyes shine with tears.

I take her hand. "I never wish to cause you distress."

My bedroom in the coven house grows clearer as I blink the strange dream away. Sara Beth, Prudence, and several other witches surround my bed. William and Jonah stare down with concern.

I focus on Sara Beth. "What happened?"

The group lets out a collective breath.

Sara Beth says, "I'll tell you what I know."

William wraps an arm around Esme. "We'll go now. I'm glad you're back, Adam. We'll check on you tomorrow."

Similar farewells are issued from the remaining witches.

Prudence pats my cheek and grins before she ambles out my door.

When there is only Sara Beth and me left, she sits on the edge of my bed, and takes my hand. "My mother was a very controlling witch in life. Since her death, she has refused to speak to me, but she still pushes from beyond when she's unhappy with my choices. She's been very unhappy these last few years. She didn't trust men, and I've allowed two to join our coven. My interest in you must have pushed her to desperation. I heard the laughter. Though it did me no harm, it was clearly paining you."

My head still rings with the memory. I cringe. "It was terrible."

Mother is with Goddess, and in life did no harm except to herself at the time of her death. She worked a spell and nearly burned down the coven house. She was killed by her own magic. I think she meant to frighten you off."

As I push to sitting, the room spins for a moment, and then stills. "She was terrifying."

"Do you wish to leave Windsor?" Is there regret in her voice?

Somehow the idea that Sara Beth would miss me softens

my near-fatal experience. "Do you think your mother will do me harm if I stay?"

"Prudence thinks Mother probably used so much energy to force her laughter into your head that it will take her a long time to recover enough to return. Perhaps I can reason with her in the meantime." Sara Beth's cheeks turn bright red, and the color travels down her neck and chest, where it disappears below the edge of her dress.

"I would like to stay in Windsor, but I don't wish to experience that again. It was like someone was hitting my skull from the inside." I shudder.

"I'm so sorry." She caresses my hand where it lies on my chest then lowers her head to press on top.

Her hair fans out on my chest. I comb my fingers through and revel the softness and this closeness that I've only dreamed of, but never really believed possible. "I'm fine, Sara Beth. I don't want to leave you or this coven. I won't run away because of fear. I'll only leave if you send me away. This was not your fault."

She shakes her head but keeps it pressed against me. "It was foolish of me to let feelings get involved. I knew my mother would disapprove. You must believe me when I say I never thought she would harm you or anyone."

Cupping the back of her head, I urge her gaze to mine. "I know you'd never hurt anyone. I don't know what your mother intended, but clearly, she wouldn't have approved of me for you."

With a humorless laugh, she says, "Mother thought men only good for one purpose, and that was getting with child. She would say even pleasure was better obtained on our own."

Drawing her forward, I press my lips lightly to hers. A million stars burst behind my eyes in an electric display. It takes me a moment to regain my breath. "When you honor me with your body, Sara Beth Ware, I promise there will be pleasure."

"You mean *if*." Her chest rises and falls with heavy breaths.

I grin. "Call me overconfident."

Shaking her head, she laughs. The sound is musical, nothing like the maniacal cackling that caused me pain. Hers is laughter I could get lost in for a thousand years. Standing, she tucks the covers around me. "You should rest now. If you need anything, just call out. Someone will hear you."

In my mind I say, *"I'll be fine, Sara Beth. This was not your fault."*

Startled at first, she calms and offers me a smile that doesn't touch those dark eyes of hers. "I'm relieved you're all right."

Despite the thrill of having Sara Beth sit on my bed and touch me, the effects of the day take their toll, and I fall asleep.

I t's dark outside when I wake, and the clatter of dishes tells me that I've either missed dinner or the table is being set.

"You're awake?" Sara Beth's voice slides into my mind.

"I am." There's something exciting about her watching over me through the connection Goddess made. However, I'd rather her walk through the door.

"Dinner is nearly ready." And as if she was never there, she's gone.

My stomach rumbles. A fresh pitcher of water is ready for me. I strip out of the morning's clothes, wash, and dress in trousers and shirt. I pull on my only coat before I join the witches in the dining room.

Sylvia rushes over. "Are you well, Adam?"

"Better, thank you." Aromas of mutton and mushrooms waft from the kitchen.

Sitting at the head of the table, Sara Beth's wears a plum dress with white trim. When she looks at me, her cheeks color. "Come, sit, and have a restorative, Adam."

I take the empty seat at her left, across from Prudence.

Sylvia brings me a glass, and the earthy scent of a magical restorative accompanies the tang of wine.

June sits on my other side. "We're all glad you were unharmed, Mr. MacNab. Esme brought the restorative, and William checked on you. Jonah and Minerva will be here shortly."

The door below opens and closes, and voices drift up the stairs before both couples tromp upstairs to join us.

Trina and two other witches bring platters of food from the kitchen.

Once Prudence thanks Goddess for the food and my restored health, the table erupts in clanking flatware and lively chatter.

Sara Beth leans toward me. "You look much better. How do you feel?"

"Slightly out of sorts from a long nap, but otherwise fine." I accept a bowl of potatoes and spoon some onto my plate.

Lamb-and-vegetable stew is ladled over the potatoes, and a large crust of bread is placed on the side of my bowl. There's twice as much in front of me than anyone else. I chuckle. "Are you worried I'll starve?"

June says, "I was not raised in this coven, but I imagine since Betty Ware's spirit did you harm, they all feel responsible. She was high priestess, and in her life, never went against Goddess. It's disturbing to think she has gone astray in death."

I'm not insensitive to the feelings of the coven, yet they put too much upon themselves. "I'm unharmed. Perhaps she only meant to frighten me off, and either misjudged the effects, or it's possible I'm more sensitive than she expected."

With a warm smile, June nods and returns to her meal.

The stew is delicious, and Prudence commands the table with stories of the coven from more than a hundred years ago. She speaks of witches long dead and some that have retired to country life. She tells a funny story about Minerva's Aunt Bellamy flooding the alley behind the house, and everyone is in tears with laughter when she finishes.

As the meal winds down, Sylvia, Esme, and William get up and begin to clear.

I stand to help, but Sara Beth stops me with a hand on my arm. "Another night, Adam. Tonight, you may behave as an honored guest."

"I don't wish to be a guest, high priestess. I wish to be a part of this family." My chest is tight with how true it is.

Her smile is warm. "I know, but humor me tonight." Hand still on my arm, she squeezes.

Warmth rushes through me. Her mind is a jumble of doubt and regret. She's normally so confident, this uncertainty from her feels strange. "I wish you would not blame yourself for what happened. It was not your doing, and I'm fully recovered."

Sara Beth's despair burns in my chest, as if I had lost someone precious. There's nothing I can say in this room full of her coven, so I send her my forgiveness and let the matter drop for now.

Once the table is cleared and more wine brought out, the witches talk of life in Windsor. A man, who I learn is Sir William's valet, Henry Dove, joins us and is welcome, despite his lack of magic. He appears to be just a man as far as I can tell.

It seems to me he can't take his eyes off Sylvia, and she

refuses to look at him at all. Most dinners at the coven house have been only three or five witches and a simple meal. This feast was made for me, and that is a first in my life.

One by one, those who live elsewhere make their way home. They each bid Prudence, Sara Beth, and me good night.

Flattered to be singled out, I hardly know how to act. I like it here. I like these witches. My feelings for Sara Beth are complicated and new to me, but I'm not willing to walk away from this or her.

June and Trina help Prudence, and soon it's just Sara Beth and me at the table. She stands, so I do the same. Staring at me a long moment, she sighs. "Will you sit with me and talk a while in my room?"

"Of course." I follow her past my bedroom door to hers. Inside the large room are three distinct areas: one for sleeping, an office, and a sitting area.

Once she sits in one of four overstuffed chairs, I take the one next to her. "You have a very nice room."

"A benefit of being the high priestess." Her smile is sad.

"I imagine there are not many." I personally wouldn't wish to have so many witches in my charge.

"I've been doing this since I was a girl of eighteen, Adam. It is my destiny. I asked you here to talk about my mother. I feel you deserve more of an explanation, even though I'm still in shock over what happened." She stares at her fingers, twisting in her lap.

Dropping to my knees, I take her hands and massage the backs until her fingers relax. "Tell me what I can say to ease your burden, dear one?"

A tear rolls down her cheek. "You shouldn't call me that."

"Forgive me. Is there an endearment I'm allowed?" Immediately, I feel her heart lighten.

"When I was a girl, I had an imaginary friend, or maybe he

was a spirit. I've never been sure. When my mother was busy with coven business, and when I was forced to wait in small rooms with no entertainment, he and I would have great adventures together." She grins, and it is as if an arrow has pierced my heart. I would give anything to make her smile like this every day for the rest of my life.

I push down the wayward thought. "What was his name?"

"Richard. He was a great deal of fun, and we sailed to the four corners of the world seeking adventure." She giggles and her cheeks flush. "Richard was a pirate, you see."

"Was he now?" I can't help laughing. "I find myself slightly jealous of this phantom from your childhood. What did Richard call you?"

"Beth," she whispers. "He called me Beth. It was a sad day when I grew too old to play those games. When I was six, Mother demanded I learn how to take over from her, and the time for imagining was at an end."

It is by far the saddest thing I've ever heard. "I mean no disrespect, but your mother was a hard woman, taking away your childhood."

"She was right. I had to learn." A lifetime of regret shines in her eyes.

I want to shield her from it all and take care of her. I've clearly lost my mind. "Don't you think there is time enough for balance in life? Goddess wouldn't have all work, or all play, any more than she believes light can exist without dark. Would you raise your daughter or son without play?"

"No," she answers quickly, and her eyes flash with ferocity as she pulls her hands out from under mine. "I doubt the question will ever come up, but my child would not have the burden of command thrust upon them. It would be the coven's and her decision. It most certainly wouldn't be mine."

"Then there is nothing to regret. You learned more than

your mother bargained for, Beth." I love the way the nickname feels on my tongue. I want to whisper her name over an over with her naked in my arms, all night.

She gestures to the chair. "Please, sit."

I do, but wish I could pull her into my lap.

"My mother was a good witch and leader. She followed Goddess's rules to the letter, never straying until the day she decided she could fight an evil on her own. She worked a spell to keep a dark witch out of Windsor. She used fire, and as I told you, it went terribly wrong. She failed and died because she intended to do harm. Yet, I know she is with Goddess now. I can't explain what happened today." She presses her palms to her eyes.

"Are you certain it was Betty Ware today?" Wanting to ease her pain, I'm looking for a way out of this.

Sitting up straight, she stares over my shoulder. "It felt like her magic, and it sounded like her laugh at first. When the noise of it became unbearable for you—I'm not sure. Her magic was still present, but I never heard such a noise from Mother. It was so rare that she laughed at all."

Her pain lances through me like a dagger. "How did Prudence stop the assault?"

Once again meeting my gaze, she dashes a tear from her eye. "Prudence speaks to Mother from time to time. Mother doesn't speak to me. In fact, that laugh was the first noise I've heard from her since her death. I often feel her magic around me and can sense approval, and more often, disapproval, but she doesn't speak. However, today, Mother refused to respond when the great mother contacted her. Her magic was angry and hard to read beyond the rage. Prudence may look frail, but she's very powerful. She called on Goddess to remove Mother until what happened can be sorted."

It must be horrible for her to have had her mother taken from her in this way as well. "I'm sorry, Beth."

Her breath catches. Arms crossed, she clutches her upper arms. "I am as well. Perhaps this will turn out to be a misunderstanding. Perhaps you are more sensitive, and Mother only made a mistake. I don't know. It all feels wrong, Adam."

"It does. I wonder that the trouble Goddess warned us was coming is not already at work." Inside, I shudder at what my being in Windsor might cost, and if it's worth it.

CHAPTER
SEVEN

SARA BETH

He calls me Beth, and I long to open my heart to him. Even so, danger rings in my head. Men cannot be trusted, and charming men are the worst of all. It's not easy, but I try to banish my mother's warnings from rolling around in my mind. "Who else might not wish for you to be in Windsor?" My cheeks heat. "Perhaps it was the nature of our conversation in the park that sparked interest from an enemy."

I've blushed more in the last week than I have in my entire life.

"I don't know why anyone, friend or foe, should care if I'm intimate with you or anyone else." Intensity flashes in his eyes.

His desire heats the air in the room. The connection allows my need and his to merge. I squeeze my knees together, but it doesn't help the sensation sparking between my legs. "Perhaps it's because I'm sworn to protect the crown. Some people believe if I were killed, the Windsor coven would be vulnerable to attack. Those people would be mistaken. This coven would survive and thrive without me. I have seen to it."

"I have no doubt." Pupils fully dilated, he looks ready to breach the gap between us to relieve my growing need and his own.

"It may look as if the witches are frivolous, but they know what to do, no matter who should fall." There's no need to defend my leadership, and yet I'm doing so with more ferocity than I ever have.

With soft eyes and a slight smile, he says, "Beth, I have only been here two weeks, and it is clear you are a great leader, and not only respected, but adored. You needn't defend your station. I can't imagine how difficult it must be to inherit such a job at a young age. No one will question your authority."

He's right. I've never been in danger of a mutiny. Prudence taught me long ago that my mother's iron fist might not be the only way to lead. Loyalty is kinder when earned. I've done my best. "Goddess connected us." I change the subject. "Why?"

"I don't know." His shoulders slump as he clasps his hands between his knees. "I asked to know your mind, but never thought it to be taken so literally. I'm sorry, Beth."

For some reason, his apology hurts deep inside me. "I didn't ask for remorse. I assume you would remove this link if you could."

Looking up, he blinks several times. "No. I would know you in all ways. I would learn your likes and dislikes, loves and hates, and I would hear every word, thought, and feeling inside that beautiful head of yours. I love the moments when I hear you, but wouldn't ever want to intrude on you. It's hard to know when to listen and when to close off when feeling your desire for me right now is so alluring."

I should be appalled that he knows of my need, but I'm

excited about it. It's satisfying to know he yearns for me just as painfully. "If I am honest, I would not change what Goddess has given us. I like the sound of your voice in my head."

He frowns, and his worry punches through our connection. "What you offered in the park..."

"Yes. I remember." Heat flushes my chest and neck, and my body tingles as visions of being taken against an old oak tree flood me.

"As delicious as the offer is, Beth, it would never be enough. I know you think one swift night to relieve our need would end this yearning, but I know you're wrong. It will only whet our appetites." His broad chest rises and falls hard and fast. "I would be honored to make love with you."

Unable to decide if it's a burden or a gift that he knows what I'm thinking, I try not to think so much. My body is on fire with desire. "I would think, after such a trying day, you might need your rest."

"Is that a no, Beth?" His voice is soft, and he sounds regretful, but he makes no move to either leave or come closer.

"What do you want from me, Adam?" I've taken lovers, so why does this feel so different?

As if I'd spoken, Adam stands and steps in front of me. He holds his hand out for me to take or reject. "It is different. We are something more. I can feel it. I could feel it the moment I saw you in the kitchen. Some part of me awakened for the first time, Beth. I don't want to lose the way I feel or see you in my world."

Can meeting someone change the world? I never thought so before Adam. He is a mystery, and I should be wary of him and his past. He's told me so little about how he came to be without clan or coven, only that some act by his brother had the family banished. "If I say yes, it doesn't mean I'll stop protecting myself or my coven from you if I need to."

"I know." Unmoving, he waits with his hand outstretched, and his piercing blue eyes focused on mine.

Drawing breath for courage and restraint, I take his hand and stand. "Pleasure can be just pleasure, Adam. It needn't have great meaning behind it."

His lips twist in half a smile. "For many, that is true." He pulls gently so I draw closer, then he wraps one arm around me. With his other hand, he threads my hair, sending dozens of hairpins tinkling to the floor.

My long dark hair tumbles over my shoulders and down my back, and he combs the last of the pins out with strong fingers.

Almost a foot taller than me, he lowers his head and presses a soft kiss to my lips. He draws my bottom lip between both of his.

Magic, static, and energy fill the air around us. Desire floods between my legs, and I clench my thighs for some relief, though it only increases my neediness. I gasp, and he slides his tongue inside my mouth.

Our tongues slip together, and our moans merge.

I clutch his shoulders and press my body flush to his. Even as a girl, I never longed for pleasure and release so thoroughly. Trapped between us, his thick shaft notches just above where I need him. "I rarely take lovers." Why should it matter?

His breath is hard, and he kisses along my neck. "I know you won't believe me, but neither do I."

A low throaty laugh escapes me. "You're right. I don't believe you. I think you can have any number of women in every town you entertain in."

Pushing my dress aside, he kisses my bare shoulder. His hand skims along my waist, and he caresses the swell of my hip. "Perhaps, but I don't, or at least haven't in many years.

The potential of breaking hearts lost its appeal when I was a much younger man."

I wrap a leg around his, pulling myself closer. "It doesn't matter."

Taking half a step back, he clutches my leg and eases it to the floor. My dress ties in the front, and he deftly releases the bow and tugs the stays free. "It does if you believe I'll go from your bed to another's, Beth."

The idea forms a stone in my gut. I pull back. "You are free to do as you please."

Adam tugs his shirt over his head and lets it drop to the chair. Reaching forward, he finds the bow at my left shoulder and tugs it free. He slides my dress down that shoulder before finding the bow at my right. "I'll not betray you in any way. I'll not seek or want another woman, and I hope you'll not look for another man."

"We have no commitment to each other, Adam. We're sharing a mutual need and nothing more." I lower my right shoulder and my dress pools softly at my feet. In only slippers, stockings, and garters, I feel sexy and also exposed. I reach across my chest to cover myself.

Taking my hands, he thwarts my modesty and places my hands on his shoulders. "Don't hide from me. You're beautiful." Kissing a path from my neck, he draws soft sighs and sends desire flowing through me once again. He kisses my chest, between my breasts. Lowering to his knees, he traces a path with his tongue around my bellybutton. He helps me out of my slippers, and even his touch on my calf and ankle is somehow erotic. He slowly rolls my stockings down. His fingers gently on my legs makes me weak in the knees, and I clutch his shoulders for support.

"Adam." His name sounds like a prayer on my lips.

His warm, wet tongue presses between the folds of my

womanhood, and if not for his arms banded around my legs, I would fall.

I have to bite my tongue to keep the scream of pleasure building inside me from bursting out and waking the entire house. "That's, oh. Goddess. So. Good."

He licks and sucks harder, then more gently, bringing me to the brink of rapture and pulling me back from the edge.

Barely holding on, I open my legs, needing just a little more. I thread my fingers through his hair.

Focused on my pearl, he circles it with his tongue and laps at my juices. His fingers press at my center, and I'm so wet, he slips inside, pumping and sucking in a perfect rhythm.

Pleasure explodes around me. I long to scream and cry from the sheer joy of it. I thrust my hips hard against his mouth, needing more, and not being denied.

He holds me as the orgasm fades, then stands, takes me in his arms, and carries me to the bed. "Feel better?"

"That was wonderful," I say as he lowers me to the bed. I relax into the soft mattress, and I could easily fall asleep satisfied. But as I drift, something is missing. I open my eyes.

Adam stands at the side of the bed. He doesn't join me. Shirtless, but still wearing breeches, he waits. "This would be enough for tonight, and I'd not regret a moment, Beth. Tell me what you want."

Lifting my hand palm up, I offer it to him. "Come to bed, Adam. Take your pleasure." I flick my wrist and send his remaining clothes to the chair with his shirt, and make room for him in my bed.

It feels larger than one night to offer half my bed. Lovers should be taken outside the coven house, Mother would say. I push her from my memories and turn into Adam's embrace.

His big hand cups my breast, and with thumb and forefinger, he worries the nipple.

Though I was fully sated a moment before, a rush of want floods through me, and I arch my back.

Lowering his head, he takes the other nipple in his mouth and sucks until I can't contain my moans. "Adam, we have to be quiet."

"Why? Will the house be shocked that you seek pleasure?" He snuggles his cheek against my chest.

Cradling his head in my arms, with our legs twined together, I say, "No. Well, maybe. I've never sought pleasure here."

Rising to his elbows, he leans over me. "I don't know if I should be flattered or concerned."

His knee is pressed into the mattress between my legs, and his thigh leans where desire has already begun to build again. I lift my hips and grind against him.

His cock between us, he moans. "Perhaps we might discuss this topic later."

"Mmm, later." I grind again as the pleasure builds.

Lifting enough to press his fingers along my slit, he teases and probes until I'm writhing beneath him. "Beth, you're so perfect. I'll never have enough of watching your pleasure."

"I need you, Adam." It's hard to get the words out, but I'm desperate to have him inside me. I dig my nails into his shoulders and bite down on my lip to keep from crying out.

Spreading my legs with his, he notches his cock and presses in an inch.

The lovely stretch forces my pleasure higher, but he pulls back. "Don't." I clutch him tighter and lift my hips.

Brushing the hair back from my face, he devours my lips and slides inside me in one gloriously slow thrust.

I explode with pleasure. My body pulses around him as my hips bounce, looking for even more of what is the best orgasm of my life.

Adam drowns out my screams with kisses, sucking my tongue into his mouth and worshiping my lips. "Easy love. I've got you."

Unable to catch my breath, I gasp against his neck, still clutching him while he remains unmoving inside me. "I'm sorry. I don't know what happened."

His low chuckle vibrates through me. "Never apologize for such a beautiful thing. Do you want to stop?"

Longing to give him at least a fraction of what he's already given me, I tip my pelvis up, and the pleasure sparks again. "I'll be very cross if you stop now."

"Thank Goddess." He slides out to the head before slowly filling me again and again.

His thick cock reaches every nerve, and with each thrust, he rubs my pearl just right. I meet every move, and pleasure builds higher and faster. "Adam. Oh Goddess."

Him speeding his thrusts shoots my rapture higher. I press my mouth to his chest and let out a long keen as another orgasm takes me. It stretches until my legs shake with it.

With one last thrust, Adam grunts and pulls out, spilling his seed between us in warm jets. Breathing hard, he kisses my cheek, neck, and along my jaw. "I didn't want to presume, Beth. We should have discussed such things beforehand."

I love his weight pressing me to the mattress. "It was thoughtful of you to be cautious." Though, the idea of a child warms me in places I thought long forgotten.

He shifts to his elbows and meets my gaze. "You would want a child?"

"This link can be a disadvantage." I push him off.

With very little force, he presses my hips back down. "Let me get a cloth."

Beautifully naked, he crosses to my basin, pours water from the pitcher, and wets a small cloth before returning. The moon lights him in hard planes and thick muscles. A smattering of hair covers his chest and makes its way to a delightful vee below his hips.

He washes his seed from my abdomen and thighs, then presses my legs open and cleans me there as well. It's the most erotic and sweetest moment of my life. I'm panting and full of desire again when he finishes. Pupils wide, he looks at me wanting before returning to the basin and washing himself.

Turing to my side, I get under the blanket. My stomach fills with butterflies. Longing floods me, and I don't want to watch him leave or think about him sleeping in the next room. "I wouldn't mind a child," I whisper, half hoping he won't hear.

The bed dips, and he presses his chest to my back. His legs cradle mine, and he kisses my back. Spreading his hand over my belly, he says, "You would be beautiful round with child."

"I think I would be big as the house and mean as a snake." I giggle at the picture I've painted.

His shaft firms against my buttocks.

Does the idea of me filled with his child arouse him?

Banding his arm around me, he draws me tight. "If you're mean, I'll soothe you."

"Ha! You'll be on the first carriage out of town." I press my hand over my mouth. I hadn't meant to say it. I hadn't even thought it until it was already coming out of my mouth, and it sounded exactly like my mother, full of bitterness and disappointment. "I'm sorry."

His warm lips press against my shoulder. "Many men might do exactly as you surmise, Beth. I don't know what happened to your father, and I don't know why your lover left you behind. I can't fathom a man walking away from you, because I'll only go if you command it."

Why would I tell him to go? "And am I likely to do that, Adam?"

"I don't know." He lets out a long sigh.

There are many questions to ask, but I don't want the answers tonight. I want to feel safe and secure in Adam's arms, even if it's all an illusion. I close my eyes. "If I were to become with child, I would be very happy, regardless of what you did or how bad my temper became."

Images of dark-haired babies with bright-blue eyes like Adam's and Mother's roll through my head, and I relax against him.

"May I stay and hold you tonight?" He brushes my hair back from my face and kisses my jaw just in front of my ear.

"If you wish."

When I wake, the moon has crossed to the other side of the house, and the room is dark. Yet, there is no mistaking the man in my bed. I'm strewn across his chest, which rises and falls slow and steady.

After untangling my legs from his, I sit on the edge of the bed. My body is deliciously sore from a night of lovemaking. I light the lamp by my bed. At my small vanity, my reflection is that of a wanton with wild hair and eyes filled with lust. I hardly recognize myself as I take the brush and start untangling my wild curls.

"It's early." The sheets rustle as he sits behind me, takes the brush and takes over my haircare.

It's lovely to have someone brush my hair. Far too indulgent, but I'm not strong enough to grab the brush away. "I always rise before everyone else. It gives me time to meditate on Goddess and settle my magic before everyone begins asking for my time."

"I can see where that would be your only time alone. Am I disturbing your routine?" He works gently through the last knot and slides the soft bristles along my scalp and through my hair.

A satisfied sigh pushes up from my chest, and my eyes close while I enjoy being pampered. "You are, but it does not follow that the disturbance is unwelcome."

Pushing my hair to one side, he kisses my neck at the shoulder, again higher, and then behind my ear. "I'm happy to hear that." He hands me my brush. "I have never had a better night, Beth. You're wonderful."

I meet his gaze in the mirror. "Then you don't feel our coming together has sated any foolish desires?"

His warm, low laughter shoots delight between my legs. "Sated is the last word I shall ever use when describing my want of you." His eyes grow serious, and his voice dips lower, as if someone speaks through him. "You and I are connected, though how or why, I can't say. Goddess brought us together. Goddess wills our paths merge. If evil be known, it will be known, but apart, there will be no peace." He blinks and looks around before shaking his head. "What just happened?"

Turning to face him, I cup his cheek. "Do you remember what you said?"

"Yes, but not as one does after making a speech. It's more like remembering a dream."

I kiss his cheek. "I think Goddess spoke through you."

CHAPTER
EIGHT

ADAM

Days later, Goddess's words still roll through my head. Are our lives manipulated by a deity, or is there a grand plan, and Goddess is only facilitating the connections? It shouldn't matter, though I'd like to think my feelings for Sara Beth are my own.

Livy Walters sits beside me where I'm thinking on her front steps. "What has put that frown on your handsome face, Mr. MacNab?"

"I'm pondering fate versus free choice." It's easier to just be honest most of the time. If the person asks, they have to deal with the answer.

She cocks her head, and a bit of unwashed hair falls from her bun. "Deep thought for a Friday afternoon. Why not think about plans with your lady for the week's end?"

I shrug. "That would be more pleasant if the lady considered herself mine, and I had any right to claim her. As it is, I'm a poor magician making my way across this grand island. What would a lady like Sara Beth Ware want with me?"

Laughing, Livy slaps my back. "There is no rhyme nor reason for why a person wants another. At your age, you should know that. As for fate and choice, I've always thought life was a mix of both. The fates push us in one direction or the other, but it's up to us to take the path."

"What if the path fate chooses is hard or even deadly?"

Livy is the last person in England I expected to have a meaningful conversation with. Yet, her insight so far is more reasonable than my own worries.

"Hmm..." She props her elbow on her knee and her chin on her fist. "You strike me as the kind of man who usually does what's right. I imagine you'll continue to do so with or without fate prodding you."

"And here I thought I was portraying myself as a reckless vagabond." I force a gin.

She nudges my shoulder with hers. "I have a way of knowing people. I know I don't look it, but I see people. I'll admit my vision was clouded about Miss Ware because of the witchcraft, but you I always saw as a good and honest man."

"You know I'm a witch as well."

"I know. Seems witches are part of Windsor and always will be." She shrugs and stands. "You might spend less time worrying over things left to fate and more time finding happiness with that lady of yours." Livy gives me a wink and goes inside. Her house is nearly finished. We've painted and papered, fixed doors, floors, and fixed the pump handle on the well at the back.

I walk toward the coven house, musing over Livy's insights. The streets are vibrant with people finishing their day's work and heading home for a day off or a good meal. The coven will gather for the Sabbath and a feast. My step quickens while I think about seeing Sara Beth. She's not invited me back to her bed, though we talk after dinner each evening. I enjoy getting to know her almost as much as holding her in my arms.

Goddess said there will be no peace if we're apart. Peace sounds like heaven. I don't know if I've ever known true ease in life. I'm always running from the past and into the future. What would it be like to live in the present?

I open the door and step inside the coven house, and I'm immediately struck by the familiar magic of my family. Raising my hands, I put up a shield while my eyes adjust from the bright day.

When my vision clears, my brother smiles from the chair near the hearth. "You don't have to protect yourself, Adam. I've come on a peaceful mission."

Sara Beth and Sylvia sit with him, having tea around a small table. Sara Beth raises her brows. "Your brother was just telling us tales about your wild childhood in the Highlands."

I'll bet he was. I lower my shield and step closer. "What brings you to Windsor, Kaden?"

He stands and holds out his hand. "I heard you were here and wished to see you."

I walk to stand between him and the ladies. "I'm sure there is more to your visit than missing me," I say with sarcasm.

"You didn't tell us you had a twin brother." Sylvia sips her tea. "When Kaden said you were twins, we didn't believe him."

"We are not identical." I state the obvious. I have red hair and fair skin while Kaden has dark hair and smooth, tanned skin. Our eyes and height are the only similarities. "In fact, other than being born on the same day and sharing parents, we have little in common."

Sara Beth flicks her wrist, and a fourth chair slides from the side of the room and stops next to hers. "Sit, Adam. You brother is telling the story of collecting frogs for some nefarious deed."

Even though the story Kaden is telling is about the harmless antics of eight-year-old boys, I wish to make everyone stop listening to him. "That's an old story." I sit.

Kaden returns to his chair and picks up his tea. His eyes flash with familiar mischief. "Adam likes to correct my storytelling."

"I'll not say a word." If he adds or lies, I'll let him have his way. If these witches believe him, they're fools. It's so obvious he doesn't belong here. I push down my anger. There's no reason to be cross with Sylvia or Sara Beth. They've only asked him for tea, and they didn't bring him upstairs, so there must be some caution in that. Holding my tongue, I listen.

"We had a fine plan to scare the high priest. He had commanded we bring him three bull frogs for his potions. Adam was already quite good at calling animals but refused to call them and send them to their deaths. It's just frogs, I told him. He wouldn't budge." Kaden smirks, as if this was ridiculous.

"My view on the subject hasn't changed," I say without letting emotion into my voice.

Sara Beth says softly in my head, *"Calm, Adam. Stay calm."*

I can't say if she used magic, but my heart slows, and my worry eases. I want to reach across and take her hand but resist the urge. Letting Kaden know I care for Sara Beth would be a mistake.

"Of course not," Kaden scoffs. "Anyway, he wouldn't call the frogs, so we had to go out to the pond at night and gather them. We were cold and muddy when we went home with our assignment complete. We put the frogs in a bucket and covered it. Mother wouldn't let us in the house until we'd washed, so we stayed the night in the barn to avoid a bath."

Joy threads around my heart as I remember my mother scolding us for not wanting to bathe, and then bringing blankets out to the barn in the middle of the night. I wonder if Kaden remembers how kind she was, or only that she wanted him to do something he hated.

"In the morning," Kaden continues. "We went to coven house with our bucket. Still covered in mud that was now dry and cracking, we looked a sight." He laughs. "I was still annoyed with Adam. I punched him, saying that he could have called hundreds of frogs with a spell and saved us from a night with the cow."

"He was mad because the cow chewed his shoe." Hearing the story brings on longing for the times when we were still innocent.

"I was." Kaden fiddles with the edge of his threadbare coat. Whatever else is happening in his life, he's not earning a wage. "I badgered him relentlessly on the walk to make our delivery. By the time we arrived, Adam was furious with me, and maybe he too regretted not using magic.

"He turned to me at the door to the still room, put the bucket on the floor in front of the high priest, and said he'd show me magic. When old Bart Stone opened the bucket, a steady stream of frogs jumped out. There must have been fifty. Bart jumped on top of the table in the still room. No easy feat, as he was hefty in the extreme."

"There were exactly one hundred frogs." I shrug. "It was just an illusion. Though, it was funny when Bart jumped on the table and screamed like a fishwife that he was going to feed us frog guts for a year."

Kaden and Sylvia laugh. Sara Beth smiles, and her warmth washes over me.

Kaden places his empty teacup in the saucer and stands. "I

wonder if you might take a walk with me, Adam. I'd like to speak with you, and I won't be in Windsor long."

The hair on the back of my neck stands up. What can he want? Whatever it is, I'm not going to like it. I nod. Turning to Sara Beth, I ask, "Can I get anything for tonight while I'm out?"

"We have it well in hand. I've asked your brother to join us for the Sabbath."

The thought of Kaden above stairs here sends rage through me. "I see."

"We have a large crowd tonight. We'll celebrate down here. After dinner, we usually invite the neighborhood to join us. It should be fun." She sends that calm through me again.

"I'll be back in time to help with preparations." I walk into the alley with Kaden right behind me.

With a wave to the baker's wife patting flour from her apron, I turn down the street. "What is it you want?"

"Brother, you are too harsh. I want to see you. It has been a long time." The sincerity in his voice just makes me trust him less.

Stopping, I face him. "You and I both know there is no length of time that will put enough distance between us, Kaden. What do you want?"

"Nothing." He spreads his arms like a knight proving he's unarmed. "It's been seven years since we caught up with you that one time. Don't you think a man can change after being on his own for so long?"

"And you are on your own?" I seriously doubt he is.

"Ariana is not with me. She left me six months after we last saw you. She tricked me, Adam. I'd never have done those things on my own. She bespelled me." Remorse shadows his eyes.

While I want to believe him, I know better. "Where is Ariana now?"

He shrugs. "I have no idea. She might be dead or found employment in a whorehouse for all I know."

Even knowing that my sister is pure evil, I cringe at the idea of her prostituting herself. Brushing those stupid thoughts aside, I ask, "How did you find me?"

"You are easy to find, Adam. You leave a trail of magic tricks behind you. I noticed several years ago that people would speak of a Scot who performed in the square. I followed the trail, and finally you stayed in a place long enough for me to catch up." He grins.

Walking on, I'm kicking myself for being found, perhaps endangering this coven.

Goddess's whisper echoes in my head. *Goddess wills our paths merge. If evil be known, it will be known, but apart there will be no peace.*

"Kaden, I don't want you here. I don't want you in my life. You poison everything and everyone around you. Tell me what you want, so I can tell you no, and you can leave Windsor." We reach the river and stop.

Hands on his hips, he shakes his head. "Brother, you will have to accept that I have changed. I will prove myself to you. Ariana tricked us, but me worst of all. She forced me to do things I will always regret. I've lived with those things for all these years. I want my only family to accept me again. That's why I'm here."

"No. Now go." I turn and walk back to the coven house.

It never had any hope of working. Kaden isn't the kind of person to accept another's decision if it doesn't match what he wants. Maybe if he'd left Windsor and said nothing more, there would be a speck of hope that he'd changed. But he's following a safe distance behind me, just as I knew he would. Whatever it is he wants will come out eventually.

When I reach the house, I say hello to June and Trina, who

stare from the long table they're setting. "My brother will return here shortly. Don't let him upstairs."

Wide-eyed, June nods.

Ignoring whoever is in the dining room, I jog upstairs, go to my bedroom and close the door. I need to settle my emotions. I can't let him get to me. Protecting this house has to be my first priority.

I know Sara Beth is outside my door before she knocks. "Come in."

Stepping inside, she watches me, then closes the door behind her. "How can I help?"

"I thought you'd want to know why I didn't tell you I was a twin."

She sits on the chair by my desk. "I have many questions, Adam. You keep many secrets, and I've known that since you came to us. I still would like to help."

"You should send me away. He'll go if I go." I could have my things packed in a matter of minutes. It's what I should do, but my heart aches at the thought.

Her lips purse. "Would he? Do you think he's come to harm you? He said he only wishes to have his family back. It's not so different from why you came here."

Fury rises inside me, and I have to close my eyes and breathe through it. "I am not like him." I get up and pace the room.

Standing, Sara Beth crosses her arms. Her dark-blue dress is a stark contrast to her fair skin. With a narrowed gaze, she studies me. "All right, Adam. Since you won't tell me how I can help, and you are clearly hiding things, why didn't you tell me you are a twin?"

"I don't want to be considered in the same breath as him." It's the excuse I've always given when my brother and I are compared.

"Because he is bad, and you are good?" Bitterness rings in her tone.

"I never said I was good. I'm the cause of him being here. I never should have stayed this long." As hard as I try not to raise my voice, it rings off the walls.

"No. I suppose you didn't." She turns and walks to the door.

Rushing over, I grab her hand on the doorknob. "My intentions are honorable, even if my character is lacking, Beth." The scent of woodland flowers and Sara Beth is a heady combination as her hair brushes my cheek.

Regret flashes in her eyes. "Go if you want, Adam. Your brother hasn't given me a reason to force him from town, but if he does, I am perfectly capable of removing him. If you are his prey, then perhaps you should go. I have a king to protect. I'll not be distracted by one brother so the other might slip into the castle."

It's like a knife to my gut. This is what she thinks of me. Why would she give herself to a man she believed capable of what she accuses? I pull my hand away from her. "I see. You take my silence on the subject of Kaden as proof of me being in league with whatever his purpose is." I hadn't expected her doubts to hurt so much, but the pain is palpable.

"You are silent on all subjects that matter. You say the link between us is a gift, yet you close me out of anything important in your past. I see the walls you've erected to keep me out." Her tone is biting and angry, and her fists clench at her sides.

Stepping back, I want to flee as much as I want to fall at her feet and beg her forgiveness. "If you wanted to know what lurks behind those walls, you would break them down, Beth. Clearly, you'd rather be ignorant. Perhaps so you might justify letting me in your bed."

She gasps, and the muscle in her jaw ticks. "I have a Sabbath to get ready for. You and I should speak when our tempers have cooled. I find I'm unable to think clearly at the moment."

Her honesty shames me. "I'm sorry, Beth."

"Perhaps you shouldn't call me that. Perhaps all of this was a mistake. Even Goddess can be wrong." Voice soft, she stares at her feet and opens the door.

Aching heart, I can't bear the idea that she thinks our time together an accident. "Magic doesn't make mistakes."

She stills. "That may be so, Adam." She looks at me, her eyes glistening. "Answer one question."

Is she crying over me? My heart feels as if it's being torn in two. "What is your question?"

"Who is Ariana?"

Every hope and dream I may have had for a life in Windsor or a life with Sara Beth collapses into a heap of misery. "Did Kaden tell you of her?"

Standing in the open door, she's half in and half out of my life. "No. I heard her name in your head when you first saw your brother."

There is no way to win. No matter what I do, the past always catches up with me. "Ariana is my sister. She is younger by six years. From the time she was a little girl, her intentions were dark. Our parents tried to save her. They sent her to the priestesses and the Order at Glasgow, but it went badly, and lives were lost."

"Your sister killed your parents, but you blame Kaden." She says it as if it's a fact rather than a theory.

"Kaden helped Ariana escape the Order. He didn't believe her capable of hurting anyone. He brought her to the new home we'd made after we were banished from our clan, and the consequence was our parents' lives. Ariana had gotten a taste for killing and found it appealed to her." I collapse on the edge of the bed. "She manipulated Kaden, and maybe she has him in thrall. I don't really know. He says he hasn't seen her in many years, but I don't believe him."

She dashes a tear away. "Why didn't you tell me?"

Feeling helpless where Ariana is concerned is familiar. "She's my baby sister. Kaden veers toward dark. I've always known. He's not without magic, but it's Ariana who holds real power. I had hoped they were left in the past, and I would never have to tell anyone about them."

"The past has a way of catching up." She backs out of my room and closes the door.

CHAPTER
NINE

SARA BETH

Sabbath goes on regardless of the drama that played out earlier. The long table stretches half the length of the lower gathering room. Most coven members are in attendance. A feast is laid with chicken, pork, turnips, carrots, and potatoes.

The crowd is lively, and at the far end, Kaden MacNab commands a feminine audience keen on his levity.

Three places down on my left, Adam scowls and eats his chicken as if the poor animal did him harm.

Sylvia's laughter cuts through the din, as she enjoys a having a new man in the house. It's probably the first time in two hundred years five men sat at the coven table for a meal.

Seated next to Sir William, Henry Dove looks ready to fight for her attention, though he says and does nothing.

More country witches than usual are present for Sabbath.

I lean toward Prudence. "Great Mother, what do you think of the addition to the group we've assembled tonight?"

"Sabbath is often a time to see how a coven melds. This coven is in transition. I see warmth." She points to William and Esme chatting with Minerva and Jonah. "Family." She gestures to June at a small table caring for the two toddlers. "Frivolity is a nice inclusion." She smiles down the table at the ladies vying for Kaden's attention.

"I don't think he's living in the light of Goddess." My gut twists with an all too familiar worry. If Kaden is dark, then what of Adam? "Perhaps not, but he's not looking to become part of our coven. I'm not entirely certain why Kaden has come."

Prudence levels her gray eyes on me. "What will you do?"

A wiser witch wouldn't have invited an unknown to her bed, but I can't regret the night spent with him. Each evening, I sense his desire to be back in the sheets with me, but I resist. Now that part of his past has been revealed, perhaps that was the smartest thing I've done regarding Adam MacNab. "Wait and see. It's better to have Kaden close and watch over him than be surprised by him."

"It is wise to keep your enemies close." She eats a few bites of mashed turnips with butter and cream.

"Are we certain he's an enemy?" Kaden and Adam are so different yet so similar.

Winnie Treacher leans over and says something to Adam.

He laughs, and his smile sends a thrill to my belly.

With a steady glare down the table, Prudence says, "He is not a friend, but I can't say for certain he's an adversary. He bears watching." She eats the last of her food. "I noticed the friendship between you and Adam has cooled. Is his brother the reason?"

"Caution is the reason." It's honest enough that Prudence won't ask any more personal questions during a crowded feast. In the past, I might have been furious with Adam for withholding vital information. The last few years have taught me that people remain silent on subjects for many reasons, and they are not all bad. Still, him having two dark witches in his family could be a sign I should remain wary.

The meal ends, and witches clear the table. The tables are moved to the sides of the room. Neighbors begin to filter in, each bringing some kind of sweet or wine. Several stand in the corner with fiddles and a bass and begin playing a lively tune.

Sylvia and Kaden start dancing, and others join in.

I take a small glass of wine and make sure to speak to each of our neighbors. Many of them have been raised next door to the coven, as had their parents before them.

The music grows soft, and Sylvia joins me by the door for some air. "You should dance, Sara Beth."

"You like this Kaden?" I ask. Sylvia isn't one to hold back, and I've always felt I could be direct with her.

She shrugs. "He's fun and full of life. Not the settling-down type though."

Smiling so the others in the room don't know the serious nature of our conversation, I ask, "Is he worth alienating a man who might be the settling-down type and certainly has shown his interest in you?"

With a quick scan of the room, her gaze settles on Henry standing like a guard by the back door. "Henry Dove is not a witch."

"No. Is that a quality that's important to you?" I feel Adam's attention on me but force myself not to look for him.

Wide-eyed, she stutters. "I never considered the—I mean, I'm not a bigot. It's only that I always assumed if I settled down it would be with a witch."

"Ideas change. Just look how much this house of ours has changed in the last year or so. If Kaden is worth losing the way Henry looks at you, then find your joy where you can, Sylvia. I only want to point out that you seemed to enjoy Henry's attention for the last several months."

Men, women, and witches all in one place and enjoying the bounty of life on a Sabbath night. It's a fine night.

Adam's warmth seeps through my skin before I turn toward him. His thoughts are blocked, but his eyes are caring. "I wonder if you would care to dance with me, high priestess?"

My pulse speeds, and I take his hand. "I would like that."

With a grin from ear to ear, Sylvia nudges me with her shoulder. "Thank you for the advice."

I step into Adam's arms, and he wraps one around my waist while taking my hand. "I'm sorry if I seemed cross earlier."

"Don't apologize, Beth. You should be cross. I should be honest. I'm so afraid to lose this new place, as I've lost others before, I may have hidden too much and caused my own troubles." Usually, his eyes are bright, but the light is dim in him.

"Perhaps tomorrow you and I might take some time, and you could relieve some of your burdens. Do you think you're ready to tell me what happened in Scotland that led to banishment and the rest?" I'm half holding my breath. I need him to trust me, but I hardly trust myself.

"You will send me away." The low rumble of fear in his voice hardly sounds like him.

I cup his cheek. "I will try to keep an open mind. I can't promise any more than that."

Turning his head, he kisses my palm, and his lips send a shockwave of pleasure through me. "Thank you."

I lean into his body, and we sway to the music.

Kaden watches from the corner, all the lively joking gone from his expression.

A shiver runs up my spine. "I'm not going to send your

brother away. I think it might be better to keep him close and keep an eye on him."

"And if he seduces half the coven before he shows his true colors?" He sighs and moves us around the room. "What then?"

I stand up straight and meet Adam's gaze. "Do you think him capable of turning good witches bad? Can he wield that kind of magic?" The horror of the spells put on the Kent witches last year still haunts me. They were possessed and in thrall for over a year. They were forced to kill and curse. Some died in the battle to save the Windsor coven and what remained of Kent. Once the demon Forrester had been banished, the bulk of the possessed witches recovered. I lost a witch in the battle and watched the lover from my youth, Orin, die that night.

"I don't know. This is the first time he's caught up to me in seven years. Usually, I can feel him coming. I must have been distracted." He tightens his hold on my waist.

"How do you feel him? Is it the same as the sense between you and me?" A niggling worry that I've been manipulated scratches at the back of my mind. I heard Goddess; he couldn't have misled me. Could he?

Shaking his head, he waits for me to look at him. "Nothing is like the connection with you, Beth. My brother is my twin. When he is near, I usually feel him like a pin prick at the base of my skull. It's not painful, but I know when he's near. Yet I didn't feel him until I was at the door today. He blocked me from knowing he'd come. He knew I'd run if I felt him coming."

The idea that he'd leave without a word is like a knife in my heart. "I hope you'll say goodbye if you decide to move on, Adam."

The music ends, forcing him to release me. He bows. "I don't want to go anywhere."

"I've recently learned that there is nothing wrong with fleeing, but sometimes one must stand and fight." A knot forms in my throat, preventing me from saying more.

"Having harm come to anyone in Windsor because of me would be unbearable." He backs away and walks out the alley door.

I go in the other direction and check on Prudence. She's holding court by the hearth. Five witches are listening to an old story about my mother and six kittens who lived in the house for a time. I've heard the story a hundred times, but it still brings me joy to hear it told.

"Will you dance with me as you did with my brother, high priestess?" Kaden's soft voice is inches from my ear.

I take a step away before I turn. "Adam and I are good friends. I will dance with you as a lady might dance with a new acquaintance." I send the thought of a reel toward the musicians and the music changes.

Kaden raises his eyebrow and offers his hand. When we reach the lines of dancers, he stands across from me. When we come together, he asks, "How long have you known my brother?"

"I hardly know. It seems the witches of Windsor have always known him."

"A very diplomatic answer." He dances well, as if he's been doing it all his life. "I wonder how he's made such a fine impression on you and the other witches. It seems everyone likes Adam."

"Are you going to warn me off him?" I fumble through the dancing as my temper rises, but I keep my emotions hidden.

He grins. "Why not? I'm sure he's warned you off me."

Somehow that makes me even angrier because of the truth in it. "Why don't you just dance, Kaden, and not speculate? Why ruin such a fine reel?"

With a slight bow of his head, he grins, and we dance the remainder in silence.

I've never been gladder to have a dance end. At the finish, instead of Kaden looking at me, he glares over my shoulder.

Adam is watching from the edge of the room. Leaning against the wall, with his arms crossed, he looks like a man at his leisure, but fire simmers in his eyes.

Minerva touches Adam's arm and says something.

The rage eases from him, and he turns to chat with her and Jonah.

Even as a fire witch, Minerva can sense someone's distress and calm them. It's one of her many gifts.

There are far too many stories and worries for a Sabbath. Once the party starts to wind down, I go to my room. The coven will put everything right before they go to bed, and no doubt Adam will make certain Kaden leaves the premises before the doors close for the night.

After removing my shoes and gown, I sit in my chemise in the middle of my bed with my legs crossed. Drawing long slow breaths, I calm my mind. I let my senses open to the house around me. Each witch, and the others too, come into my consciousness. One by one, I feel them exit the house. Each has a light associated with them, and the colors are myriad blues, whites, yellows, reds, and greens. Auras tell much about each person.

My instinct carries me to Adam, who glows a buttery gold with the flicker of green, blue, and red. The nature of his magic churns like a rainbow within his aura. At the threshold of the front door, he stands with Kaden, who glows a muddy red with a hint of green trying to push through.

A person's aura can change over a lifetime of decisions. I wonder if Kaden's wasn't once the green of an earth witch but has been muddied by the darkness of his choices.

As he strides away, he turns back once before continuing out of the neighborhood.

I return my attention to the house, and the calm of coven witches cleaning up rolls through me. Peace and joy reside within the witches after a lovely Sabbath.

Protection spells already cover the coven and castle, but I send fresh magic and the strength of the goddess within me into the night for added security.

Kaden MacNab has done nothing to create my trepidation, but part of me must trust Adam enough to be cautious. Joy flickers inside me at that realization.

I watch the house in its sheer energy within me. Prudence took to her bed hours earlier and sleeps peacefully. Duty complete, Sylvia leaves for the night with Henry Dove to walk her home. More witches leave for their homes as Trina and June sit near the hearth talking. Minerva and Jonah have gotten distracted by something in the still room.

Slow steps on the stairs draw my inner gaze to Adam as he climbs and turns down the hallway. He stops at his door but doesn't enter.

My heart pounds, but I do nothing to dissuade or attract him. Calming my breath, I let Goddess's comfort flow around and through me.

He continues down the hall, and finding my door unlocked, steps inside. "Should I leave you, Beth?"

I long for him in ways I never thought I'd long for another person in this lifetime, and I can't make myself send him away.

The bed dips, and Adam sits behind me. He wraps his arms around me and cradles my legs with his. "If you wish me to find my own bed, I will go. I only needed to hold you." His lips press lightly on the back of my neck.

As he moves to leave, I stay him with a hand on his knee. "Don't go."

His hand tightens under the curve of my breast and the other over my abdomen. My sheer shift is no match for the heat vibrating off him. "Seeing you sitting like this with the hint of flesh showing takes my breath away. You're the most beautiful sight I've ever gazed upon. You should send me away, but you don't. You should banish me and my family from Windsor, but you don't. I confess, I don't understand you, Beth. And I long to know what is in your mind."

Closing my hand over his, I ease it over my breast. "One day, perhaps we shall have the kind of trust that allows our connection to flow openly." I sigh as he squeezes and molds me to his rough hand.

Lightening his touch, he grazes my nipple, pulling a soft cry from my lips.

Desire pools between my crossed legs. "I want you, Adam."

"I've never wanted anything or anyone as I do you, Beth." He nips the flesh just behind my ear and traces a path with his tongue to the crease of my shoulder before kissing his way back up and circling my ear.

The sensation is too much. Longing for relief, I clutch between my legs.

As my body lightens and lifts from the bed, soft fabric traces an erotic path over my hips, waist, back, breasts, and I raise my arms as it floats away.

His magic is light and gentle. His arms band around me as if he can't let go. Pressing a finger between my thighs, he whispers, "Let me."

Still sitting with his legs cradling mine in a meditation pose, I'm completely open to his exploring fingers as I settle back to the bed. Pressure on my pearl sends waves of pleasure through me. I arch and press my head back against his shoulder.

His slips two fingers through my folds. "So wet and beautiful, Beth."

I want to hear him say my name every day for all my lives. Its prayerlike quality folds around me, luring me in for more of him. My hair falls from the braided bun and unwinds with his gentle magic. "Your magic is lovely." The words barely get out of my mouth as a soft cry of pleasure accompanies them.

His fingers press inside me while teasing my sensitive pearl, bringing me closer to my release.

Relentless, he tortures me with pleasure. Cupping the back of my head with his other hand, he turns my head, covers my open mouth with his, and thrusts his tongue inside. Our tongues slip together. His fingers press harder and faster.

I scream into his mouth as my orgasm crashes down around me.

His fingers still, and I grind against his hand while my body shakes with rapture. Kissing me softer and more thoroughly, he sighs. "You are spectacular."

"Have you bespelled me, Adam?" I'm half serious.

He stills. "No more than you have me, Beth. Believe me, I have never longed for anyone as I do for you. When you say my name, I'm lost in a lifetime of possibilities. Even though I know it's not likely I'll be able to stay with you. Even though I'm certain I should leave and pray my brother follows me away from here. I can't leave while you don't demand it. Tell me to go. Command me to get out of your bed, your house, and this town. Make me do the right thing, my dear one."

I turn, forcing him to his back.

Thick and long, his shaft stands at attention. I lick the very tip, and I let my body skim over his until we're face to face. "Tell me you'll stand and fight whatever evil threatens the king or this house."

"I will never let harm come to you or those you protect." His eyes are wide, as if his answer surprises him.

CHAPTER
TEN

ADAM

I would die for her. Have I ever thought that with regard to anyone else? I would die for this woman and the things that are important to her. Lifting my head, I kiss her full mouth and suck her tongue before giving her mine to do the same.

She groans and bends her knees to straddle me.

There are so many things I want to tell her, so much I long to promise, but as she lowers her body onto my cock, I can focus on nothing but pleasure. "*Beth.*"

Gripping her breasts, she presses her knees to the mattress and rides me like a goddess off to battle. She rises and falls, pulling me deep within her perfect body. When she falters, I grip her waist and set a steady pace.

My body thrills with the coming little death. My legs tingle.

She quickens her pace, and I press my thumb to her bud,

bringing her over the edge. Inside, her muscles pulse, drawing my orgasm hard and fast.

Thrusting up, I hold her hips, ready to pull her away the moment before I spill my seed.

"No," she commands and presses her hips down to keep me within her. Hard and fast, her pleasure stretches beyond mine. I pull her chest over mine and muffle her cries with kisses.

Her hair spreads over my chest like black flames. Her back rises and falls with each heaving breath.

Clutching her to me, I want to stay connected for as long as Goddess will allow. I love being inside this woman. I love the niggling of her mind so close to mine. As she suggested, one day, I pray we shall have the kind of trust needed to open ourselves completely.

She presses her palms to my chest, and still intimately connected, looks into my eyes. "I needed to feel all of you."

"It was wonderful." My cock jerks to life despite being spent a moment earlier.

She shifts to deepen our connection. "Should we talk of important things or leave those things for the morning?"

Gripping her tight, I roll her to her back.

She wraps her legs around my thighs. "I'm guessing you're in no hurry for a long talk."

"Nothing would please me more than talking, but you seemed determined for pleasure first. I can deny you nothing." Though I said it to be light, I immediately realize I mean every word. I would give her anything she asked for, so why not the entire truth?

Going still beneath me, she cocks her head. "What thoughts took you away from me just now?"

With a heavy heart, I pull from the comfort of her body.

"We should talk, Beth." I grab my trousers from the floor next to the bed and pull them on before sitting again.

She grabs her white robe from the bedpost and wraps it around herself. "Is it because you spilled within me? Do you worry there will be a child?"

An image of Sara Beth full with our child floats through my head. Pleasure so bright floods me. "I would revel in the greatest joy if I could be a father to our child."

She sits next to me. "What an odd way of phrasing that. Have you plans to leave even if you are accepted here?"

"I have little faith that you will want me after I tell you the full story of Ariana and Kaden." My chest aches with the pain of leaving her and Windsor.

"Tell me or don't, but don't let the past poison every moment of our time together," she scolds.

The sun begins its assent, and we've had no sleep. This is bad timing, but it can't be helped. "It might be best if we wake the great mother, and I tell you both."

She closes her eyes, and her worry lines ease. Looking at me, she says, "Great Mother is already awake. She's taking her morning tea in the dining room, and she is alone."

Any hope of a few minutes to gather my wits dies. I tug my shirt over my head. "I'll just go to my own room and wash up. I'll meet you in a moment."

Expression stern, and with a deep worry line between her eyes, she goes to her basin. Her back is straight and rigid as a pine.

I walk to her side and kiss her cheek. "Should this end badly, know that I am sorry, Beth."

Without waiting for a reply, I go to my room, wash, and put on fresh clothes. The small mirror reveals a man I hardly recognize. Where is the magic man who entertains crowds for coin and keeps those around him laughing? Have I finally met my match in all things? Has Sara Beth's serious nature subdued my frivolity? Could I bring lightness to her formal ways?

Looking around the room, I wonder if this is the last time I'll see it. My brain screams, run as fast and as far from here as you can, Adam MacNab. You have no business among good witches. My heart speaks of loyalty and family. I look at my empty bag next to the wardrobe and consider readying it for travel but dismiss the idea. If I must go, I'll have time to pack. When everything you own fits into one bag, there's little fuss in the leaving.

Drawing a full breath, as if it might be my last, I step into the hallway, and then I walk to the dining room.

Sara Beth's hair is braided once again and pulled into a tight bun. She leans in and speaks in hushed tones with Prudence.

The great mother nods, her expression solemn but not angry or disappointed.

They both turn as I enter. "Good morning." I sit across from Sara Beth so that I can face them both. If the inquisition is to come, I shall meet it head on.

"Would you like tea?" Great Mother asks.

"No. If I said yes, it would only be to stall. I've withheld my past long enough. I am sorry for misleading you both." My chest is so tight, I have a vain hope I may die before I tell the story.

Prudence pats my hand on the table. "The funny thing about the past is that while it haunts us, it need not define us."

Surprise rockets through me. "Are we not all products of our past?"

"Yes, but it does not stand that we become one thing or the other based on it. I would assume you and your brother lived a similar childhood. You grew up in the same home with the same parents. You were both six years old when your mother birthed a daughter." Prudence stares with her brows raised in a knowing way that is unsettling.

My hands shake, and I clutch them together. "You know about Ariana. You knew before you invited me here?"

With a hint of a smile, she says, "I know a great deal about the witching world on this island and beyond. I have lived a long time and corresponded with a great many old friends."

Thinking of the elders of my birth clan and coven, I wonder who spoke of my family to Prudence. "Why did you correspond with me, Great Mother, when you know what I am?"

"I know nothing of that." She sighs. "Tell your tale. Let Sara Beth hear what haunts your past. It is not for me to decide the coven's business."

I look at the door just off the dining room where Trina sleeps.

"She was up until almost dawn. She'll not disturb us." Sara Beth sips her tea, keeping her eyes leveled on me.

My heart may pound out of my chest. "I suppose, I must go back to when we were exiled from our clan. Kaden and I were eighteen. Ariana was only twelve but had already begun to dabble in dark magic. The right hand of the high priest caught her bringing a cat back to life. She'd claimed that killing the cat had been an accident, but the magic was forbidden. Pressure from the coven pushed my mother into writing to the Order in Glasgow."

The sound of my mother's weeping still rings in my ears.

"The Order sent three witches to evaluate Ariana. With their black robes and dour faces, they were terrifying to me.

"At the full moon, they made a sacred circle and placed Ariana in the center. They threw spells at her to see if she would block them. I remember that one caused a rash. Ariana didn't cast against them, but she healed her itching skin with ease. They flooded the circle, cast fire and a whirlwind. Each spell dissipated when met with Ariana's magic." The memories grate on my mind. All the things I've tried to forget flood back as if they happened yesterday.

Drawing a long breath, I pray for Goddess's strength. "Perhaps they grew angry at her for her power, or perhaps they were desperate. I don't know, but the spells became more harmful and vicious. Ariana continued to fight the spells, and then cast one against a witch. It was a simple air spell that only pushed the witch back three steps.

"When that didn't stop their assault on her, Ariana ripped through the veil with magic. I think she intended to escape through the other side, but it wasn't Goddess's arms she lurched for. What I saw in that hole was evil and full of horror."

I have to stop and close my eyes to shake off the images that haunted me for years. Sara Beth presses her hand to my shoulder. "If this is too difficult, we can talk again later."

Shaking my head, I look into her dark eyes for strength. "No. I'll tell the rest." I sit up straight. "The holy order deemed her evil but savable. They bound her magic and took her away that night.

"For the Inverness coven, our clan, our family, it was too much. No one could have guessed that Ariana would search out enemies of Goddess for protection. The high priest listed everything any of us had ever done to offend him right back to the frogs in his banishment of our family. He gave us until the new moon, but we left while the moon was still bright."

"Where did you go?" Prudence's eyes are kind and full of sympathy.

"We traveled south to be closer to Ariana. Mother hoped that she would be healed and returned to us. We settled a few hours' ride from Glasgow. Mother wrote to the Order weekly but was told each time that Ariana had not improved.

"We didn't know Kaden also wrote directly to Ariana and

had his letters delivered by a pigeon he'd enchanted. Ariana convinced him she was fine and had repented all her dark ways. He was so convinced, that on Ariana's fourteenth birthday, he went to Glasgow and helped her escape the holy order." My gut twists with regret. I should have known what Kaden was doing. I should have stopped him. But after what I had seen in that evil place, his support of Ariana angered me, and I kept my distance from him. Maybe if I'd been a better brother, Kaden would be in the light.

Swallowing my guilt isn't easy, but I've spent years perfecting it. "Ariana could have just walked out with Kaden's help. From what I know, there was no resistance as the witches were in prayer. It wasn't enough for her. She entered the sanctuary and killed three of them.

"When Kaden arrived home with Ariana, we knew nothing of the murders. My parents were overjoyed to have her home. She was happy and sweet. Kaden was ashen and refused to speak to me of his troubles. Honestly, I didn't try very hard to get him to open up. I didn't think a witch who would run into hell should be in our midst, even if she was my sister.

"A few days later, Father received a letter with the horrors of Ariana's exit from Glasgow. When he confronted her, she grew ugly with fury and slit his throat with fire magic. Mother ran to stop her, and Ariana set her aflame." I'm shaking with the memory, but I need to get the rest out before I lose my courage.

Sara Beth takes my hand. In my head, she says, *"I'm with you."*

That reassurance is more than enough to calm me. "I threw a blanket over my mother and put out the fire, but it was too late.

"Kaden stared wide eyed until Ariana took his hand. She said they had to leave, and he followed her without a word.

She told me to come with them, but I stayed and buried my parents. After I'd said all the prayers I could think of, I ran the other way."

Calmly, softly, Prudence asks, "Did you ever see your siblings after that?"

I nod and wonder if I'd have been better off if Ariana had killed me too.

"No," Sara Beth whispers softly in my head.

There is comfort in her caring that I live. "A year after she killed my parents, they found me working in a potato field. We made arrangements to meet the next day as I had the day off. They both looked as if nothing had ever gone wrong. They were clean and well dressed, without a care in the world."

"You didn't meet them the next day." Sara Beth squeezes my hand.

"No. I ran that night and have kept ahead of them for the last seven years since. Yesterday was the first time they caught up to me again." Exhausted, I finish my story and wait to be banished from Windsor and Sara Beth.

CHAPTER
ELEVEN

SARA BETH

The terrifying tale sends shivers through me, but also relief. I tug his hand, so he looks me in the eye. "What you have told us is one of the most dreadful stories I've ever heard, Adam. You know you are not to blame. If you've told us the truth, and I sense no falsehood from you, you are not at fault. Your guilt is understandable but unwarranted."

His shoulders straighten as he stares at me and then looks at Prudence. "You're not sending me away?"

"No," I say.

Patting his cheek, Prudence smiles, revealing a few missing teeth. "You are not to blame for the actions of your sister. I even feel sympathy for Kaden, though his path has not been totally in the light. I'm not convinced that path isn't determined by Ariana." She shrugs her thin shoulders. "That is not as troubling as why they keep trying to gain access to you."

"I don't know," he says, and his gaze is faraway. "I have felt them approach in the last few years, but I have always run away before they reached me."

"You've thought about it though?" I prod him for more, but gently. Reliving this terrible past has taken the warmth from his cheeks.

He combs his fingers through his hair and rubs the back of his neck. "I've tried to find some reason they would want me to join them. Other than being siblings, I can't imagine any cause to follow me for so many years."

Prudence sighs and pats our hands. "Go and get some air. Then you should both rest. I will make a few inquiries. There are smarter witches in the world." She laughs.

Without an argument, we head downstairs hand in hand. Air sounds like a good idea. I cast a protection spell around us before we step out the front door.

"How will the great mother contact these smarter witches?" He draws my hand through his elbow but keeps it in his opposite hand. We might be an old married couple strolling together toward the park if I didn't know better. The idea of that sparks joy inside me.

The tingle of my mother's magic niggles at the back of my skull. Not the angry disappointment I'm used to from her, just a sense that she's with me again.

It's comforting.

I say, "Probably through the fire, but she shooed us away because whatever she plans or whomever she'll speak to, she doesn't wish to be witnessed. The great mother is quite remarkable in her friends and her powers."

"So I'm coming to understand." He looks at the ground as we enter the park. "I thought you would send me away. I was certain my blood being the same as Ariana's would force you to banish me."

Disliking the fear in his voice, I lean into him, passing him my admiration as I do. "You've done nothing wrong. I'll not lie. It worries me that they have pursued you all this time. I don't know what your sister wants, but I would guess she needs you to obtain it."

"Bringing danger to Windsor is not what I want. Yet I know Ariana is near, and she is most definitely dangerous. If I am what they need, I should leave here and never come back. It's too much of a risk to have me here with you." He drops my hand and steps a few inches away.

"If you want to leave, you are free to do so." It's impossible to keep the hurt from my voice.

As we walk into a stand of trees, he steps in front of me and faces me. "If it were up to me, I would never be more than an inch away from you, Beth. I would follow you to the ends of this earth. I don't want to leave. I want you, and I want to be a part of your coven. However, I don't want to be the cause of more pain and suffering. The witches of Windsor have endured so much over the last year. Would you bring them into another war?"

Everything he says is true. My family of witches has endured more than most. They have also risen to meet every challenge with magnificence. I'm so proud to lead these witches. Love and pride fill my heart.

He must sense my emotions. His eyes narrow. "I need to know what you're thinking, dear one."

"I think if trouble must come to England, that I'd rather fight it at home than have to find you in a week, a month, or a year to fight by your side. My witches are fierce and strong."

"How can you ask this of them? How can I ask this of you?" His pain permeates my heart.

I consider his questions. "You didn't ask me. I will stand by you, Adam. I will know if you are in danger wherever you are." Perhaps this was too much to declare. It's not like me to share feelings, or even have them, where a man is concerned. That niggling at the back of my head is back.

"What is that?" Eyes wide, he backs away from me. "Is that your mother?"

"You feel that?"

He nods, and his panic is clear from our connection and the way he looks ready to bolt. "I felt it when we arrived at the park, and now again. Is she about to attack me again?"

The niggling softens. "I don't think so. I'm sorry, my mother doesn't speak to me. She only lets me know she's here, and this is the first time I've felt her since Prudence blocked her."

He lets out a long breath and pulls me into a hug. "I'm happy you have your mother back, Beth, but she does not like me. I don't want to be laughed into unconsciousness again."

Glad we're hidden by trees, I relax into his embrace. "I don't want that either. I feel no animosity from her. Just her presence."

He relaxes, and his arms tighten around me. "I'm happy to hear that."

Pulling out of his embrace, I take his hand. "Let's walk. There's a gardener's cottage at the center of the park. It's protected."

He grins. "Why is the gardener's cottage protected? Is he a witch?"

"Not that I'm aware of. I think Minerva protected it. The gardener rarely uses it." I act as if none of this is important. Actually, it isn't, but I like the arousal I sense building inside him, and it fuels my desire.

"Are you hoping for a tryst, Beth? I don't mind, but I would have thought you too serious to steal away in light of the danger I've revealed today." He's grinning.

It's hard to resist his joy. I love the way it rolls through me like a gentle spring rain. What I don't like is how right he is about me. "As lovely as that sounds, Adam, I was thinking about the bench outside the cottage as a good place to rest. Perhaps if we talk, we'll divine what your sister and brother want with you."

His smile widens. "Of course."

Part of me wants to tear down the walls I've erected against the bond between us and know everything he's thinking. Mother's magic niggles, reminding me of a lifetime of lessons where men are the enemy and will steal everything you have.

Outside the simple stone cottage is a lovely view of the wooded section of the park. A small grassy hill is about to bloom with wildflowers, and a soft breeze skims the earth, making everything breathe with life. We sit on the rough wooden bench set between two stones.

Adam takes my hand and kisses my knuckles. "I've wondered for years why they pursue me, and I still have no idea. I'm not sure sitting here with you will change that, but I'm willing to do almost anything to stay near you."

I should scold him for his pretty words. Men use compliments and flirting to lure women in. I need to stay in control of our relationship. It would be easier if I didn't like hearing his sweet words so much. "Tell me about your relationship with your siblings before Ariana was sent away."

Keeping my hand in his, he lifts his shoulders in a heavy sigh. "There's not much to tell. Kaden and Ariana were very close. He was taken with her from the day she was born. Not to say that I didn't love my sister. I did. For Kaden, she was perfect and needed him. He helped Mother each day after our lessons by caring for the baby while I took over much of his chores around the house and farm."

"Did you resent their relationship?" I'm digging for some morsel that will help us fight these people if need be.

With a cock of his head, he says, "No. It was special, and I recognized that. I was still figuring out my magic, and with no other elemental witches to help me, father gave me whatever instruction he could."

"What kind of witch was your father?"

He releases my hand.

The sense of him slips out of my mind and I spin toward him.

Head slumped with his shoulders slack and his eyes closed, he might have fallen asleep, but the way he disappeared from my mind tells me this is not natural. Touching the side of his neck, I feel the steady beat of his pulse, and relief floods me.

I cast an additional protection spell before rising and watching the woods around us. "Are you going to show your-self? Clearly, you wanted to speak to me alone, and now you have my attention." I prop my fists on my hips, hoping it looks like a show of strength while my heart beats wildly.

"You are prettier than I imagined," a woman answers, her voice melodic and feminine.

The oddly worded compliment requires no response but does succeed in annoying me, which I'm sure was the purpose.

She says, "My brother said you were past marrying age. I expected someone with lines around her eyes and mouth. How old are you, Sara Beth Ware?"

"Is that why you took the trouble to render your brother unconscious and get me alone, because you wished to ask about my age? I'm a witch. What difference does it make?" In the shadowy woods, beyond the grassy patch, I glimpse a hint of her figure.

"Come into the clearing, and I'll join you there," she says sweetly.

"So that you can have your henchman snatch up Adam? I don't think so." I stand closer and open my mind a crack. *Where are you, Adam? Fight your way back.*

I feel nothing from Adam.

The girl who steps into the clearing is beautiful, with bright blue eyes and shining red hair. She's dressed in a pale-green dress with butter-colored ribbons flowing from the high waist and fluttering in the breeze. "I will wait for my brother to come to me. He will come. It's only a matter of time. His destiny lies with me and Kaden, not with you."

"What do you want, Ariana MacNab? Why did you want to speak to me alone?" I like being in the shadow of the trees while she is out in the clearing, but her stare tells me she can see me just fine.

She crosses through the grasses to the edge of the woods, looking as if she means to close the rest of the gap. The edge of my protection spell forces her to stop.

I can't help the bead of pleasure that gives me.

Shifting her loose hair from her shoulder to her back, she grins, as if the blockade means nothing. "I thought perhaps we could talk woman to woman and sort this out. Men can be so tiresome, don't you think? Even if those men are my brothers. I asked a simple favor of Kaden. Find Adam and bring him to me for a talk, and he couldn't even manage that."

"Kaden told Adam he wasn't with you. He said you might have become a whore to survive. Did he tell you that?" I make no attempt to hide my disdain, and it rings in my voice. "Now you're here confirming that he lied, and I doubt every word that comes out of your mouth."

She smiles, showing straight white teeth. "It's not surprising you're smart. I understand you became a high priestess at only eighteen. You see, I asked around about you and your coven. Oddly, many people in Windsor know all about you. It's a wonder you and yours aren't burned at the stake by these creatures you live among. I could rid you of the burdens with the flick of my wrist, Miss Ware. No more peasants to protect would make your life so much easier. I will take Adam from here, and you will be free to rule this part of the country, while I take the rest. After all, this is my destiny. It's only that you helped me so much by keeping poor Adam in one place long enough for me to show him the error of his ways. I will gift you Windsor and the surrounding countryside." She waits primly, fussing with the ribbons.

"It's a fine offer, but I'll have to decline. Release Adam and get out of my town, Miss MacNab." I collect magic at my fingertips. *Adam, wake up.* I open my mind farther, and the hint of his consciousness presses back.

Ten feet to Ariana's right, Kaden steps out of the shadows. In brown trousers, coat, and a white shirt, he looks like a servant compared to his sister in her fine dress. His dark hair is dull, and the light in his bright blue eyes has gone. He stops at the edge of my protection spell, touches it, and pulls his hand back as if burned. "Nice magic. I thought you witches only protect the king. Why do you have a spell that bites back?"

Bashing down the remainder of the wall I had erected to keep Adam out of my thoughts, I open my mind fully. *"Pull yourself out of this trance this moment, Adam. I need you."*

Adam blinks awake, and he looks at me. *"I hear you."*

"Your siblings have paid us a visit."

Jumping to his feet, he draws a fireball into his hands. "What do you want?"

Ariana keeps her gaze focused on me. "Impressive magic, high priestess. You are the first to wake someone from one of my trances. How did you do it?"

"It's time for you to leave Windsor, both of you." My wind magic swirls to life, contained in my hands.

She laughs. "You don't have the power to remove me. I'll have you drowned or burned by the very creatures you protect before the week is out." She shifts to look at Adam. "As for you, brother, you will fulfill your destiny, or I'll destroy every witch or human who has ever meant anything to you."

"Why, Ariana? What drives this evil inside you?" Adam asks.

"That is our destiny, Adam. It's what we three were born to do. I was created by those people you loved so much for the purpose of dominating the world. I'll admit, it's taken me longer than I expected. You see, there is power in blood, our blood, together." Ariana lifts her hands, and the air fills with smoke that seeps through my magic.

Gagging, I let loose my air and blow the poison back in her face.

She coughs and doubles over.

Kaden roars and throws his body against my ward. The magic bashes him back, and he lands on his backside. He conjures a fireball and hurls it at us.

It's not strong enough on its own to penetrate my magic, but nothing is unbreakable. The trees catch fire.

With a flick of his wrist, Adam removes the air from the fire and area surrounding his siblings. "You will leave this place."

The fire snuffs out.

Ariana's eyes are wide as she gasps for air. Even so, she beats back the magic with a dark cloud. It's magic I've never seen before. It looks as if her magic has a life of its own, and it pushes back Adam's magic to allow Ariana to breathe again. Whatever it is, as soon as she's safe, it retreats back inside her. "You can't kill me, brother." She gets back on her feet. "Our lives are intertwined. There is no you without me."

Kaden walks to his sister and wraps an arm around her.

Dark rings mar the undersides of Ariana's eyes, her skin is ashen, and she leans against Kaden to keep her feet.

"She's injured by either your magic or her own, Adam. This is over for today. Let them go for now." With my strongest wind ready to help them leave the park, I will Adam to stand down.

Narrowing his eyes, Adam studies his siblings and lowers his hands. "You should leave Windsor before I'm forced to prove you wrong about destiny, Ariana. I don't wish to kill you or Kaden, but I will if you harm anyone in this town."

Her laugh is hollow. "You would kill me over the peasants who bake bread and make shoes? What has happened to you, Adam? Magic is to be used, not hoarded. Become the man you were meant to be."

Warm feelings flow from Adam to me. He shakes his head. "Go away, both of you. Take your evil with you and leave Windsor as the high priestess has commanded. Don't make me force you out."

With a weak laugh, Ariana turns and pads across the clearing. She calls back, "You don't have enough magic to make me do anything, brother. I'm not a little girl anymore."

CHAPTER
TWELVE

ADAM

"**H**ow did she entrance me?" I remember talking to Sara Beth on the bench, and then nothing. Despite the openness of her mind, I speak out loud. "How did you reach me?"

"Through our connection. Once I completely took away the wall I built, you were right there and fully open to me." Body tight, she's hurrying out of the park, toward the coven house. She's worried that Ariana may have struck there.

I know it, but I need to talk. I need to know what was said when I was unconscious.

"I will tell you everything, or you can look in my memories for the information, but I need to see my witches are safe."

Of course, she's worried. What a fool I am. Taking her hand, I pull her to a stop. "If you'll trust me, I'll have us there in a minute to two."

"How?" Her eyes narrow.

I draw my earth magic to me, wrap her in my arms, and ask, "Trust me?"

Wide-eyed, she holds my shoulders.

"Hold on. This may be a bit unnerving for you." I call on the spell to give me the ability to move faster than any man or beast and run through the streets of Windsor. People on the street see only a blur, like a shadow from the corner of their eyes. When they turn to look, we're already long gone.

Within two minutes, we're standing at the back door to the coven house. I lightly place Sara Beth back on her feet. "Are you all right?"

She wobbles for a moment before a wide smile spreads across her face. "One day soon we're going to sit down and talk about all your skills, Adam."

I run my knuckles along her jaw. "You are part of me now, Beth. Look inside me and see all there is. I'll hide nothing from you."

For a moment, I feel her joy. Then it's gone, and she bounds into the house. "Great Mother? Sylvia? June?"

Footsteps on the stairs bring June down with an apron covering her light blue dress. "Is something amiss, Sara Beth?"

Sara Beth walks to the back door and looks out before closing it again. "Is the great mother all right?"

June opens her mouth and stares with shocked eyes as she fusses with the knot tying her apron. "She's sitting at the table upstairs. All is calm here. What happened to the two of you?"

I was so riveted by her moment of happiness at the idea of being a part of me, I didn't even notice her hair sticking out in all directions from speeding through town. Patting my own hair down, I laugh. "We're well, but there is much to tell."

Sylvia stands in the still room doorway with a hand on one hip. "Do I need to call the coven, high priestess?"

With a long breath in and out to calm her nerves and keep

her words even, Sara Beth says, "Not all, but those who I'll need for a consensus."

Sylvia pulls her hair tight and knots it at the back of her head as she rushes inside the still room.

My questions about how she's going to call anyone must slip through our bond. Sara Beth says, "Sylvia is a telepath. She'll contact Esme, Minerva, and Winnie. That will bring the witches we need to explain things."

Upstairs, Prudence stares into her tea. "Trouble is upon us?"

"I'm afraid so, Great Mother," Sara Beth says, sounding resigned to the inevitable.

June asks, "Should Trina and I leave, high priestess?"

Shaking her head, Sara Beth gives the two young witches a small but warm smile. "You should hear what is afoot and decide if you wish to remain for what is to come."

Trina steps in from the kitchen, where she'd been hovering on the threshold and listening. "I'll not leave my sister and brother witches to save myself."

Sara Beth holds up a hand to stop any more declarations. "You'll listen to what we face and what we know, and then you can decide what you wish to do. No witch will be forced to face danger. We've all been through enough. I want everyone to have the opportunity to be safe."

I have brought this trouble upon this coven and this town. "Perhaps if I leave Windsor now, they will follow me. It might be better for everyone if I just pack my bag and go."

"Are you leaving, Adam?" Jonah asks from the top of the stairs. For a giant of a man, he moves very quietly. He's frowning and looking from me to Sara Beth.

Minerva steps around him. "I hope we haven't chased you away, Adam. Tell us what we must do to encourage you to remain in Windsor."

"I'm only bringing the subject up as a possible solution to our problem." My heart is lodged in my throat. I don't want to leave, but I don't want anyone to be harmed, or worse, because I'm selfish.

"You're not selfish," Sara Beth scolds in my head.

More stomping up the steps brings Esme, William, Winnie, and Henry Dove.

Esme says, "We came as soon as Sylvia called. What's happened?"

Sylvia troops up behind them. "I've locked the doors and added some protection to the house."

"Thank you. Please, everyone, sit. Adam and I have a story to tell you. Once you've heard it, we'll discuss how the Windsor coven should go forward." Sara Beth waits while everyone finds their seats at the long table.

Once they are all quiet, Sara Beth recounts what happened at the park. She explains every detail but reveals very little of my childhood to the group. When she's finished, a long silence settles.

Winnie clears her throat. "Forgive me, Adam, but do you believe your siblings capable of harming others?"

"Yes," I say. "Ariana has killed. I'm not sure about Kaden, but if she asked it of him, I believe he would murder."

Jonah traces a path in the grooved wood of the old table. "She said she wanted to destroy the people of Windsor. Did she mean to kill the nonmagical population too?"

"Yes, Jonah." Sara Beth takes a deep breath. "I understood her to mean she wants to rule this entire island and beyond. She takes no issue with killing anyone who stands in her way. She offered me domain over Windsor and the surroundings if I hand Adam over to her."

"Out of the question." Esme's places a cup of tea in front of Prudence. Her shoulders are stiff and her voice sharp. "We'll not trade a good person, witch, brother, or otherwise, for an empty promise. Whatever she plans with the help of her brothers will not bode well for England and the crown. We've sworn to protect this country."

People nod and reply in a flurry of agreement.

Sylvia bangs her fist against the wood. When the room quiets, she asks, "Why couldn't they cross the protection spell, Sara Beth? Did you cast a circle through Goddess?"

I hadn't even thought about that. A normal protection spell might have kept us hidden from prying eyes. A nonwitch might have walked right by without noticing us. Another witch might have seen us but not taken enough interest to stop. The spell should have diverted Ariana from finding us, but once she did, she should have been able to walk right through even, if her magic was stilted.

"I'm not sure. Maybe Goddess was watching. I'm thankful for the gift, but it would be nice to know if they're not capable of crossing my protection." Sara Beth shrugs.

Trina shakes her head. "Kaden has already crossed your protection. You protect this house, and he's been here twice."

"True." Sylvia narrows her gaze. "I think we must assume today's gift was from Goddess."

"Even so," William says, "our enemies don't know that. As far as they know, Sara Beth can cast a ring that they can't cross. It might be a strategic advantage."

Without anyone actually saying so, it's obvious this coven intends to fight my siblings. I have to give another option. "You could turn me over to her and save Windsor, or I can run far and as fast away from here tonight, and they will give chase."

Still and silent, they all stare at me.

A long twenty seconds pass before June says, "That is not our way, Mr. MacNab. If you wish to run, I don't think Sara

Beth will force you to stay, but you have been accepted. You are liked. We protect our own as well as the crown."

"Well said, June." William pounds the table. "If you want to go, Adam, that's another story."

My heart is bursting. It's hard to form words. "This is the first place that has felt like home since I was eighteen years old. Leaving is not what I want, but it might be what's best."

Several witches shake their heads, but it's Prudence who speaks. "Stay and fight, Adam MacNab. We will be your home and your family. If we die, we die together, but we've won more than one battle in this house."

My throat is too clogged with emotion to speak, so I nod.

Sylvia clears her throat and dashes a tear away. "It would help to know what your sister needs you for, Adam."

"I wish I knew."

Prudence says, "I may have an idea about that."

Everyone's attention turns to the great mother.

She sips her tea then puts the cup aside. "I spoke to an old friend earlier. She's even older than me." With a rough chuckle, Prudence grins. "She reminded me of an old text from a book they say was written by the gods of old. A passage tells of three brothers who tried to kill a god. They used the power of their sibling bond to join their magic and force the god to submit. In the end, the gods joined forces and won the battle, destroying the witches."

"Great Mother, I know this tale. My mother used to tell it to me as a bedtime story, but I thought it was a fable. Are you saying the brothers Donnoble were real?" Sylvia shakes her head, as if to clear away a lifetime of belief.

Esme clears her throat. "It's a children's tale, to be sure. It's in a book my father brought back from Ireland. My parents read it to me as well. How can it be real?"

Everyone starts talking at once.

Prudence smiles over the loud debate.

Never having heard the story they're on about, I have nothing to add.

"It's a children's story." Winnie's cheeks are red.

Minerva nods. "I know, but that doesn't mean the story didn't come from somewhere."

"I don't know this story," William says.

Glad not to be alone, I say, "Neither do I."

Prudence raises a hand, and the room grows silent. She blinks slowly before settling her gaze on the young witch with long brown hair and light-brown eyes. "Trina, please go to my room and get the book from my dresser."

Trina jumps up and rushes down the hallway. A minute later, she returns with an old book, its cover worn to gray, and its pages frayed. She hands to book to Prudence.

"Thank you, child." Prudence opens to a page in the middle of the book marked by a green ribbon then turns the book toward me. "Adam, will you read the tale aloud?"

I do as I'm asked.

EVIL BORN

With three, there is power. With three linked by blood
    and magic can doom prevail.
Three to take the world.
Three to shadow the light.
Three to crack the veil.
Evil born were the brothers Donnoble. No light shone
    in their hearts. From birth cursed. Once men, they
    plotted and planned to take over all the land, and
    the world of gods as well. No others had ever dared
    seek power beyond the veil.

From town to village they traveled, leaving destruction
in their wake as they gathered knowledge and
power to further their plans. Dark magic fed them,
and their magic grew greater than any other.
On the third day of the third month in a year of three,
they climbed the old tower and made their sacrifice
of three, three, three. Blood rushed down the
tower's walls, and the river ran red, then black.
As one, they cast against the veil, and fired rained down
upon the land.
The gods fought back but would not join forces, as it
was not their way.
When night fell, bodies lay in waste upon the land in
every corner. Death was all they knew.
The heavens cried for the loss they did not prevent, and
as one, joined their magic to smite down the three.

I close the book, and my stomach is in knots. "You tell this tale to your children?"

Sylvia sighs. "The one my mother told me was not quite as graphic, but it's a warning that not even Goddess is unbreakable."

Shaking off the doomsaying of the story, I still don't understand. "If the tale is true, why is this the only evidence? Where are all the bodies?"

"People tend to explain away what they can't understand." Minerva looks me in the eye. "The black plague destroyed much of the population, and there have been other times when death covered the world. Any of those might have been caused by the three brothers."

It's all too much to believe, but we have no other ideas.

Sara Beth stands. "Let's, for a moment, accept that the

story is true, and these witches have plans to recreate what the Donnoble brothers attempted. Why does Ariana believe she can succeed where they failed?"

"Goddess is the last who can travel to this world." Esme stares at the table. "If she doesn't have the help of those gods who have long been replaced, how can she fight such a force?"

"That doesn't mean they can't help, only that they may not," Jonah says.

I can't believe I'm buying into this madness. "Even though I can't fully believe the premise yet, if I do as the high priestess says and accept the story as truth, I have a theory."

Sara Beth's admiration floods me.

"Tell us." Sylvia grins. "A theory is better than all this arguing."

They may think me mad, but this entire thing is insane. "Ariana believes she can kill Hecate, and by doing so, rule all witches. If she succeeds, she will likely use nonmagical people as slaves and witches as her army. She could then rule on both sides of the veil. Clearly, her plan is to get me to join her madness. Is it possible that Goddess manipulated me to come to Windsor, where the coven is strong and sympathetic? Surely another coven would have sent me away as soon as my sister's evil was revealed. This is the only place that would rather face a threat head on. Most covens want to live simple lives, practice kitchen magic, and go unnoticed. They hide what they are from their neighbors for fear of repercussions. There is no town like this. I have traveled across the island and asked many covens to take me in, but they have pushed me out as soon as they learned the truth about Kaden and Ariana's past."

"Smart boy." Prudence pats my hand.

"Maybe Hecate can't defeat an onslaught like what the Donnobles attempted. Maybe that's why she brought me here, where a coven would protect me and the world on both sides of the veil. This coven has protected a country for many hundreds of years. There are few who can make that claim."

Henry Dove is the only man in the room without magic. Dressed as a gentleman in a black coat and crisp white cravat, he clears his throat. "The men and women of this community will stand by you, Miss Ware. You are well respected."

Eyes weary, Sara Beth forces a smile. "Mr. Dove, I hope it will not come to that. I'll not ask anyone to risk their lives."

"We can't let them attack Goddess." Jonah seemed a gentle giant, but there is no doubt of the passion in his voice.

"I will stand with Adam and defend with my last breath if need be." Sara Beth looks down the table into my eyes. "I can't ask any of you to do the same."

Her devotion is more than I could ever hope for and far more than I deserve.

William stands. "I will stand with Adam and Sara Beth."

"As will I." Esme stands.

One by one, the witches around the table declare they will join this insane fight against my brother and sister.

It's been so long since I felt part of anything. I have to brush a tear away before I embarrass myself. Still, my sister will kill them, and I can't bear that. My immediate thought is to leave.

Anger mixed with sorrow hits me all at once, and I know Sara Beth hears my plans.

The conversation turns to visiting the other coven witches and letting them know what is happening. As the danger is grave, each will be given the option to stay away.

When everyone is in agreement about who will visit whom, the meeting breaks up.

Prudence claims she's tired and retreats to her room while June and Trina go to the kitchen to begin preparing dinner.

Being alone with Sara Beth should make me incredibly

happy, but she knows my heart, and she is not pleased. Somehow, that also makes me happy. I round the table to her. "We are no closer to knowing how to stop Ariana. She has gained the ability to put me in a trance. If she reaches me, she may know how to use me to further her plans. I have to go."

"If leaving is the only thing you know how to do, Adam, then go you must." She turns on her heel, storms down the hall, and disappears inside her room.

THIRTEEN

SARA BETH

Goddess, this is not fair. I waited my life for a man I might have feelings for, and you bring me one who has no ability to stay.

My bedroom door opens and closes. I gaze out the window at the street below, busy with people rushing to finish their day. I consider erecting the wall between us once again.

"Please don't, Beth." As he moves behind me, his heat warms me through our clothes. "I don't want to leave. "I would stay with you a hundred lifetimes if it was safe. You and these witches of Windsor have embraced me as no one else ever has. Believe me, I want to stay. Tell me how I do that without risking all of their lives."

My chest hurts, and it's hard to breathe. "Where will you go?"

"I don't know." He lets out a long sigh. "Another town, and then another. If the legend is correct, I need only escape them until after March third."

"She could still find you and keep you for another ten years when it is again a year of three, or maybe the year need only be a multiple of three. Perhaps a six or a nine would do as well." It's all so unfair. I want him to stay, and I know he cannot. "There is no way to know what the story means or if it's even true."

"I know." He cups my cheek and presses a gentle kiss to my lips. "But it's all we have. Even if it's not true, don't you think it's likely Ariana believes it? Goddess set her chess pieces in place many years ago. I've moved from place to place to come here and learn what I now know just a few weeks before the date described in the doomed fable."

"If she brought you here, Adam, what makes you think leaving is the right course?" I'm never desperate. I don't need anyone. That's what I keep telling myself, but the pain in my chest has grown, and I wonder if my heart is going to explode.

He pulls me into his arms. "I'm sorry, Beth. The last thing I ever wished for was to hurt you. I..."

Though he stops short of saying it, I feel his regard. It makes no difference. He's leaving, and I'll probably never see him again. I put up a wall inside my mind, blocking him from me and me from him. If I hear more of his desire for a life with me, I'll burst into tears, and I'm not that kind of woman. I'm strong. Pushing back from him, I step away. "I'm a grown woman, Adam. You've no power over me."

Anger and sorrow are clear in his tight lips and soulful eyes. "I don't want power, Beth."

"Go then, and good luck to you." I walk out of my room, stride down the hall, and down the steps. I'll go to the river and think. There are too many people around the coven house to hear my own thoughts. Actually, there's only one too many.

"Where are you running?" Minerva asks from the front door, where she's standing as if she just stepped inside.

"I thought you and Jonah had gone home." Minerva is my truest friend, but I want out of the house. I want out of my thoughts.

She walks to me, and takes my hand before drawing me out the door. "We were halfway out of the city when I realized what was happening. I made Jonah turn around."

"What's happening?" I don't know if I can bear more worries right now, but it's my duty to help my coven sisters. I squeeze her hand. "How can I help you?"

Leading me toward the river, Minerva smiles sadly. "It's not me who needs help, Sara Beth. It's you."

I snatch my hand from hers. "I need nothing."

Letting out a long sigh, she resumes walking and says, "Of course you do. It hit me as we were riding home, that Adam must leave here to avoid his sister until after the third day of March. He's not the kind of man who would risk other witches' lives no matter what we all vowed at the table. He's going to leave. Am I wrong?"

"No." It's as if my heart is being ripped from my chest. My mother's voice yells to protect the coven, while my head and heart long to be with Adam and protect him.

"You will let him go alone?" She walks faster as we near the river.

"I can't make him stay. I'm not even sure he should stay. Maybe it will be safer for him after the date passes." My throat clogs with emotion. Why would he ever come back to Windsor? He'll go and be glad to have this place behind him.

At the bank, she turns toward me. "Go with him, Sara Beth. He needs you, and while you think you need no one, you need him too."

The idea is too absurd. I laugh. "Leave? I'm high priestess. I have responsibilities. This coven is my duty, as is protecting the king, in case you've forgotten."

With a warm grin, she takes my hands from on my hips and gives them a tight squeeze. "You will come back to your duty, and we will continue to protect the king. Jonah and I will move into the coven house until you return."

"I can't go." Doubt creeps up my spine. Is it that I can't leave, or that I'm afraid of what lies beyond the limits of Windsor? "I promised to watch over this coven."

A friend since the cradle, she pulls me into a hug. "You are a fine leader, but you are hard on yourself, my dear friend. Adam MacNab will love you for a lifetime. Maybe longer. He's leaving to keep you and the other witches safe. He's leaving to save the world and the world beyond the veil. Would you let him make his way alone? Would you give him no support when he needs you most? It is not our way to wash our hands of trouble and let others take the risk. We face darkness with our eyes open and fight for right. Or am I mistaken?"

Is that what I'm doing? Would I let him leave alone out of fear? "If I left, you would lead in my stead."

Minerva will take care of this town, its witches, and the crown. With a wide grin, she says, "Of course. Sylvia will help, as will the others. Jonah has gone to William to get two horses for you and Adam. Come, we should return and pack. It's best if you leave tonight." She grips my hand like a vise and drags me back the way we came.

"I haven't agreed to anything, Minerva. I'm only considering the idea." Somehow, though, the notion has lifted a weight from my heart. Fear of the unknown doesn't sound so terrible if Adam is safe and by my side.

"You will. I know you, and you'll not leave him to the wind. Even if you were not in love with him, you'd protect him. It's the love that's clouded your judgment."

Feeling like a child being dragged home after a scolding, I jerk free and stop. "I never said that I love him."

Minerva crosses her arms and narrows her gaze at me. "Will you lie to me now?"

"Love is not meant for Ware women. We have no use for men who'd bully us and tell us where to go and what to do." My mother's words fall from my lips with ease, and I feel her presence as a tingle at the back of my skull.

Minerva sighs and lifts her hands, palms up. "I loved your mother very much, Sara Beth, but what was good for her is not necessarily good for you. Witches are strong people. None of us require anyone else to make us complete, but I can tell you from my own experience, there is nothing like finding your perfect match. Jonah is the other half of my soul. I can't tell you if it is the same for you and Adam, but I can see love in your eyes when he is near, and there's no doubt he was in love with you at first sight. He looked as if he'd been struck by lightning when he walked out of the kitchen that first night. Honestly, he looked the same today at the meeting. He'd stay if he could, but he can't. The question is, will you go and protect him as he protects you?"

She's right of course. Minerva is rarely wrong.

"When did you start giving speeches?"

Without waiting for a response, I take the lead to get us back to the coven house before Adam leaves without me. "I have a few items I'll need while we travel." I wish I had time for a list and thoughtful packing.

When we arrive, Johan is holding the reins of two saddled horses, one black and one gray. Both are fine looking and stomping with an urge to be gone.

My heart stops at the sight of Adam holding his pack over his shoulder.

"It was kind of William to send a horse, but what do I need with two and two saddles?"

Running toward them, I grip my stomach to catch my breath. "The second is for me."

Minerva pets the black, and the horse calms immediately then nuzzles her shoulder.

"Beth, what are you talking about?" He drops his pack to his feet.

"I only be about ten minutes gathering a few things we'll need. It will be twilight soon. It's a good time to slip out of town unnoticed." Without waiting for him to respond, I open my thoughts to him. *"I'll not let you face this alone."*

Adam's mind is a jumble of emotions, but he's not repelled by the idea of me leaving with him. He looks to Jonah for clarification, but only receives a shrug. He says, "Who will protect the coven?"

"I am not essential to the safety of this coven or this town. There are many who can take my place. Perhaps, though—" I step so close we're nearly touching. "I am needed to keep you safe, Adam."

His chest rises and falls with quick breaths. "And keeping me well is important?"

"Vital." Staring into his eyes, I let the love inside me ease out. "But not just to me. You are needed to save Goddess and this world."

When his mouth opens but no words come, I add, "Give me a few minutes."

At the top of the stairs, Prudence waits. "You'll go with him?"

"I must." I draw a long breath.

She shuffles closer and holds out her hand. "Take this." She places a shard of blue crystal in my hand. "For protection and strength."

"Thank you, Great Mother." I hug her and fill with worry that this will be the last time I see her.

Patting my back, she laughs. "Goddess isn't calling me yet, child. We shall meet again." Threading her arm through my elbow, she walks with me to my room. "There are witches who are in the light all over the land. Use them for safety."

I pull a bag from my wardrobe and a change of clothes and my money purse. I fill the purse with the money I keep tucked in a drawer for emergencies. With this, we can eat, and I can use magic to mend and wash. Taking my grimoire and some healing salves, I don't have time to sort through all we might need. I can make things as we go, and with that in mind, I put three vials in my bag. "I won't want to put anyone in harm's way."

"I know, but they are witches in the light and will want to help. You must stay alive, as must Adam. I can't say how I know, but the day will come when we'll all need you. There are none in the light who would not die to save our Goddess."

She's right, I know, but I still will only stay a day with any family or coven. Letting Ariana and Kaden catch up with us could lead to disaster. "We'll keep moving."

"There are places that will keep you hidden as well. Ancient places, where centuries ago our people worshiped Goddess. Look for them when you need to rest." She dashes a tear from her eye.

I think of the place Minerva told us about where she and Jonah were blessed by Goddess. It wasn't visible to those under the demon's control. Ariana is no demon, though she may as well be. "We'll come back in a few weeks. The mild weather is a good sign for us. We'll not freeze to death."

She shows her gapped teeth and pats my cheek. "An early spring is always good fortune. Now, be safe and well, for I know you'll be wise."

One last hug, and I bundle my bag in my arms and rush down the steps.

Trina hugs me, and teary-eyed, runs up to her room.

June smiles, but it doesn't reach her eyes. She hands me a pouch, and the bread and cheese within smells wonderful. "It's time for an adventure, I see. We'll care for Great Mother while you're away."

I hug her. "I know you will."

Sylvia waits by the door. Her face is an emotionless mask. "You know I'll do all I can to help Minerva. Any instructions?"

It's not that she's cold or indifferent. Like me, she keeps her emotions tightly corked. I appreciate her directness and lack of tears. "Be careful and keep our leaving town quiet for as long as possible. If Kaden comes snooping, shoo him away. If there's trouble, you know how to defend this house and this town."

She gives me a curt nod. "I do. The king is in London, which is a blessing. Even so, we'll defend Windsor and all within her borders."

I give her hand a squeeze and rush out the back door to the alley.

Minerva must have cast a spell to keep prying eyes away. The local folk would normally be interested in two fine horses held in the small alley for so long with witches standing by. They'd want to know who was taking a journey. However, no one seems to even notice the witches or the horses.

Already mounted, Adam won't meet my gaze. "That was fast. Are you sure about this?"

"Of course." I hook my bag to the saddle.

Jonah lifts me as though I'm featherlight and places me in the saddle.

I'll ride sidesaddle until we're out of town. No need to look suspicious if anyone sees beyond the spells and protection.

Jonah says, "This girl is called Zephyr. The black is Pilot. Be safe, high priestess. Keep Adam safe too."

"I will. Thank you, Jonah." I look down at my dearest friend. "Minerva, I'll pray to Goddess to keep you safe."

Reaching up, she takes my hand. "I'll pray the same for you. The blinder spell should keep prying eyes away from you to the city's edge, but beyond that, I can't be sure."

The sun dips below the horizon. "It's time."

Adam still hasn't looked at me since I mounted, but he turns his horse, and we walk through the streets away from coven house to the main road out of Windsor.

When we're out of the city, it's mostly dark. "Even in the dark, I know you're avoiding my gaze, Adam."

"I'm afraid, Beth. I could bear to leave you behind to keep you safe. I don't think I will survive if you come to harm." His mind opens to mine.

"I understand, but I couldn't let you go alone. I need you safe just as much."

The depth of his emotion is almost too much to receive. "The horses can see, but how do we keep them on the road to wherever we're going?"

"Throw your leg over the saddle, and we'll let fate take hold of us, sweetheart." He guides his horse closer.

"How do I stay with you?" My nerves bubble to the top. I've never left Windsor for long or gone away with no destination.

Even in the dark, his eyes are bright. "Perhaps this moment is why Goddess linked our minds. Stay with me." He points to the side of his head.

Inside, I feel his warmth. "Maybe you're right." Somehow the idea that our link might be for practical reasons, and not emotional ones, hurts. Pushing that aside, I say, "We'd better go."

He kicks his horse into a trot and is soon out of my sight.

Panic boils to the surface.

I nudge my horse to follow, but I don't see him.

Then his voice is in my head. *"Don't be afraid, Beth. I'm right here."*

Excitement flows through me as I nudge my mare into a gallop. Adam is just ahead, and no one else is on the dark road for miles.

Twenty minutes later, he slows, and I pull back on the reins. "What is it?"

"I think we should trot a while. Then we'll get off the road before daylight. Maybe find a place to rest for a few hours at dawn." He touches my knee. "You ride well."

"It would be a shame if I didn't, and you haven't thought to ask until now." I laugh as we fall into a comfortable trot.

I hear the words in my head before he says them. "I suspected you'd have said if it was a problem."

I also hear his faith in me. "I don't ride often anymore. I suspect I'll be sore tomorrow." My thighs are already aching from the gallop. "How long before Ariana and Kaden find us?"

"They won't find us if I can help it. They'll probably realize I've left Windsor within a day and start looking. They'll check towns and ask around for me and my tricks. I'll have to change my patterns. Maybe take a break from the stage." Worry seeps through his light tone.

"I have enough money to get us through for a while. If we have to stay away longer than a few weeks, I can heal people for extra money."

He's silent a long time, but he's holding something just out of my hearing. Finally, he sighs. "You didn't have to come with me. You'd be safer in Windsor."

"If you don't want my company, I'll keep away from you. I can follow and protect without being in your way." My heart balls up like a stone in the center of my chest.

"That's not what I said. I want you safe, but you coming

with me is the most generous thing anyone has ever done for me." The last words are tight.

It takes a few deep breaths to find my voice. "I did it for more than just you. The world and Goddess are at stake." My pulse pounds. "And I didn't want to lose you," I whisper.

CHAPTER
FOURTEEN

ADAM

As the first gray of daylight makes its way over the horizon, what she said still bothers me. Lose me. She thinks she could lose me. How can she not know that I'd have come back when I was able?

Moving off the road and into the woods, we wind slowly to the Northwest. "The horses need rest, water, and food."

"So do I." She sounds weary.

The scent of burning peat forces me to a stop. "Do you smell it?"

"A hearth fire." She stops beside me. Tiny strands of hair have come loose of her tight braid, and she pulls her cape close around her throat.

Spring has come early, but a chill is in the air nonetheless.

"Shall we see if the owner of the hearth is willing to give aid?" I ask.

"I'd risk a lot to get out of this saddle for a few hours." She walks Zephyr forward. In the saddle of the big gray mare, she looks like a fairy princess. Even worn out from the ride, she's stunning.

As the woods lighten, we come upon a small stone house with a thatched roof and a smoking chimney.

Magic simmers in the air.

Sara Beth holds up her hand, and a silver ball forms in her palm. She whispers a spell, and the light dances around the house like a fairy looking for someone to play with. She grins. "I feel you are in the light, friend. May two who are also children of Goddess rest in your home?"

The heavy wooden door opens, and a man in his twenties steps out. Warm brown skin, black, curly hair, eyes dark as night, and staff in hand, he studies us. "You have business here?"

"It's a long story, but I know your heart is pure. If you'll help us, I'll tell our tale." Sara Beth drops to the ground, and her knees give a little. She steadies herself against the horse.

The man rushes to her side and grips her shoulders. "You've been in the saddle a long time, madam?"

"All night." She smiles, steadier on her feet. "I am Sara Beth Ware, and this is my friend Adam MacNab. We need a safe place to rest, and the horses need care and rest."

Climbing down from my saddle, my legs shake a little too. I take my pack from the back of the saddle and step closer to Sara Beth.

Eyes wide, the man bows his head briefly. "High priestess of Windsor," he whispers. "I'm honored. I'll care for the horses, and my home is yours." He steps back and takes the reins.

"And you are, sir?" Sara Beth asks.

He tugs at the frayed sleeve of his homemade coat. "Jasper Lyon."

"You don't sound French, Mr. Lyon." Sara Beth removes her pack.

I take it from her and watch our host and the surroundings. He seems a nice enough man, but I'm concerned about stopping in a place where Sara Beth is known. Perhaps her name is known by witches far and wide in England, but here in the middle of nowhere, worries me.

"My father was French and my mother English. She brought me here when he died. I was very young. She died last winter. This house will be safe. Mother built it with strong protections in every stone. Most people pass it by without ever noticing it's here." Taking the reins of my horse as well, Jasper smiles, showing straight white teeth. "Your need must have been great. Go inside. There's bread and fresh milk. Make yourself at home. I'll tend these beasts."

We stand and watch him walk through a stand of trees and into a paddock, where a pair of cows and a donkey trot over to see the new arrivals. At the far end is a chicken coop, and a pair of bee boxes dot the south corner.

"This is a well-planned home." I take her hand and lead her toward the front door. "What did he mean by our need being great?'

Legs unsteady, she stumbles along. "I suspect the house is charmed, and those charms keep him safe from outsiders who might do harm to a solitary man with a well-planned home. His dark skin might put him in danger in a cruel and foolish world. His mother must have held powerful magic to keep this house hidden from anyone who is dark or without need. Any spell that continues beyond the caster's death is mightily impressive."

The house is one room with a curtained bed in one corner. The yeasty smell of bread makes my stomach growl. Leaving my bag, I cross to the table near a wash basin and cut two pieces of the crusty treat. "Eat, Beth."

She takes the bread and nibbles then drops into one of two chairs near the hearth. "I may be too tired to eat."

The house is warm and comfortable. As small as it is, I could live happily in such a place. Knowing Ariana would find me and foul such a treasure, I brush the thought away. "Try to eat a little," I command, despite her drooping eyelids.

She appeases me with two bites before setting the bread on a small table next to her chair.

The window by the basin looks out over the paddock, where Jasper is brushing down the horses. He appears to be talking to them at length while they munch from a grain trough.

The moment Sara Beth falls asleep, I feel her mind ease out of mine, though not completely. It's as if she's busy with her dreams, and I've been set aside while she sleeps.

The donkey curiously sniffs around while the cows have lost interest and are chewing on grass several feet away.

I make no attempt to hide my curiosity as Jasper finishes with the horses and walks to the house.

Stepping in the back door, he grins at me, and then removes his heavy boots. "Fine horses."

"Thank you for the bread." I pop the last of my slice in my mouth.

Seeing Sara Beth, Jasper frowns. "Will you put your lady in the bed? She'll be stiff sleeping with her neck like that."

Slumped to one side and fast asleep, Sara Beth looks peaceful, but Jasper is probably right.

With a nod, I lift her and lay her on the bed.

Jasper pulls the curtain around her. "The curtain is charmed. She'll only hear outside of it if there's danger. What are the two of you running from?"

"What makes you think we're running?" It's a curse to always be suspicious, but it's also a habit.

He sits at the table, cuts more bread and slathers jam from a small pot over it. Offering me a seat and the other slice of bread, he sighs. "You may have reason to be mistrustful, sir, but you're not in danger from me. Maybe I can help."

"Why would you want to help us?" Even suspicious, I can't reject the offer of what looks like a fine jam. I spread it on my bread and sink my teeth into it. Pops of berries and honey spark on my tongue. "You're a fine host, Mr. Lyon."

"The bees do most of the work." He grins but looks down at the table. "I would help anyone the house admitted. My mother wouldn't let anyone in whose purpose wasn't noble."

"You said your mother had gone to Goddess." It's a small house. If another person was inside, I would see her.

Sorrow darkens his eyes. "She did, but she left her mark on this house. Her magic reigns here, and the house will not let anyone dangerous or dark see it. I'd help your lady just because of who she is. Sara Beth Ware was little more than a child when she became high priestess, and word travels about her deeds. When I heard she'd allowed men into the coven, I hardly believed it." He gestures with an open palm to me. "Now I see it's true with my own eyes."

Am I a member of the Windsor coven? Nothing formal has been said, but I feel they have accepted me even if I left them. "We are avoiding my brother and sister, who wish to use me for the power to destroy Goddess and take over our world and hers."

Jasper flinches. "And here I always wished for siblings. Perhaps I'm better off alone."

I laugh. "I thought that too. So, I ran from them for eight years. Then I went to Windsor and found a kind of family not defined by blood, but by something more. Now, I want to go back, but that would put them in danger."

"And her?" He points to the curtain.

"She wouldn't let me go alone." My heart expands so far that it's hard to speak. I eat my bread with jam and wait for my emotions to settle.

Fed and tired, I accepted Jasper's offer of his bed and slid in beside Sara Beth. It's midday when I wake up to an empty bed. Regret and panic assault me, and I sit up so fast my head spins.

"I'm here. I'm well."

Her calm voice in my head eases away all the tragedy I'd imagined. I take several long breaths before I stand and pull back the curtain.

Sara Beth and Jasper sit, drinking tea and eating cake as if all is good in the world. They look like old friends. Her dress is clean, and without a hair out of place, she looks content.

Feeling a bit rumpled, I run my hand down my shirt and trousers and use magic to clean up. A real bath and wash basin would be better, but this will do for now.

"Would you like some tea?" Jasper asks, taking a cup and saucer from the tray on the table.

"Thank you." I sit beside Sara Beth and let our fingers touch under the table.

Smiling, she lifts her hand and cups her tea in both. "You slept well?"

"Too well," I admit and thank Jasper for the strong, hot tea. "You are very kind, Mr. Lyon."

"It's Jasper, please. I rarely get company at all, and you have both been very nice companions today. One can only talk to animals for so long before people think you mad." He lifts the plate with a slice of cake on it and passes it to me with a fork.

"Thank you, Jasper. Has Sara Beth told you more of our story?" The sweet light cake is divine.

"She tells me you rode all night and let the horses decide your path. I find it interesting that path led you to me." He cocks his head.

"You suspect a deeper meaning than fate or good luck?" I eat the cake like a starving man and place the plate back on the table.

"I suspect Goddess led you to me for a safe place to rest and stay if you choose." Jasper goes to the fire and adds wood. His shoulders lift and lower in a long sigh. "I wish I had more to offer you both, but what I have is yours."

Sara Beth's eyes are glassy with emotion. She leans toward Jasper, draws a long breath, and smiles softly. "You cared for the horses, gave us your bed, and fed us. It's more than we deserve. Should you ever wish to move from this lovely place, you will have a home in Windsor, Jasper Lyon. You shall be as our brother if you wish it."

CHAPTER
FIFTEEN

SARA BETH

My offer was genuine, but even I can't believe how easy it came to me to offer a man I barely know a place in our coven. Still, I meant it, and Jasper would be welcome.

We were led by Goddess. There's no other explanation for finding his home. Not only is it safe, but Jasper is an animal healer, and the horses needed his hands on them after such a ride. I suspect the days to come will be worse. "You have been more than generous, but you must realize we can't stay. We are safe for now, but Ariana is strong and determined. She will find a way to locate her brother, even through your mother's fine magic."

"You may be right," Jasper admits, but his brow is tight, as if he's considering something. "Goddess sent another from Windsor here when I was a child. She was old and wise but needed my mother's help."

My heart beats faster. "Do you remember who it was or what she needed?"

He sits and stares over my shoulder, as if picturing the scene from the past. "She didn't have a name. Mother called her Great Mother and spoke with extreme reverence."

Meeting Adam's stare, I hear his thoughts. "*Perhaps Goddess did bring us here, but for what purpose?*"

I wish I knew the answer. "The great mother is our treasure in Windsor. She never travels alone now, but perhaps she still did when you were a boy."

"I think I was six or seven, and that's twenty years gone by. Mother was honored by the visit. I remember her speaking of it for weeks afterward." Jasper draws a long breath and looks at everything but us. His eyes are thoughtful, and he fidgets.

"Is there something else?" Adam asks.

With pupils fully dilated, Jasper looks from Adam to me. "She said someone would come, but she didn't know who or exactly when. She believed there would be two, and they would need help. She hoped Mother would care for them and warn them that the fate of worlds rests in their hands. She said not even she would know when the wheels of peril would begin to turn. Only Goddess showing them the way here would be the sign that they were chosen. Goddess had tasked the great mother with putting in place the first of three tools the pair would need. The first is here." Jasper rises and goes to his bed. He pulls a trunk from underneath and rummages inside.

"Beth, do you believe we are the pair, and this wheel of peril is my sister?" Adam whispers, but the house is so small, there's little doubt Jasper can hear him.

"I don't know, but here we are, and worlds are at stake." My pulse is so fast, I draw long breaths to try to slow everything down.

"Wouldn't the great mother have told us we had some kind of quest other than avoiding Ariana and Kaden for a few weeks?" Adam sounds angry, or maybe he's fearful.

I can't blame him for being afraid. I am too. "Evidently this visit to a hidden house of a kind witch is how we were to be told and the proof we are to undertake this quest. Perhaps she couldn't be sure unless Goddess led us here."

"I really hate being manipulated by deities," he mutters under his breath.

"Ah!" Jasper grips a roll of black silk cloth. It's about a foot long and perhaps an inch in circumference. He carries it to the table. He looks at me, and then at Adam. "I think this is for you, though I can't say why. It's just a feeling." He places the rolled cloth on the table in front of Adam.

Magic vibrates from the bundle in a way I've never felt before. As Adam reaches for it, I touch his hand. "It's not aligned with light. Whatever it is, it's neutral."

With a nod, he carefully unrolls the silk until a long slim piece of black crystal catches the fading sunlight despite not being polished. "A wand. I know no witches that use a wand." He touches the matte stone. Wide-eyed, he jerks his hand away. "Did you hear that?'

I shake my head. "I heard nothing, Adam. What did you hear?"

"It said, 'For you.'" He touches it again. "It's so clear."

The wand is cool beneath my touch, and its magic is not familiar, but not dark either. "I hear nothing. It's full of power. Power meant for you. Power created by Goddess I think."

"If this was delivered here twenty years ago, I was only a child. How can this have been left for me?" He lifts it from the end that's slightly wider. It's not perfectly round, but it does taper to a point.

"I don't think Goddess and those in her sphere are constrained to time to the way we are." The air pulses.

Jasper lets out a short sigh as his eyes close, and his head slumps to one side.

I jump up and feel his pulse at his throat. "Only sleeping."

"He does not need to hear what I have to tell you." Goddess is stretched out on the bed, as if she's been listening the entire time.

Still holding the wand, Adam faces her. "What am I to do with this?"

"That is your destiny, Adam MacNab. You may use it for good or evil, light or dark. It is not for me to tell you how to live your life."

Adam throws his arms up in the air and turns his back on her. "Deities! Why must they always be so cryptic?"

Appalled, I say. "He is only scared, Goddess. He means no insult."

She laughs. "I know all he is and is not, and I am not offended, Sara Beth Ware. Do not fear for him. It is never easy to be the hope of worlds."

My heart lodged firmly in my throat, I ask, "What do you need of us, Goddess?"

Despite his complaint, Adam stands by my side and takes my hand. "Forgive me, Goddess."

"Dear one, there is nothing to forgive. You have a long, hard road ahead of you." She rises from her repose and floats above the slatted wood floor. "After the brother Donnoble's attempt to rule this world and that of gods, hallows were made should another rise to try again. In this time, she comes, and you, Adam MacNab, are her third." Goddess smiles warmly at him. "But her brothers are not dark, and so she must make them so. She will come for you, but you must resist until you must not."

"What does that mean?" Adam huffs. His shoulders are tight and the muscle in his jaw ticks.

She acts as if he hasn't spoken and looks at me. "You will need two more items. I made the wand, but it is not enough to stop her once she has both of her brothers."

My chest aches. Adam will turn and betray me, just as Orin did. I have to swallow twice to ask, "What are the other two?"

"A staff of Birch, white as pure light. The crystal you bear makes it whole. The shield staff is made by my father's hand. He can protect but not interfere."

Adam squeezes my hand. "I'll never betray you."

Unfazed, Goddess smiles. "The third is a shard from the sacred hart's antler. He is a creation of the fae. He shan't give a piece of himself if you are not worthy, children." She gestures to Jasper. "Go before this kind soul is in danger. His part is done for now."

"And where do we find these items?" Annoyed, Adam narrows his gaze.

"Go north to the hills, then west to the sea. The beasts know the way." She shimmers out of sight.

Once she is gone, Adam drops my hand and stomps his foot. His knuckles are white where he grips the wand. "Why can't she just give us what we need and tell us how to use them?"

"Because she's vowed not to interfere in the lives of mortals."

He shakes his head. "I know, but her life is at stake as well. I don't understand this divine right of half helping, full of riddles and half stories. Either she should help or not."

"I share your frustration, but there's no sense worrying over what we don't know. We must use what she did tell us to keep our world and Goddess's safe." What she did say was that

Adam would go with his sister, and that leaves a knot in my gut.

Dropping to his knees before me, he takes my hand and kisses it. "I will not betray you, Beth. She's wrong about that."

"Goddess is never wrong." I pull my hand away.

"Then it's a half truth. Even if I must go with Ariana, you have to believe in me. I won't do anything to harm you, this world, or the light." He bows his head and sits back on his heels.

My heart aches for him, and if he goes with his sister, it will break. Still, he means what he's saying now. Leaning down, I kiss his forehead. "I know, and I will try."

As I move to walk away and gather my bag, he grips my hand. "I am not like the man from your youth. He should have stayed and fought for you. Maybe you should have left with him. I will not abandon what we have together. My pledge to you, Sara Beth Ware, I'll never betray you. I love you, and my heart is true."

The last man to tell me he loved me left at my mother's order and did not return. Orin was little more than a boy at the time. After he left, he looked for power in dark magic, allowed a demon to possess him.

Adam comes from a family with darkness in it, yet I know he means what he says in this moment. He loves me.

I drop to my knees and cup his cheeks. "I love you too. I know you believe every word, but Goddess is never wrong. You will go with your sister."

Pressing his lips to mine, he devours me. His arms wrap around me, and full of desperation, he deepens the kiss.

Heart pounding, I open for him. I would give almost anything to allow my mind and body to be his for all time.

Breaking the kiss, he presses his forehead to mine. "If

Goddess is right, then I will go to Ariana. Still, you must know, I will be with you."

I want to believe him. I want to love him for a hundred lifetimes. My heart believes him, but my mind says to be cautious. "I will try, Adam. It's the best I can offer you at this moment."

A sad smile tugs at his lips. "You said you love me, and that will carry me for a lifetime if need be. Your love is more than I ever dreamed of."

At the table, Jasper stirs, letting out a soft sigh.

I stand, cross to our host, and whisper in his ear. "Thank you, dear friend. We shall meet again. I feel certain of it."

Before Jasper comes to full wakefulness, we gather our meager belongings, leave him money for the food and care of the horses, and quietly leave the hidden stone house.

CHAPTER
SIXTEEN

ADAM

Zephyr is determined to head due north. Goddess said the horses would lead the way, so we give them their head.

"I don't know why we can't ride northwest. That's the direction Goddess said the staff was in." Even sounding petulant, inside I'm brimming with joy. Sara Beth loves me. What more can I need in life? Nothing.

"She said to ride north, then west, and to let the horses lead. There must be a reason."

"Why are you so apt to follow her blindly?" I nudge my horse to ride beside her where the path widens.

Looking at me, she says, "Not blindly. If the path brought us directly into danger, I would alter our route. I have faith, and at the moment, there is no danger. We ride quietly through the woods on an old path. We've not seen a soul, and the day is fine. Why are you so apt to work against her directions?"

It's a fair question. I do want to go some other way. "Ever since I began communicating with the great mother, I've felt a tug. It's as if someone were pushing me this way and that. I'd been running from Ariana for years, but where I would land each week was aimless. I had no destination, only backward was forbidden."

"How did your letter writing begin?" The path narrows, and she trots in front of me.

I check that the protection spell is still in place around us then pat my breast pocket, where I've placed the black wand. Finding all as it should be, I stay close on her heels. "There was an advertisement on the back of a pamphlet in Edinburgh that caught my eye. It said Windsor seeks you, and you should come."

Stopping her horse, she turns in the saddle to look back at me. "What on earth does that mean?"

Shrugging, I can't help how her snappish tone amuses me. "I have no idea, but it caught my eye. I thought about it all day, and in the afternoon, went back to the shop where they sold the pamphlet to buy it and see if I could make sense of it. But there were none left.

"I tried three more shops before I found one copy left, but the odd advertisement wasn't there. The back was blank."

"How odd." She urges her horse to walk on.

"I thought so, but soon forgot about the incident. Edinburgh is large enough to distract me for some weeks and hide for a long time. It would be difficult for Ariana to find me with all the noise and other attractions.

"I took rooms at an inn. It was delightful to have the ability to bathe and eat regularly. I kept my wits sharp by searching the area each night for signs of my siblings. I scried for them regularly but found nothing. So, I stayed and enjoyed the city."

"It must have been nice for you to be in one place." The

path widens again, and she falls back to walk beside me. Her warm caring washes over me, making me wonder what took me so long to follow the signs to find her.

"It was." Closing my eyes, I see those neat rooms and the street below. "I made friends with the butcher who delivered chickens to the inn. One night, he invited me to listen to a speaker at the college. I'm not much for politics, but it was something to do, and I hoped it would lead to having an ale at the pub afterward." A chill runs up my spine at the memory.

"What happened?"

"As with these types of things, there was a young man standing on a soapbox, talking about rising up and that kind of thing. Suddenly the air grew still. I thought for sure Ariana had found me. Every soul in the square froze in place except for me. I searched for the danger I was certain was coming.

"The fellow who'd been spewing his politics looked me in the eye. 'Prudence Bishop of Windsor. Windsor seeks you.'"

"My word," Sara Beth breathes.

"A moment later, everyone was normal again. The fellow on the box was telling them what to do to join his cause. Shaken, I excused myself from the crowd and went back to my room." I let out a long breath. It's the first time I've told the story. I was sure anyone would think me mad.

She whispers, "What did you do?"

"I addressed a letter to Prudence Bishop in Windsor and asked her to write to me if she was real. I didn't expect to hear back, but what else could I do?" I lift the reins helplessly.

"But she did write back." The road opens in a field, and in the distance, the hills rise and roll on for miles.

"She did. The letter arrived the day before my scrying found Kaden lurking to the north of the city. I packed up, and letter in hand, moved on from Edinburgh. It wasn't easy to get mail, but I did manage to receive a few more letters from the great mother in the weeks to come. Each one told me that I would be welcomed to Windsor and that my destiny would never begin if I didn't come."

Her smile holds no joy. "She never said a word about you until the day you came to dinner, and she gave no information. Sometimes I think Prudence is in constant contact with forces beyond the veil. Perhaps it's her age, but she knows things and does things that seem impossible most of the time."

"You're upset that she didn't tell you she went to such measure to invite me to Windsor?"

She puts one hand on her hip while holding the reins with the other. "No. She can invite whomever she wishes. Her rank grants her that right. I'm upset that she knew something rather extraordinary was about to happen, that I would be a part of it, and would be leaving Windsor, and she didn't even give me a hint." She kicks her horse into a gallop.

I follow and enjoy the wind and energy of the run.

When we reach the wooded stretch before we begin the climb, we are forced to slow, and the air tingles with magic. *"Beth do you feel that?"*

With a nod, she casts a spell to keep the horses silent. We walk into the shadow of the trees and stay still.

Pressure from a searching spell shimmers against our protection spell. Someone is looking for us, and it's safest to assume it's not someone from the coven.

"Ariana?" Sara Beth asks silently.

With the protection spell in place, I can't tell. At the rate the spell is wavering, it won't be long before we're found. The wand vibrates in my pocket. Pulling it out, I focus a new spell through the crystal wand. Magic flows from me, through it, and feeds the existing spell. The wavering stops, and the bubble of magic around us glows dark blue.

Whoever was looking for us passes by. The pressure eases and disappears.

I've never seen magic like that, and I have never produced a spell that could firm up a spell cast by another witch.

"How did you do that?" Sara Beth asks.

"I have no idea. I was thinking that your spell wasn't going to hold, and it needed to be stronger. I conjured my own spell, and this is the result." I gesture to the glowing bubble around us.

We walk deeper into the woods. The sun is setting, and we'll have to fully rely on the horses to take us north through the night. The magic moves as we do.

"It's possible the coven was looking for us." My hope to return there and be safe, and more importantly, to see Sara Beth safe, feeds my statement more than any real possibility.

I hear her *no* in my head before she speaks. "That felt too aggressive for a friend. They would find a more sensible way to contact us. A way that wouldn't make us hide."

Despite knowing she's right, I pray Ariana and Kaden are far away, looking in the wrong place.

"I hope so too," Sara Beth says.

I touch my chest where I've hidden the wand again. "Can we assume they know nothing of the items made to defeat them?"

"I wish I knew, Adam."

For hours, the horses continue on.

I am dozing in the saddle and wake when they walk toward a dense shrub. "Beth."

She startles awake and pulls the reins, but Zephyr shakes her head to gain more lead and barrels right through the center of the greenery.

I stop.

Pilot blows air and stomps in protest.

Heart hammering, I can't see Sara Beth. Loosening the reins is all it takes, and my horse walks right through the center of the shrub.

No branches or brambles touch me, and a moment later, I'm on the other side. A bright half-moon lights the clearing with thick grass inside a circle of trees and a clear pond that shimmers in the moon's glow. It's warmer by at least twenty degrees in this little patch of beauty.

Sara Beth slides from her saddle. "Goddess. I thought I'd be torn up by stickers, not brought through to an oasis."

The bubble of protection vanishes, and panic bombards me.

A touch from her mind, and I'm calm. She says, "It's sacred ground. Only those in the light and their magic can enter here."

Tentative, I drop to my feet. "Let's get the tack off the horses and let them find something to eat. We'll have to settle for the bread we have left. Maybe some berries are in the bushes."

She uses magic to unsaddle Zephyr and Pilot then removes their halters the same way. Everything she does is with ease and grace.

I love to watch her magic and her movements. She's beautiful and strong at the same time. If I were a poet, perhaps I could do justice to describing her. As it is, I'm only a mesmerizer and illusionist. I hardly deserve her. Still, she loves me. My heart swells with the truth of it as she walks to the water's edge.

The horses rear up playfully then trot to a patch of grass where they munch away.

One last look that the horses are safe, and I join her. "I don't know about you, but that looks like a fine place to bathe."

With a wicked smile, she calls her pack from the ground

next to the saddles. It floats across the empty space as if it were meant to do so then settles on the ground at our feet. Crouching, she opens it and pulls out a cake of soap. "A bath would be welcome."

"Do you want me to join you, or wait until you're finished?" It's only a bath, but my heart pounds with fear she'll reject me.

"And I thought I worried too much." She shakes her head and hands me the soap. Untying the front laces of her dress, she never takes her gaze from mine. "If I didn't want you to join me, I would have told you to watch the horses or turn your back." Once the garment is loose, she lets it fall to the grass.

For the long ride, she's also wearing breeches and some kind of binding around her chest. She bends to remove her boots, but I stop her.

"Let me, Beth." I drop to my knees and tug the leather over the buttons. Her ankles are slim, and I let my hand graze the stockings.

Gripping my shoulder, she steps out of one then the other before loosening the fall of her trousers and letting them drop.

As she unwraps the binding like a bandage, I roll her stockings down her legs. She's the most beautiful woman I've ever seen. What she sees in me, I'll never know.

With a toss, the wrapping lands on her pack, and gloriously naked, she cups my cheek and draws me to stand in front of her. "I see a beautiful man who has been through more than most people could survive, and stayed in the light. I see strength and determination, despite your anger. Most of all, I see love, Adam."

Threading my fingers through her hair, I pull her into a kiss.

Her lips are soft and strong, just like the rest of her, and she presses against me, gripping my shoulders.

I'm breathless when my need to be naked forces me to end

the kiss. "I must monitor my thoughts better. Clearly you hear every word I think."

"I do, but you have nothing to hide." With a light kiss on my nose, she draws away and walks into the pond without looking back. Her pale skin glows in moonlight, and the arch of her spine calls to me to touch and kiss every bone down to the swell of her hips and the curve of her ass.

I'm gripping the soap when a magic tug causes me to release it, and it floats toward her.

It's a wonder my clothes don't tear, I pull them off so quickly. As soon as my toes hit the water, the calm of sacred waters soothes me. With a leap, I dive under headfirst.

The water sings in soft tones. I open my eyes, searching for the source, before I sputter to the surface and scan the area. Nothing is amiss.

Visible under an unusually bright half-moon, the horses are still munching grass.

Sara Beth stands with only her head and shoulders visible. Expression pinched, she watches me. "Is something wrong?"

"I heard singing." I look around again.

She cocks her head. "Do you hear it now?"

Shaking my head, I say, "No. But it was clear when I was underwater."

Without any hesitation, she dunks her head under the surface.

I do as well, and the singing rolls melodically through the water. I swim closer and think, *Do you hear it?*

"It's lovely." She smiles.

Rising, I wipe water from my face. Once she's above as well, I ask, "What is it?"

"I have no idea. Goddess's way of soothing us after a tiring day? A mermaid? Something else? This water is blessed, of that

I'm certain." Sara Beth wades closer and takes the soap floating a foot away from me.

I feel the calming effects of the water as well, but that doesn't mean I like not understanding. "There is no such thing as mermaids. Doesn't it trouble you not to know what's singing?"

She soaps her arms then swims to the pond's edge and stands. Water sluices down her curves, and I'm unable to look away.

My cock is rigid and has been since she first walked near this charmed water.

She soaps her body from head to toe then turns and dives under the water.

Unable to help myself, I duck my head under. The singing is louder as she moves through the water. Her body is fluid, and bubbles gently float from her nose. I swim toward her, and when we meet, we rise as one to breach the surface. Wrapping my arms around her, I devour her lips.

She kisses my cheek and my neck and whispers in my ear, "I don't care about the source of the singing because I have faith we are meant to be here."

"How do you know?" Gripping her bottom, I pull her tight against me.

She arches into the pressure between her legs. "We rode due north rather than a more direct route, Adam. Do you think those horses found this by accident?"

"To be honest, it's hard to think of anything besides giving you pleasure at the moment." I squeeze her tight and push my pelvis forward.

She wraps her legs around my hips and moans. "Then you should go make use of that soap while I have a little swim."

With a reluctant groan, I let go of her.

Laughing, she stretches out on her back and floats away.

At the bank, I take the soap and wash. It's nice to rid myself of the grime, and the lavender in the cake is soothing. "I wonder how Ariana and Kaden found us. We kept off the road and were always under protection."

"Your sister is very powerful. She uses the dark arts to her advantage. Who knows what demons she can call upon to seek you out? Or perhaps it's me she's targeting. She must know by now that I am with you. She can't be pleased about that. Maybe she believes if she were to remove me, you would have a moment of weakness where she could control you." Breasts high and nipples tight, she works her way around the pond, stops at an outcropping of rocks, and climbs out of the water. Like a cat, she scales the boulders and disappears around to the left. "This is lovely."

Soapy from hair down, I dive under the water and swim directly across to the rocks. I find the small foot holes where she obviously climbed what seemed impossible. There's a path of sorts, and I make my way up and follow.

On the other side, Sara Beth sits in a stream of moonlight that seems to glitter with magic. "Adam, this is some kind of restorative." She arches her neck and drops her head back on the deep green grass. Her fingers curl into the blades, and her breath causes the rise and fall of her breasts.

Restorative or not, I scale to the bottom of the stones and kneel at her feet. "Beth."

Rising to her elbows, she watches me with eyes that invite more.

The glittering light touches the top of my head, and the aches and pains of riding ease until they disappear. Impossibly, my shaft gets harder still.

Lifting her foot, I kiss the curve of her ankle and along her calf. "I love you, Beth. I've never been so sure of anything or anyone in my life."

CHAPTER
SEVENTEEN

SARA BETH

"I love you, Adam, and I never thought to love any man." My body aches to have him touch more than my foot and leg. "I need you."

"Is this all Goddess's doing? Is she using us to get what she needs?" His doubts are valid, but they don't stop him from kissing the inside of my knee.

Opening my legs for more, I let the soft blades of grass caress my skin. I experience every tickle and touch both from this world Goddess created and from the man I love. "She brought us together, but she is forbidden from forcing us to love. Love is beyond even her magic. Only disaster can come from that kind of interference. She's sworn to always give us free choice."

With his tongue, he traces a path along my inner thigh.

My womb tightens, and my center yearns for more. I arch and let my legs fall wide, lest he mistake what I want and need. "Adam."

Licking a path through my curls to my center, he growls my name. The way he sucks and licks until I'm writhing beneath him is magical, and my pleasure builds. He cups my bottom and lifts, then traces a path up and down my slit before latching on to my pearl.

Unable to control my pleasure, I cry his name and arch my back as rapture erupts within me, spreading to every inch of my body. I feel it in my toes and fingers. My legs shake with ecstasy, and I roll to my side and curl up for some relief from the joy of it.

While the orgasm still shakes me, Adam holds me. "I've got you, sweetheart." He kisses my neck and shoulders.

Slowly, I come back to myself as he traces kisses down my spine and up again. Hard and twitching with need, his shaft rests against my bottom.

As good as my pleasure was just moments before, his desire sparks mine once again. Reaching back, I grasp him and work my hand up and down his rod. "I want you inside me, Adam. I need you." As I look back to see his loving eyes full of passion, the moon glows a bit brighter. I push him to his back, straddle his hips and draw his length deep inside me.

"Goddess, you feel so good." He holds my hips to keep me still a moment.

When I lift, he releases his grip. Pressing my hands to his chest, I ride him. With each plunge, his shaft rubs my pearl, bringing me to the height of pleasure. It's so good I lose my pace.

Adam clasps my hips and sets a rhythm.

Throwing my head back, I scream as pleasure crashes around me.

He grunts as he pumps up into me, stretching out my orgasm.

He's going to pull out. I hear him calculating the moment in his head. "Stay, Adam."

Wide-eyed, he acknowledges my plea and calls my name as he spills inside me.

Warm jets fill me, heightening my rapture. I pulse around him again, and unable to catch my breath, collapse on his chest.

He wraps his arms around my back. "Beth." Gasping, he says, "That was—the—thank you."

I can't blame him for his lack of words, as I have none to offer in return.

As he lifts me off, I let out a long groan of pleasure and pain. My thighs ache deliciously. Lying on the soft grass, we soak up the moon's healing light. "If we live, I hope we made a child here tonight." My voice is sleepy.

His arms tighten, and he kisses my cheek.

While I sleep deeply, it doesn't last more than a few hours. There is much to do before true rest will be available to us again. Lying in Adam's arms on the cool grass under the stars, I'm tempted to forget duty and just be.

"You could never do that," he responds without me ever voicing the thought.

I still wish it. "Could you?"

Kissing my cheek, he tightens his arms around me. "Maybe before I knew what was at stake, I could ignore my sister's obsession with me. Now I can't. Now there is too much to lose, both personally and in the bigger picture."

The moon has passed beyond the trees that shroud the sacred clearing where the light of the goddess moon restored us. Making love in such a place is rare and beautiful. Lit by only the stars, he looks at me with love and hope, and I'm drunk on his gaze. "You know, we may die finding those other two items."

"It's possible, but if I die, Ariana fails, and I'll still have no regrets. I never dreamed I'd find you, Beth. I expected to go through my life running, hiding, and stealing pleasures where I could. Since knowing you, every moment that led me here has been worth it."

A tight knot forms in my chest. "I'll be very vexed if you die without me. I feel certain we'll have other lifetimes, but I can't wait forever to be in love again."

Rising on his knees, he looks at me with narrowed eyes. "You have a coven that needs you. No one will miss me. You have to survive."

I stand and draw him with me. Naked in the starlight, he's hard and angular. A fantasy really. "The witches of Windsor will survive with or without me. I'd prefer we both live, but we shall live or die together."

Pressing his forehead to mine, he closes his eyes and lets out a sigh. "Then we head west at first light?"

His acceptance of my share of whatever we might face is warm and comforting. Mother said men thought themselves superior to women, but she must only have known a few and assumed they were all alike.

"Perhaps it was what her mother told her and her mother before that." Adam reads my thoughts ever so gently. There's no anger toward my mother or grandmother. He only hopes to ease my burden.

"It's possible. No men were in the Windsor coven or others in England for many generations. Mother told me once that there had been a battle between witches, where men tried to shift power in their favor. I wonder why they were not content with sharing. Were they dark or just foolish?" Ever since I allowed William and Jonah to join the coven, I've wondered about this. They are both big, physically strong men. William is a powerful witch, perhaps more powerful than any other I've ever met. He doesn't seek my seat at the table, only a place there. Jonah has made Minerva even more powerful, but he would never withhold his unique magic to keep her from achieving whatever she wishes. With Jonah's size, he could overpower her when she is vulnerable, but he never would.

Why did the witches my mother told me about try to take control?

Despite my not voicing the question, Adam responds, "I don't know. We may never know."

"Am I setting the stage for history to repeat itself?" My worst fears are known to him now.

He cups my cheek. "No, Beth. You are making decisions based on each witch without bias. You have pushed prejudice aside in Windsor, and it sets a fine example for the rest of the world."

Resting my cheek on his chest, I let his heartbeat soothe me. "I suppose we had better dress and get the horses ready. It won't be long before daylight."

We find a path around the pond to where we left our clothes. Unable to stop myself, I watch him dress and find my desire for him fully heightened again.

"Stop," he commands. "If you keep thinking that way, we'll never leave this place." Despite his harsh tone, his shaft is fully erect, and he's grinning.

I pull my trousers on and then my dress over. "Fine, but who knows when we'll be safe and alone again." I tease as I snug the laces at my waist.

Once I have my boots on, I head for the edge of the clearing. "I'm going to see if there's anything to eat."

As if on cue, a fish jumps in the pond. I'd not noticed them earlier.

Adam laughs. "You had other priorities. I'll see if I can catch one if you'll build us a fire."

With full bellies, we head west. Staying off the roads makes the travel harder and longer but may keep us safe from Ariana and Kaden.

Above us, a hawk cries, and my heart leaps. "Can your sister control animals?"

"She couldn't when we were children. Honestly, I don't know what skills she's acquired over the years. If she's capable of stealing magic, she could have almost any gifts and use them for any number of malicious acts. I do know she has no kindness in her heart. She killed our parents without sparing a thought despite their love for her. I saw no remorse in her afterward."

His pain sears through me like a dagger. I can't tell if his sorrow includes the loss of his siblings or if he mourns his parents still. It doesn't matter. He's suffered so much and had no one to comfort him.

I'm ashamed that I wanted to send him away when he first came to Windsor.

His beautiful lips turn up in a soft smile. "You didn't, Beth. Don't regret what did not happen."

"I might have treated you like every other coven leader

you've encountered in your years of running." Ashamed or not, it's better to get it out.

"But you didn't. You were cautious, which is smart. Ultimately, you welcomed me into your home and your heart." His thoughts return to the sacred pond and our lovemaking.

I fidget in my saddle. "Perhaps it's best to change the subject since your thoughts go to places unfit for our current task."

His laughter, and the way he too must adjust his seat, brings me more joy than anything I've had in my life.

"Where do you suppose we should begin looking for a staff made of birch?" He nudges Pilot into a trot.

"I have no idea. Perhaps we'll find a birch forest on our way and ask the trees." I can see why he gets annoyed with Goddess's clues. They are rather vague.

He scratches his chin where a few days' beard, a few shades redder than his hair, has grown. "Perses is her father, and she said that he made the staff. Where would a witch go to find a staff made by a god who married a nymph and gave life to the goddess of magic?"

"The peaks were made by gods and are west of here. Perhaps Perses made them too, and we'll find what we need there." I shrug. "There must be many trees in those hills."

With a shrug, he says, "To the Peak District we go then. It's a lovely place at least. Perhaps it will remind us of what we're saving, even if it doesn't produce a staff of pure white."

"How long will it take to get there?" The water and the sacred little clearing where we made love healed me, but new aches have already begun.

His broad back expands with a deep breath. "Six days without a change of horses. We don't want to kill these two beauties." He pats Pilot's shiny black coat.

"That long." I calculate the date and wonder if we'll find

what we need in time. "What do you think happens if we can't find the staff and the hart in time? Even if we find the hart, who's to say he'll hand over a piece of his antler? So many things can go wrong. I don't even want to think about what I'll have to do if Ariana finds us and takes you."

Stopping his horse, he faces me and forces me to stop as well. His eyes are dark and serious. "You will let me go. Goddess has already told us she will take me. You must trust that I will not betray you or this world."

My heart is pounding so hard it's difficult to think of the right words to say. Sidestepping my horse so our legs touch, I want to rage at him, but my heart is too full to get angry. "She could bespell you and make you do things you won't be able to live with, Adam."

"If she could truly control me, she would have done so in the park. She put me in a trance, but she was not able to make me leave your side. She was not able to force me to get up and walk to her and Kaden." He closes his eyes and breathes. When he looks at me again, calm is back in his gaze as well as love. "She needs me to be willing. She'll use you or someone else to force me to go with her, but she'll not have my heart, Beth. She can never have that, because it already belongs to you."

Gripping the reins in one hand, I reach across, and he takes my hand. "I never expected my heart to be this full. I thought I would grow old and not know this kind of love. I trust you, Adam. I will do what is right."

"Will you promise me you'll not try to get me back when she takes me?" He grips my hand tighter.

"No. I cannot make that vow." I shake my head to stop whatever argument he's about to make. "I will do what is right and appropriate to the situation. Nothing will keep me from saving you if possible. I can promise I will put this world first.

Even my love and future cannot come before the fate of witches and nonmagical people in this world."

"What about Goddess and her world? Is that not just as important?" He skims his fingers along my cheek, as if I'm made of porcelain, and he might break me if he touches me too hard.

"Goddess is important, but I'm not pledged to protect her or the other gods and creatures who live in her world. I'm pledged to protect Windsor and England. I've vowed to do my best to keep the witches in my coven safe. I've extended that to other covens when it was needed, and I'm willing to do whatever it takes to keep this world out of the hands of a dark witch."

"You worship Goddess, Beth. I don't see how you cannot protect her," he says so softly that I strain to hear him.

"I will do what I can for her world, but if the choice is you or Goddess, she can fend for herself. You are a witch in this world and under my protection. I've lost witches in the past. Each time, a piece of my soul goes with them across the veil. I'm willing to die for this quest to stop your sister. I know you're willing to do the same. However, losing other witches for the sake of deities is not part of my commitment to magic. Let us assume that if we do all we can and find the items Goddess provides, she can take care of herself." Giving Zephyr a kick, I trot ahead, and I'm a little surprised when I sense only amusement from Adam.

A moment later, he's beside me. "A fine speech."

"You're making fun of me." I hear amusement in his head as well as in his tone.

"No. I'm impressed. You mistake my joy for folly."

"What do you have to be joyful about?"

"You love me more than you love Goddess." His adoration is like a warm blanket on a cool morning.

I wish we had ten thousand cool mornings to sit together with hot tea and watch the new day come to life. I push the horse faster to clear my mind of what I cannot have.

Inside my head, he says, *"Don't lose hope, my love. We may still have all you dream of and more."*

As unlikely as it is, the fact that he still believes it possible and longs for the same future heals my aching heart.

CHAPTER
EIGHTEEN

ADAM

Despite the long days, and sometimes nights, of riding, Sara Beth never complains. She's a rare person, as I wanted to complain every moment other than when she slept in my arms. I've been running for eight years, and my body aches in places I didn't know existed. It's all worth it for the look on her face as the Peak District rolls out before us.

The road leads us over a hill, and the valley below is awake with a dozen shades of green. The peaks are dotted with the jutting rocks the area is famous for. There's a reason people holiday in Derbyshire.

"This is spectacular," she says on a breath. "Should we get off the road?"

I shrug. "I can't imagine Ariana knows we're here yet. We've not stopped in a village, so word could not have spread. Besides, I saw a sign for Birchover not long ago. That seems like the kind of place one might find a staff made of birch." It amuses me more than it should, but I'm tired, and my mind and body desperately need a safe place to rest.

She smiles and continues down the road. "We should see if there's a coven to shelter us in Birchover."

"How will we know if they're in the light?" The idea of exposing Sara Beth to danger lodges a knot in my gut.

She rolls her eyes. "I'm not weak, Adam. I can take care of myself and more. Don't become one of those men who thinks he must protect his property when you're thinking of me."

Is that what I'm doing? "I only wish for you to be safe. I would never think of any person as property. Do you not wish to keep me from harm?"

Her shoulders rise and fall sharply. "I do. I'm sorry. It's only that I'm tired. I think and also hope, I will know if the Derbyshire coven is in the light."

The animals are as tired as we are. They need a good rest and something more than grass to eat. As we enter the village, heads turn. At the center of the buildings lining the main street is an inn.

A boy carrying a chicken under one arm slows, and wide-eyed, he stares. Blond hair pokes out from under a threadbare cap. Magic tingles in the air before he runs down the street with the chicken clucking as they go.

Jumping down from my saddle, I look up at Sara Beth. "I suppose we'll know as soon as that boy gets to his high priest or priestess and alerts them to our arrival."

She swings her leg over the horse's back and lets me help her down.

A round man with thinning black hair and a dishtowel in his hand rushes from the inn's double doors. "Welcome!" He raises his hands with his towel flailing around joyfully. "You are most welcome. Will you be staying with us?"

"If you have room for us and a place to have our horses tended, good sir." I hold out my hand for shaking.

Pumping my hand as if water might spring from me, he grins, showing off yellow, crooked teeth. "Of course. I'm Wyatt Bule. Jillian!" he calls to a girl of perhaps sixteen who is leaning on the side of the building.

Blond hair plaited on either side of her head, Jillian runs over. Breeches peek out from beneath a brown skirt. "I can take care of those animals for you."

"Can you?" Sara Beth studies the girl while she unties her bag from the saddle. "They need some rich feed, as they've been worked hard and only had grass for several days. I'd like to see them have a good rub down, then rest."

Jillian stares at Sara Beth then looks at me before returning her gaze to Sara Beth. "I'll see them properly cared for, madam." Without another word, she unties my bag, hands it to me, takes the reins of both horses, and trots around the building and down an alley.

Still grinning, the innkeeper says, "We have a stable at the back. Won't you both come inside? I have a fine mutton stew, if you're hungry, and a room already made up if you're tired."

"We're both, Mr. Bule. I'm Adam Drummond, and this is my wife, Elizabeth."

"Excellent." He bows to Sara Beth. "Come inside. We'll see you fed and rested."

We take our bags up to a nice room with a large bed and a copper tub.

Sara Beth gasps at the sight of the tub. "Mr. Bule, would a bath be possible after we've eaten?"

"I'll have it filled, madam."

Before he can say more, a boy of no more than ten runs in. "Papa, Miss Pinkerton is here, and she wants to see them."

Bule's smile falters, and his eyes grow wide. "I didn't realize." He smooths his hand over his balding head then fiddles with his towel. "Do you wish to meet with her here or in the common room?"

Sara Beth looks at me. The high priestess, I'm guessing.

I'd hoped for a full belly before this introduction, but it's not to be. "We'll come down. We wouldn't wish to put Miss Pinkerton to any trouble."

As it's in between lunch and dinner hour, the common room isn't crowded, and if my calculations are correct, it's Tuesday. Two men are having ale at a long bar, and a tall woman is setting a table for two.

As soon as we reach the bottom of the steps, the boy who first saw us arrive points from just inside the door. "There. That's who I saw."

"Thank you, Isaac. Go take care of your chicken. I'll be fine here." Miss Pinkerton is strikingly beautiful with black hair pulled back in a tight bun and brown skin. Her features are such that she might be carved from stone for masses to witness her beauty. Straight nose, bright teeth, full lips and high cheekbones. When she meets my gaze, her light-brown eyes are dazzling.

She crosses the common room and stops a few feet in front of us. "Forgive the intrusion, Wyatt. I heard you had new guests, and I admit I'm curious."

"Not at all, Laura. You know you're always welcome here. May I introduce Mr. And Mrs. Drummond. Sir, madam, this is Laura Pinkerton." As soon as he bows to all parties, Mr. Bule scurries away to help with setting the table.

Sara Beth gives a short nod to Laura. "We would have made our arrival known, Miss Pinkerton. Though we'd hoped to fill our stomachs and have time to rest before an intro-duction."

A genuine smile lights Laura's marvelous eyes. "I'm glad to

hear that you have good manners, Mrs. Drummond. Have you been traveling long?"

"Some time," Sara Beth says. "We travel in the light, as I see you do. We mean no harm in Birchover. We are only stopping on our way."

"On your way where, if I might ask?" Laura leans on the newel post.

"I'm afraid that not even I know. We travel at the will of Goddess." The truth of it almost makes me laugh. I could actually cry with equal verve.

"Interesting. Does Goddess often send you on quests, madam?"

"Thankfully, not often. We have an object we must retrieve, and then we'll be on our way. I admit I'd hoped to stay a day or two to sleep."

I'm constantly amazed at the way Sara Beth can be truthful without telling anything.

Laura Pinkerton is not as impressed. She frowns and stands up straight. Holding out her hand, she asks, "May I have your hand, Mrs. Drummond?"

With only a moment's hesitation, Sara Beth places her hand in Laura's.

Closing her eyes, Laura breathes deep, and as she lets the breath out, she smiles. "You are welcome here in Derbyshire. I don't know what you seek, but I'll help you if I can."

"Don't you want to touch my hand, Mrs. Pinkerton?" I ask.

Her laugh is warm and deep. She gestures to Sara Beth. "If you were not in the light, this woman would not be with you. Her heart is pure, with a glow that shines white."

"You read auras," Sara Beth says.

Laura stares a moment before pulling her cape around her shoulders. "We can discuss the gifts of Goddess when you both come to dinner tomorrow night. It will be informal, with just my sister, nephew, and the three of us." She inclines her head to Isaac when she speaks of her nephew. He didn't leave as instructed, but stands just outside the doorway, peering in.

"We will be delighted." Sara Beth bows.

"I'll send Isaac to direct you." She wraps an arm around Isaac's shoulder. In a lower voice, she says, "Perhaps you'll be inclined to tell me your real names when the setting is more private."

I like this witch. She's direct without being rude and cunning without scheming. "Perhaps," I say.

Her expression remains pleasant as she bids us good day, then calls out to Mr. Bule and his wife where they're still fussing with the table.

Once Laura is gone, Mr. Bule hurries over. "You have fine friends. Miss Pinkerton has saved this town from..." He frowns and fusses with his towel, as if he said more than he meant to. "Well, we're all grateful to her for her kindness."

Sara Beth takes pity on his blunder, whatever it was. "The stew smells wonderful, Mr. Bule. May we sit?"

Arms and towel waving, he smiles wide. "Oh, yes. Please sit. My wife, Tilly, was just setting your places. I'll fetch the meal."

I hold the chair for Sara Beth. "So, Mrs. Drummond, what do you think of Lara Pinkerton?"

"I like her. If she's not in the light, she has more magic than I can detect. Tomorrow night should prove interesting." She places the napkin on her lap.

"Will you ask her about the shield staff?" My gut twists. It's not that I don't trust Miss Pinkerton, but that I lack trust in anyone.

"I can hear your thoughts, Adam." She sighs and remains quiet as Mr. And Mrs. Bule bring two bowls of stew and a crusty loaf of bread.

The aroma of rich mutton and vegetables makes my stomach growl. The yeasty bread smells nearly as good. "This is wonderful. Thank you, both."

After several bites with her eyes closed, Sara Beth lets out a long, satisfied sigh and looks at me. "If we don't find the staff on our own before we go to dinner tomorrow, we can discuss how much is wise to reveal. I don't know if I trust her either, but we may have no choice. She may be our only hope of finding this needle in a haystack."

The joy of waking in a soft bed cannot be measured. Rolling over, I feel across the soft sheet, hoping to draw Sara Beth into my arms. Her space is empty. I open my eyes.

"I'm here. Don't panic." Her voice is soft and comes from across the room, where she's leaning over the small writing desk. In just her blouse and trousers, without her dress overtop, and with her hair falling all around her face, she's adorable.

"What are you doing?" I swing my feet over the side of the bed and sit combing my fingers through my hair.

"Come and see."

After dragging my breeches on, I groan over the cold floor and cross to her.

Leaning over a salt circle she's made on the desk, she dangles a lavender crystal from a rope.

I sit in the chair across from her and look at the symbols of north, south, east, and west. "What exactly are you scrying for?"

"A general direction of the staff." Her eyes are closed, and her face is softened by the calm required to perform a scrying ritual.

My heart can't help but beat faster just looking at her. "You look very fetching in trousers."

"I'm glad you like them." Sarcasm bleeds from her statement and makes me laugh.

"I do like them. I would have liked it better if you had stayed in bed to keep me warm on a cool spring morning."

The crystal shimmies.

"Let me concentrate." Voice soft again, there's no heat behind her request.

How is it possible that with my sister and brother hunting me, and an impossible quest ahead of us, I'm happier than I've ever been in my life? I would slay a dozen dragons to be near this glorious woman.

Letting out a long breath, she flops back in her chair. "It's a good thing there are no dragons left in the world, as I can't even find a simple piece of wood carved by a god."

"By a god." My thoughts flit to the wand Goddess made. "Maybe the wand would be a more appropriate crystal to search with." I get it from my bag and bring it back to her.

While I'm holding it out, she doesn't take it. "You would part with a gift given to you by Goddess?"

How can she ask such a thing? I take her hand and wrap it around the wand. "I would give you anything, Beth. Whatever I have is yours."

Love cascades from her and covers me like the softest blanket. I could die happy at this moment. She presses her lips to mine, and the warmth turns to heat as she closes the gap between our bodies. Breathing fast and hard, she breaks the kiss and presses her cheek to mine. "We should find the staff. Lovemaking can wait for now."

As right as she is, lovemaking is all I can focus on, and my cock aches to be inside her. Reluctantly releasing her, I close my eyes. "You are stronger than me by far, my love."

Smiling, she loops the rope around the wider end of the black wand and pulls the knot tight. "Not stronger. I'm just determined to have a life where lovemaking doesn't have to be put off because of danger."

The image of a little girl prancing up steps to wake us in the morning flashes through my mind from Sara Beth's imagination. The child has Sara Beth's hair and my eyes. "Is that what you dream of? You want to fill a house with babies that will interrupt our lovemaking regularly?"

A warm blush travels up her neck and face. "It's not a bad dream."

Taking her hand, I kiss the knuckles. "It's a lovely one. I wouldn't mind a dozen little girls that look like you."

She laughs. "A dozen! Perhaps one or two that look like us would do."

I shrug. "Perhaps a baby already grows inside your beautiful body."

Eyes wide, she cups her belly. "I don't think so. Not yet."

"Do you think you would know so soon?" It's strange that I'm disappointed. I never even dreamed of children until I met Sara Beth, and now, I want to fill a house with them.

She rubs her abdomen. "I think if a witch grew inside me, I'd know." She shrugs. "But perhaps not." With a smile, she closes her eyes and hangs the wand over the circle on the desk.

Slowing her breath, she holds perfectly still while the wand swings in small circles. It jerks down, pulling the rope from her hand and stabbing the table a quarter inch deep.

Sara Beth gasps and opens her eyes.

I stand. The wand impaled the circle at the southwest edge. The circle glows bright orange, and a steeple appears before it vanishes, taking the salt and glow with it. The wand clatters to the desk.

I have to catch my breath. "That was different from any scrying I've ever seen."

"Or me. I suppose we should look for the steeple and see what we find." She hands the wand back to me and walks behind the dressing screen.

I wash up and pull on my shirt and boots. "What do you think would make the wand react so violently?"

"I don't know." Fabric rustles behind the screen. It's adorable that she's gone back there to dress when she slept naked beside me an hour ago. She steps out with her dress hiding her masculine clothes. "It's as if it was impatient for us to find the staff."

Pulling on my jacket, I walk to the door, and then I hold it open for her to pass through first.

Her mind is full of possibilities and worries, but I push them aside in search of her love for me. It's my reason for staying and fighting. Goddess may command as she likes, but I answer only to Sara Beth.

"What you're thinking is blasphemous." There's no shock or censure in her tone. She sounds more amused than offended.

I shrug. "Perhaps. It's the truth."

"Regardless of your reasons for following this path, it is the right thing, Adam. I'm sure of it." At the bottom of the steps, she slips her hand through the crook in my elbow and lets me escort her out of the inn and down the street. As soon as we're outside, the gray steeple with a belfry is visible. I feel magic rising around me like a bad omen. "My sister may have already found the staff." I run to keep up with Sara Beth. We turn down several streets, keeping the steeple in sight until we come around the last corner.

At the edge of the cemetery adjacent to the church, Ariana and Kaden stand in front of an old birch tree. Kaden's eyes are black as ink and his arms are crossed. Dressed all in black, he looks like her henchman rather than her brother. His skin is far too pale for good health.

Rage burns in Ariana's blue eyes. Her hair is pulled away from her face, and a long red plait hangs over one shoulder. "Brother, I've been waiting. You didn't honestly think you could avoid me."

"I would prefer to do so for the rest of your life, Ariana. If I wanted contact with my family, I'd seek you out." I move to put myself between them and Sara Beth, but she takes my hand and stands beside me.

Her mind screams, *"Together."*

"I suspected I should have killed this witch in Windsor. I'm far too kind for my own good." As she lifts her hand, a bolt of red lightning flashes across the air.

Sara Beth lifts her hand and blocks the magic with a wave of blue light. "I suspect if you could have, you would have."

Ariana's laugh grates on my ears and dies as quickly as it started. "Why come this far? What are you looking for?" She looks around the church grounds.

"She doesn't know what we're after." I step forward. "What are you talking about? You know why we left Windsor. Do you think Sara Beth wants her coven in danger from you?"

Ariana steps closer, winces, and stops.

Kaden walks around her and continues toward us. His eyes are dead, and his skin is sickly. He raises his hands as if to push something back.

"What have you done to him?"

The protection from evil spell should keep him at least six feet away from us, but he's getting closer.

"Kaden is a part of me. He understands what's at stake. If

you would come back to me, where you belong, Adam, you would understand as well. Why must you be so stubborn?" Ariana pouts.

I lift my hand and push Kaden back with wind magic.

He lowers his head and fights against the gusting wind.

Sara Beth pulls water from the church well and creates a wall of water between them and us.

The wand is inside my jacket, but I can't let Ariana know that we have it. I'm not entirely sure why, but I feel certain her knowing would be a mistake.

CHAPTER
NINETEEN

SARA BETH

Something about me seems to keep Ariana at bay. Just like in the park, she can't get any closer. I worry that they'll take Adam away, but so far, he's fighting well. It's wise that he not use the wand in front of them until the moment is right. They might figure out what we want and get to the other items before us.

Ignoring me, Kaden pushes through wind and water and continues toward Adam. His eyes are black, like he's possessed. It's clear that he acts at Ariana's will and not his own. Why would she manipulate him this way? Has he had a change of heart? Did he threaten to leave her to protect his brother?

At the moment none of my questions are relevant. I cast another protection spell.

Kaden hesitates a moment before pushing through. His face and shoulders blister from crossing the magic. It must be excruciating, but still he comes.

Forced to back up, I cast magic of all four elements at him.

Ariana advances as our resistance begins to weaken.

"I'm sorry, Adam. I can't hold them off."

"It's not your fault. Just remember what I promised." He shoots fire, burning Kaden. Adam winces at the sight. "Don't make me do this."

Emotionless, Kaden continues forward.

From across the cemetery, green and blue bolts of magic shoot at Ariana.

Ariana screams and holds her shoulder. "Kaden."

On a roar, more animal than man, Kaden runs back to his sister, scoops her up, and they vanish in a black cyclone.

Trudging toward us through the line of headstones are Isaac, Laura, and a blond woman.

Laura looks as calm and stunning as she did in the inn yesterday. "It's a good thing my nephew saw what direction you were heading. When I felt the dark magic, I grew concerned we'd not arrive in time to assist."

"You're timing is quite good," Adam says then puts his hands on his knees and draws several long breaths.

When they reach us, Laura points to the blonde, "My sister, Lynda."

After a quick introduction, I say, "I need to look at that birch tree, High Priestess. May I have your permission?"

Folding her arms at her waist, she slips her hands inside the opposite sleeve of her emerald-green dress. "You come to work for a higher calling than mine. Though, I appreciate the request."

Reaching out for Adam's hand, I'm relieved to find his grip strong and steady. I know harming his twin wasn't easy for him, but he did what had to be done. We can only hope that Ariana's magic extends as far as healing, and Kaden will not have to suffer the aftereffects of burns.

We walk through the graves to the left and stand in front of a twenty-foot birch tree. Its white bark shows no sign of the staff we hunt.

"What is special about this tree?" Lynda asks. Her voice is softer and gentler than her sister's.

I step closer to the tree. "I don't know. Maybe nothing." Reaching out, I touch a large black knot a foot or so above my head.

The tree vibrates with magic.

Lynda gasps.

"Hmmm?" Laura hums.

Worry for me and curiosity mix with Adam's excitement.

His feelings mirror my own. When I place my other hand over the same spot, the knot loosens. Light flashes and covers me in fierce magic unlike anything I've ever felt before. Clearly the magic of Perses feels nothing like Hecate's.

The light fades, and a smooth staff of pure white is in my grasp.

Adam grins proudly at me.

The other three witches gape.

From the pouch at my waist, I draw out the blue crystal Prudence gave me the day we left Windsor and hold it to the broader end of the staff. The stone grows hot and seems to melt into the wood. Another flash, and it's as if stone and staff had always been one. The lapis blue lodged inside the shield staff catches the sunlight.

"I thought it was just a children's story." Lynda's mouth is wide, as are her eyes. "Mother told us of the brothers who tried to take the world. She told us of the items left behind to keep the next attack at bay. She never said one of them was here in Birchover."

Running my hand along the staff, I'm as in awe of it as anyone. "Perhaps she didn't know."

"Even if she had, she might not have said." Laura smiles. "Mother loved her secrets, didn't she, Lynda?"

"Aye, she did. We should go home and talk about this. Someone was bound to have heard or seen some of what happened in the last twenty minutes. When they come to inquire, we'd be better served to be absent." Lynda ruffles her son's hair and walks out of the churchyard.

Isaac and Laura follow. After a moment, Laura looks back. "That invitation was meant for the two of you as well. Unless you have other matters to attend to?" Her grin is mischievous.

With a chuckle, Adam holds out his hand for mine, and we join them on the walk to their coven house.

The one-story stone house sits at the west edge of town. Several people wave and bid the witches good afternoon. The small wooden door is thicker than I expect.

With a wave of her hand, Lynda opens the window shades and lights the wood stacked in the hearth.

Isaac rushes to take the kettle from the hook and goes out the back door with it. He returns a minute later and swings the hook and kettle over the fire.

"Thank you, Isaac." Lynda beams.

Laura invites us to sit with her at a grouping of six chairs that surround a round low table.

Sitting, I lean the staff on the chair next to me. It's hard to keep my gaze from the marvel. When I look up. Adam is smiling at me.

Our hostess is patiently waiting.

They saved our lives. Goddess, I hope this is what you had in mind. "Our names are not Adam and Elizabeth Drummond. This is Adam MacNab, and I am Sara Beth Ware."

Laura's eyes widen. "High priestess of Windsor's coven." She lets out a breath. "May I ask why you lied about your names?"

Clearing his throat, Adam sits forward with his elbows on his knees. "The witches at the church are my brother and sister. They've been hunting me for many years. We believe they plan to use me as one of three and attack the world of man and Goddess. If they succeed, they would then likely create an army of witches and turn the nonmagical into slaves."

"It is the woman who is in charge. That man seemed possessed." Lynda stands at her sister's right hand.

Nodding, Adam says, "It did look like Ariana had Kaden bespelled in some way. The last time we saw them, his will seemed not his own. I don't know what's changed that she's keeping him in thrall."

"If the story is to be believed," Laura says and shakes her head, "time is running out for Ariana's plot. The coming together of threes is soon at hand. Do you have the three weapons?"

It's hard to see the staff as a weapon. "We have two of the items Goddess sent us for."

Cups rattling on his tray, Isaac brings the tea and sets it on the table. "The great hart will be in the fae woods. It's a half day's ride north of here."

"How would you know that?" His mother frowns and props her fists on her waist.

"I read the stories, Mum. The hart serves the fae king. Everyone knows the Northshire Woods hold the door to the fae world." He rolls his eyes.

Laura laughs. "As impertinent as my nephew is, he's not wrong. There are dozens of old stories about those woods disappearing for a hundred years and then coming back. They've been there for all my lifetime, but Mother said there was not one tree there when she was a girl." She shrugs.

"What would the fae king care about any of this?" Adam asks.

It's a fair question, but he's not going to like the answer. "Balance. All these powers like balance in the worlds. Witches in the light also like balance, and so they don't disturb that which should be. Your sister wants all the power for herself. If she gets the power here and in the world of the old gods, there will be little to stop her from searching for ways to attack the fae world next. I don't know how many other worlds exist, but one is bound to lead to the next and the next."

Laura's eyes fill with sorrow. "When everything is so out of balance, it will all crumble. This sister of yours may think she's winning, but literately, she and all she's conquered will fall. What will be left behind will be rubble."

Sitting on the arm of Laura's chair, Lynda says, "From the rubble, they shall all begin again. We're talking about the end of the world. At least the world as we know it."

As I suspected, Adam is not happy with the ideas we're putting forth. "So, if the world will rebuild, why should we mess with it? I can run, so I have no part in Ariana's plan. If we're lucky, we survive until she collapses this world. Then we rebuild. Why are the other worlds any of our business?"

With a wide smile, Laura watches Adam. "It's interesting Goddess would pick a doubter as her champion."

"Isn't it?" I say, then take Adam's hand. "It could take thousands of years for this world to rebuild, and the foundation would be shaken. The children of this world, like Isaac and ours, if we're so blessed, would be left to grow in darkness. There are no guarantees any light would survive the fall of worlds."

He looks from my eyes to my abdomen where he wishes a child were growing. "I want our children to live in the light of your magic."

"I know you do." My heart fills with love from him and for him.

"I suppose we have no choice but to go to the fae king's woods and find the sacred hart."

I love this man so much; I wish we were alone at this moment.

Laura clears her throat. "I don't want to ruin your moment, but how did your sister find you, and how will you keep her from finding you again? The hart is sacred in all worlds. If it chooses to reveal itself to you, you're bound to protect it.

"I imagine the fae king will be more than a little distressed should his hart be harmed by your sister and brother."

Letting go of Adam's hand, I sit back against the deep brown overstuffed cushion. "She didn't know about the staff, that much was certain."

Looking equally deflated, Adam adds, "But she was suspicious about us being here."

"I hit her with my strongest spell, and she slumped." Isaac stands taller.

"My spell got through as well." Laura goes to the fire and adds a log. "She only protected herself against the two of you. Quite arrogant of her. I'm sure we hurt her, and Kaden too. They'll need time to heal and recover."

I stand. "High Priestess, I'm sorry to decline your offer of a meal, but I fear we must leave right away."

Standing, Adam rubs the back of his neck. "We'll settle up at the inn and get the horses, but Sara Beth is right. Our best chance is to go today before Ariana is healed."

"We will pack and head toward Windsor," Laura announces.

"Why would you do that?" I'm astonished and not sure what else to say.

She pulls her shoulders back and might be a queen, she's so

elegant. "If this world and others in the light need defending, this coven will stand. We'll gather our witches and the other covens along the way. I wonder that the standing stones might not be the true destination." She seems to say the last more to herself.

Of course. The stones have been doorways to other worlds. That's why the old gods put them there. "They've not been used in centuries, but I think you're right, Laura. We'll come as soon as we have the item. If we're not there by the third of March, we've been defeated."

Laura takes my hand and pulls me into a brief hug. "You will be there."

My heart thunders, and I feel more courageous from her belief in me. "We will do everything in our power to succeed.

When she releases me, she stares at Adam a long moment. "You may have to kill your siblings before this is over."

"I know." He keeps his gaze on her, but I feel his sorrow at the likely outcome for the MacNab children.

After another long look, Laura nods then pulls him into a hug. "Be well. Take care of your lady and yourself."

Sad and resigned, he looks her in the eyes and says, "I will."

Lynda packs a basket and gives it to him. "Food for the trip. You'll be starved by the time you reach the Northshire woods."

"Thank you." He takes my hand. "We'll need to stop on the way to have Jillian saddle the horses and bring them around. That will give us time to settle our bill and gather our things."

With another round of goodbyes, we leave the coven house and rush back to the inn.

Thirty minutes later, we're headed out of Birchover with the shield staff tucked into two loops on my saddle. The blue stone catches the light like an animal blinking out of the darkness.

I'm so engrossed in the staff I almost miss Adam speaking.

"How did she find us?" he finishes.

There was something about our having turned direction, but I missed most of it. "I don't know. She must be able to sense you through our spells. Could that mean she's gaining power?"

Picking up his pace, he leads us off the main road, but we stay pointed toward the fae forest. "It's possible."

Through the spring leaves starting to fill in the trees, the sun catches the stone at the top of the staff. I pull the staff out and examine it. "Maybe that's why we need this staff. Maybe it will do as its name indicates and shield us from our enemies."

"Perhaps you should cast a new spell and direct the magic through the staff." He stops beside me.

Pilot throws his head and puffs at being forced to stop.

Zephyr moves her head, rubbing Pilot's neck, and it appears to soothe the beast.

I hold the shield staff at the halfway point and raise my arm. "Goddess magic of the light, make our path unseen. Should our enemies search our flight, leave our markings clean. None shall find those with me, as I will, so mote it be."

Clear white light rises from the top of the staff and expands like an inverted bowl around us. It spreads above the trees and wide until we can't see it. However, the magic tickles over my skin.

"That was something one doesn't see often." Adam stares up at the sky where the dome of magic is like a clear film.

I wonder what else the staff can do.

My thoughts must have been loud. Adam says, "Time will tell, my love. Just as time will likely show us what the wand is capable of."

"Perhaps this is all about what we're capable of. These items are only tools." It would be better if we could defend our lives without tapping into items we don't truly understand.

With a sigh, Adam kicks his horse to a brisk trot. "If we didn't need them, they would not have been provided. I know how you feel, Beth, but we have seven days to find the hallowed hart, be gifted part of his antler, and get to Stonehenge. We can only hope that's the right location."

It was lovely to be out of the saddle for a day. Now I wish I could have more time. I'll never complain about walking again. My bottom and thighs ache like I've been beaten with a stick. Pushing the horse into a lope makes it slightly more comfortable, and the animals are happy to run.

Rather that yell over the pounding hooves, I think, *"The stones feel like the right place."*

"Perhaps."

"You know, wherever you go is where Ariana will make her attempt. Stonehenge was built in the light. It's an advantage for us. And it just feels right."

"Stonehenge it is then." We find a small path through the woods, and Adam pushes the horses harder.

When the horses finally stop at a break in the forest, every inch of my skin, muscle, and bone aches. At least, I hope we're stopping. So far, in these woods, every tree has looked like the others, and I've noted no change in the magic around us.

The rising moon lights a strip across a stream in front of us. On the other side of the stream is a field.

Adam searches left and right.

"What is it?"

"The woods should be right there." He points across the stream. "If the directions were correct."

"They said it doesn't always appear."

"Perhaps we're not worthy of the fae king's gift."

We cross the shallow stream. I can't ride another minute tonight, so stifling a groan, I slide to the ground. "It's a long way to come only for him to hide himself."

A low chuckle carries on the breeze.

Stopping, I listen. "Did you hear that?"

Adam dismounts beside me. "There was something," he whispers.

"I am everything," the wind replies.

A few feet ahead, a forest shimmers into existence.

Standing dumbly, I gape at the woods that were not here a moment before.

CHAPTER
TWENTY

ADAM

It's difficult not to laugh at Sara Beth's wide eyes and mouth. Of course, my own heart is pounding with similar shock, but her tone was petulant toward the fae king just before he spoke.

Now his woods are here, and we stand mutely looking at them.

"I think we must enter, my love."

"Yes. Come, and be welcome." He sounds arrogant, even when he's trying to be polite.

A deep frown pulls at Sara Beth's lips as she steps into the woods. She looks from side to side and up before narrowing her gaze. "Show yourself, if you will. I'll not chat with a disembodied voice."

It's hard not to chortle at her annoyance. She tolerances the same behavior from Goddess, but from this fae, it angers her.

She turns on me. "I heard that, and it's not at all the same. I know Goddess. I was raised with her, and she has come into my life on many occasions. I'm invited into a wood that was hidden, probably as a joke, and now our host is still hiding."

I try reason. "Perses didn't show himself when we collected the staff."

"Because he can't enter this world." She crosses her arms, tucking the reins into the fold.

Behind an ancient oak, a man emerges. He is tall, lean, and even from my perspective, far too good-looking. His face is more angular than a human's and his cheekbones higher. White hair hangs straight to his shoulders, and his eyes are blue. Nothing about him can be confused with a human man.

Sara Beth's eyes are even wider than when the woods first appeared. "You are the king of the fae?"

He bows. "I am Midhir. You are quite lovely for a witch."

Frowning, but at least not looking at him as if he were for the taking, she curtsies. "We are in need of the hart's antler. Will you provide it?"

In little more than a loin cloth, he crosses his arms over his hairless chest. His muscles tighten.

He reminds me of a wild animal about to pounce.

Eyes narrowed, Midhir shakes his head. "It is not for me to give. The sacred hart must find you worthy, witch."

"I suppose if he doesn't, we're all in trouble," I say flippantly, but the king's sharp look makes me wish I'd kept quiet. In all the old stories, fae are not kind. They do what amuses them. If that's dispatching me, that's what he'll do.

"Your people are the problem. You might just kill these witches and be done." Midhir leans on the tree and studies his fingernails.

"That is not our way. Goddess commands we do no harm." I make a small bow in deference to his rank and power.

He laughs at this. "That is exactly what your goddess told me. She said that the easy way is not always the right way. I think she believes if the problem is not dispatched as we promised so many years ago, another will rise to take their place."

If magic is always right and never makes mistakes, Goddess is right. However, whoever rose would not be our problem. I only have two siblings. My gut is in a knot. Will they die on the third of March? As evil as Ariana is, and as misguided as Kaden might be, they are my only family.

Sara Beth takes my hand and squeezes it. "Where will we find your sacred hart, King Midhir?"

Pushing away from the tree, he waves his hand and a path glows in the underbrush. "I will see to your beasts."

We tie the reins to a limb, and leaving the horses behind, follow the winding route deeper into the woods.

Looking back, I find no sign of Midhir. "We have seen some remarkable things on this journey, Beth."

She chuckles. "That is an understatement. If this path is true, we are about to see something no living man or woman has ever laid eyes on."

Still hand in hand, we wind around various trees, never straying from the glowing way set before us. For all we know, he's toying with us. "I thought all those stories my mother and gran told us as children were fiction. Part of me even doubted the existence of Goddess, though at least I felt connected to her. The stories of the Tuatha De Danann were amusing, but never did I think them real."

"It's far better for them if we don't go hunting for them. Our host here probably prefers if our kind thinks him fictional." Sara Beth stops.

"What is it?" Scanning the woods, I search for danger but see only tree after tree and our glowing path.

She closes her eyes and breathes deep. "I feel strong magic."

Gathering my power, I let go of her hand. "Ariana?"

"No. I've never felt this kind of magic before." Threading her fingers through mine, she walks quickly.

"What do you feel?" If this goes wrong, I'm ready to cast enough fire to burn these woods to ash.

"I can't explain it, but it's the purest magic I've ever felt. You'll not need to defend us, Adam."

In moonlight, we step into a clearing. A stream runs through the middle, and the water shimmers with light. Grass and moss are so green there's no doubt we've stepped into the fairy world.

Even I can feel magic in the air.

Fireflies swirl around joyfully.

A frog jumps from the bank and splashes in the stream.

Hand in hand, we step closer to the bank. On the other side, an oak that must be five hundred years old has limbs that spread across the width of the clearing and almost to where we entered. It would take ten men with arms outstretched to complete the circumference of its trunk.

The breeze stills. Animals rustling brush quiet.

A huffing sound comes from the tree, and a hart as white as snow and as tall as a man steps around the giant oak. He looks at me and then at Sara Beth. Lifting his massive rack high, he grunts, crosses the water and stops directly in front of her.

Letting go of my hand, she takes half a step forward and makes a low curtsy.

The hart moves one leg forward and lowers his head.

Sara Beth reaches out and touches him between his keen eyes.

Nothing in my life has ever been as beautiful and pure as witnessing this sacred animal approving of the woman I love. I have not purpose here, but I bow from the waist and pray my family tree does not impede our quest.

A grunt forces my head up.

The hart looks me in the eye before lowering his multi-pointed antlers. Each dark-brown point is tipped bright white. He turns and crosses back to the oak.

We follow mutely. Ignoring the wet seeping through my boots, I help Sara Beth across.

On the other side, the hart walks to the tree and thrashes his antlers against the trunk.

The noise is so sharp and loud, a bird flies out of the tree, and Sara Beth gasps.

A three-inch tip breaks off his tallest point and rolls to the mossy ground.

Looking at each of us one more time, he grunts, then strides around the tree and disappears.

Hand shaking, Sara Beth picks up the piece of antler. "This was—I don't know how I shall ever explain this to the great mother." She giggles and clutches the shard with both hands.

"Do you feel something special from the gift?" I long to touch it yet know I'm not worthy of it.

She reaches toward me and opens her palm. "You're wrong, Adam. The hart wouldn't have gifted us had you been unworthy."

"He gifted you. Your heart is pure." Magic radiates from the hart's gift.

Closing the distance between us, she takes my hand and wraps it around the antler. "He knew your heart and was not put off. What Kaden and Ariana are doing is not your fault. Men are not guilty by association. You have become a man of honor despite difficult circumstances. Why is it that you are the only one who cannot see it?"

The hart's magic doesn't reject me. In fact, it seeps below

my skin as if exploring my power. "What do you think we are supposed to do with it?"

"Hopefully we'll know when the time comes." She wraps her hand around mine and we stand with our foreheads touching.

It was cool when we entered the woods, but the clearing is warm like a summer eve.

Magic sizzles behind us, and we turn to find Midhir standing at a table laden with food. "Eat and sleep. No harm will come to you in this place. When the sun rises, I will hide these woods until they are needed again. I think in the days to come you will be glad to have had one night of peace." Without another word, he vanishes.

Roasted fowl, potatoes, and vegetables make my stomach grumble. It's been a long time since we ate Lynda's thoughtful bread and cheese. "He's right about needing rest and food."

Leaving the tree behind, we sit at the wooden table that was not here when we entered the clearing.

Sara Beth picks up a grape and eats it. "It feels and tastes real enough."

"It smells like perfection." I hold the chair for her to sit before sitting across from her.

She takes a leg from the fowl. "I feel a bit guilty for being so cross with Midhir when we entered the woods. This is very kind."

Always thoughtful, even about her own behavior, is just one of the reasons I love her. "He provoked you. This kindness is because even the sacred hart has chosen us for this task. Perhaps our host didn't believe we were the right people for the job when we entered."

"It's possible he just enjoyed a bit of foolery at another's expense." She bites into the meat and closes her eyes with a hum of delight.

"Also a possibility." I wish we could stay in this clearing forever. It would be perfect to remain just as we are without any worries. "What if we wait until after the third, Beth. If she doesn't have me, she can't work her magic as she pleases."

Before Sara Beth can reply, Goddess appears three feet from the table. "I wish it was that simple, child."

I stand then bow. "Why isn't it, Goddess? Ariana needs me, and here she can't find me."

Hair and diaphanous gown billowing in a nonexistent breeze, she floats a few inches above the ground. "When your sister's attempt to capture you at Birchover failed, she found another to use in your place. The girl is not a perfect match, as you would have been, and the dark magic will probably kill her, but the attack could still work. She will take her brother and false sister to the great stone circle and open a gate as soon as the sun leaves the sky on the third day of the third month in this third year. When the gate opens, she will use the darkest of magic to kill all that live in the world beyond."

Sara Beth says, "Why don't you stop her, Goddess? Take her magic from her or bind it so she can harm none."

Sadness dulls Goddess's eyes. "Perhaps when she was a child, I could have done this. Her magic was still mine to take. I thought—perhaps it was only hope. I hoped she would use her gifts for good. I wished the priestesses of the Order would show her the way to the light."

I'm torn between not wanting to know and having to hear the truth. "What happened while Ariana was with the Order?"

"What has never happened before. She opened a path to a world of dark magic. She changed her alliance. She gave him all her light, and in return, the dark one funneled his magic into her. I cannot bind her magic because it is not from me. The Order nuns tried to bind her when they saw what she'd willingly become. Your sister killed them." Hecate closes her eyes and floats toward the stream.

"I don't think I can kill her, Goddess." My soul feels as if it's being ripped from my body.

Stopping over the spot where we crossed the water earlier, Goddess stares at me. "I only ask that you try to stop her from destroying my world and yours."

"How do we do that?"

She floats closer and opens her arms. "Three powers have given you tools for a task that has never been completed by a mortal. The fourth comes from the two of you."

I'm about to ask for more clarification when she shimmers out of existence. I close my eyes. "Why is she always so vague?"

With a short laugh, Sara Beth falls back into her chair. "Because she's Goddess. She's not supposed to interfere. I think her vagaries are to keep that promise while still helping us."

"Rubbish! It's all a lot of rubbish, Beth." I sit and tear a piece of meat from the fowl. "We're to go into battle with weapons we don't know how to use against a magic we can't understand to save beings that have lived for millennia from my sister. Is it me, or is this a ridiculous quest?"

"When you put it that way, it does sound unlikely." She eats and grins.

"It's not funny," I say around a mouthful of food.

She nods and eats with a silly smile lighting her face.

It's impossible to stay annoyed when she looks so pleased, so I eat my fill and enjoy looking at Sara Beth while I do.

As the first light of day crests the horizon, I'm sorry to leave the clearing. It was the best night's sleep I've had in years, and I wish again we might stay forever in Midhir's woods.

We find the horses happily eating grass just outside the woods without their saddles or bridles on. Those items hang neatly on the branches of a large tree.

I pet Pilot's nose. "It looks as if you were well cared for."

Sara Beth slings her saddle over Zephyr's back. "I never doubted. The fae are noted for their love of beasts and disdain for men."

Once both horses are saddled, I look back at the woods and long for more time in the peace of the fae world.

"It will all be lost if we don't stop Ariana, Adam. You know that as well as I do." Sara Beth swings into the saddle and watches me.

"Yes." I mount. It does no harm to imagine a perfect world where I can live happily with Sara Beth for eternity. "I know. We'd better make our way to Stonehenge."

We head southwest with the sun rising behind us. Sara Beth's thoughts are less organized than usual. She flits from the lovely night in the clearing to missing her coven.

Strangely, I miss them too. I love having a large family group to laugh and chat with. At least we're heading back in their direction.

Sara Beth smiles. "It will be nice to see them all again. We shouldn't have any encounters with Ariana and Kaden. If she's found someone to take your place, they'll be heading to the stones as well."

"Who do you think she's taken for such a task?" Goddess said that the dark magic channeled through her would kill her.

My heart hurts at the idea that my life will cost someone theirs.

"We'll know soon enough." She frowns and kicks her horse into a gallop.

For five days, we ride, sleep, and ride again. On the morning of March second, we wake before the sun. I think about the miles ahead of us and pull Sara Beth into my arms. Ready to run, the horses stomp and grunt. "We're not going to get to Stonehenge in time."

"I know." She holds me around the waist and presses her cheek to my chest. "You might use the magic that speeds your progress."

"I've never used it for such a distance. Would we leave the horses behind and hope they find their way home? I'm not even sure I could carry you for such a stretch of miles." My mind is racing with all the things that might go wrong attempting such a spell.

She cups my cheeks and presses her lips to mine. Once I'm calm, she looks me in the eyes. "The wand enhances magic. I think if you alter the spell so that the horses move at the increased speed, and we stay on the main road, it will work."

"It might get us there early enough to rest before the coming battle." We might be seen or hit something. What would such a spell do to the horses? I can cast to avoid obstacles and people. I've never been injured by using the spell over short periods. I can monitor the animals and make sure they are well. In truth, I can see it's the only way we can arrive in time to stop Ariana. If we fail, no animal, man or beast, will live in the darkness my sister can bring.

I take the black wand from my pocket and let out the breath I've been holding. "We had better mount and hold on. I imagine this will be very uncomfortable. Whatever you do, Beth, don't fall off the horse."

Once we're both in our saddles, I try to convey to the beasts what I'm going to ask of them. It's hard to tell if they understand, but they paw the ground and make no signs of distress.

I pat Pilot's neck. Lifting the wand, I cast my spell with the words changed to indicate the horses, that we all stay together, and not come to harm, or harm any on our way. I envision the circle of massive stones that will be our destination and set my will upon the task.

We nudge our mounts into a trot and then a gallop. Within a few seconds the scenery is whipping by so fast, I can barely make out the trees and houses. Everything is a blur as we move at impossible speeds down the road.

Through my connection to the horses, I sense only their joy.

"Beth, are you all right?"

"A little nausea, but I'll be fine. It's remarkably smooth, considering."

She's right. It feels as if we're flying down the road and hardly touching hoof to dirt.

As the sun reaches its peak, we slow. The Salisbury Plain comes into view, awe-inspiring on its own with the standing stones rising up from the plateau, but the multitude of people camped around Stonehenge takes my breath away.

Sara Beth sways in the saddle, closes her eyes, and opens them. "I hope we never have to do that again."

CHAPTER
TWENTY-ONE

SARA BETH

Adam's agape. "Who are all these people?"

Sylvia stands at the edge of the crowd, shielding her eyes from the sun. Waving, she calls over her shoulder.

"These are the witches coming together to save this world and Goddess, Adam." My heart is fuller than I'd have thought possible.

"I never dreamed there would be this many." His voice is tight.

We dismount. The horses seem no worse for wear, though I expect they'll need good food and water as soon as we can arrange it.

Zephyr is breathing hard, but no harder than she might after a good run. I pet her neck as we walk uphill toward the masses of witches.

Windsor coven has gathered beside Sylvia, who immediately pulls me into a hug. "I've missed you. Are you well? We thought you might stay away until the day passed."

"Fine. We could not stay away. Goddess told us we are needed."

Minerva rushes to the front and grabs me as well. "I was worried you might not make it or that you'd come to harm." She lets go of me and hugs Adam with equal enthusiasm.

Grinning, Adam pats her back like an affectionate brother. "I've only ever moved myself with that spell until today."

Minerva pats his cheek. "We're all relieved you've come. We called the Kent coven, and they brought two covens with them. Then your friends from Derbyshire arrived with three other covens. Others have been arriving for three days. We don't know how so many heard of the trouble."

With June beside her, Great Mother approaches. "Perhaps Goddess told them."

The covens are arranged in tents around fires. I hug Prudence. "Should you be living so rough, Great Mother?"

"I'm not a child, and I'll not miss what's to come," she scolds. Then softer, she says, "I'm guessing you found all you'll need?"

I nod. "We have the items, but no instructions for how to use them."

Looking around and counting in his head, Adam frowns. With panic in his voice and in his heart, he asks, "Where is Trina?"

I search the crowd as well. Katrina Davidson would not be left behind. No witch would be excluded from such a gathering. A knot tightens in my gut.

Eyes filled with worry, Prudence sighs. "She disappeared a week ago. We looked everywhere. I even scried for her. Wherever she is, my magic cannot go there."

Sir William and Henry Dove come and take the horses to be cared for. "Glad to have you both back," Sir William says.

I don't want to say it or even think it, but there is no way around it. "It's her who has taken your place, isn't it, Adam?"

His face is a mask of pain. "You told me once that she had been possessed by a demon. That's probably why Ariana chose her. Even as good as Trina is, darkness leaves a mark."

"What is this?" Prudence places her hand on Adam's arm.

He shakes his head and stares at his feet.

Somehow, I find the strength to speak. "Six days ago, we considered not arriving in time, thereby keeping Adam away from Ariana and her plan. Goddess came to us and told us Ariana had taken another to fill Adam's role and that she would not survive the dark spell."

"And Trina is this replacement," Prudence says. She closes her eyes. "There is no time to change what is."

"I will do all in my power to save her, Great Mother." He scans the hundreds of witches. "If I can, I will save us all."

Taking his hand, she leads us to the fire. "Come and eat something. You need to take care of yourself and not think you are alone in this." She gestures to the crowd. "Any one of these witches would die to save this world and Goddess's."

I sit beside Prudence and accept a cup of hot tea from Sylvia. "Great Mother, it is more than two worlds at stake. We don't know how pervasive this magic will be, but we met the fae king. He was equally concerned, though with a different way of showing it."

"Can you show us the items you collected?" Prudence asks.

"No one said to keep them to ourselves," I think.

Adam shrugs and draws the wand from inside his coat. "It focuses and bolsters my magic. It's how I was able to get us here in time."

Without touching the wand, Prudence moves her hand

over its length. "That's what it is, child, a drawing wand. It draws magic and increases the vibration, like when a pebble hits a still pond and the rings get bigger as they move from the center."

"I still don't know what I'm supposed to do with it." He puts it back into his coat.

I pull out the staff. "She called this the shield staff and said her father made it. When I matched it with the stone you gave me, Great Mother, the two became one."

She holds the staff, and power rolls from her and the item made by a god. "This will come in handy when things from other worlds try to come through." She hands the staff back to me.

Deep in the magic pouch I keep tied at my waist, I dig and find the hart's antler. I hold it out in my palm. "This was from the world of fae. While I suppose Midhir is the creator, the sacred hart offered the gift."

June crouches and stares at the piece of horn. "You saw the hart." Her voice is breathy. "My mother's mother used to say that only one with a soul purely in the light could ever witness an animal so good."

I close my fist around it and put it away. "I'm not sure about my worthiness, but seeing the hart was humbling in ways I cannot explain. He is the most majestic and magical creature I've ever encountered."

With her typical voice of reason, Sylvia asks, "How do we use these things to stop your sister, Adam?"

"I don't know," Adam admits with slumped shoulders.

"She cannot be stopped." Great Mother's voice is strong and sure.

"Then we've already lost." It feels as if a knife is embedded in my chest. "Why did Goddess have us traipse all over the country if we had no hope of winning?" I long to run as fast and as far from this place as I can, but I can't leave my coven without their leader another day, and I'm too exhausted to run. Without meaning to, I find I'm standing.

Prudence takes my hand and turns me to face her. "I didn't say we can't win, Sara Beth. I said we can't stop her from casting her spell. She will cast it. I have seen it. We shall fight the battle against dark magic, not the woman wielding it."

The link between Adam and me feels distant.

He only smiles. "We have to fight the magic. With wand and staff and pure hearts."

"What if she actually opens the gates of hell? How do we fight thousands of demons? It was deadly when we only had to kill one." I look at my Witches of Windsor and worry about who will be lost in the coming battle. It would be far easier if it were I who fell.

My mind is so filled with worry I can't make out what Adam is feeling or thinking.

Minerva says, "Come and eat. We'll worry later. For now, we have our high priestess back among us, and we have that to be thankful for."

There's an exuberant round of agreement, and Jonah begins carving a leg of lamb roasting over the fire.

After the meal, all the witches gather at the center of the standing stones. Laura Pinkerton approaches with her nephew, Isaac. "I'm very pleased to find both of you well."

"Thank you." My tone is solemn, as is my mood.

Adam ruffles Isaac's hair. "It's good to see you again. I trust your journey was uneventful."

"It went well. We gathered many witches as we traveled.

More still arrive." She points to the road where carriage full of witches and a cart filled with supplies has just arrived.

Have I brought all these souls here to die? Would Goddess be so cruel? "Great Mother says there is no way to stop the spell from being cast. The gates will open, and evil will pour in both directions."

Even frowning and living rough on the plains with only dotted firelight, Laura looks elegant. "I suspected as much." She grips my arm. "Do not lose hope, Sara Beth Ware. We will fight with every ounce of our strength to defeat anything dark that comes into our world. United, we shall find a way."

"I wish I had your confidence."

She smiles. "You need to rest. Take her to her tent, Adam. Things will be better in the morning."

With a nod, Adam takes my hand, and we cross to a tent our coven has set up for us. The tent is evidence that our sister and brother witches never lost faith that we'd arrive in time. I should take solace in that fact.

As Adam opens the tent flap, I look back at the milling forms of so many witches having gathered on this ground that will be a battlefield tomorrow. "I wonder if so many have ever come together before."

Laughter erupts from the center of the crowd.

Adam smiles. "People will write tales about this."

"If we live past tomorrow, I'm sure they will."

Pulling me close, he brushes stray hairs from my cheek and stares into my eyes. "Why have you suddenly become so pessimistic?"

Despite my worries, being held by Adam still makes my stomach flutter. I push back and move the two feet away that the tent will allow. "All this time, I thought we could prevent the gates of hell opening, or whatever your sister is about to unleash on us. Knowing we cannot win breaks my heart. Why are you not just as dismayed?"

He blinks slowly. "No one said we were going to lose this battle."

Had he not been listening? "Both Prudence and Laura said Ariana would open the gate. Goddess said that Trina will be killed." Tears blur my vision. "I can't save anyone. This world will fall to darkness, and we will stand and watch it happen."

Dragging me into his arm, he shushes me. "No. Beth, that is not going to happen. We may not be able to keep her from casting her spell, but we can fight and win for the light."

"What if we fail?"

Adam wipes my tears away. "We won't, but I'm willing to die to save this world, to save you. I know you'd die for the witches in your coven. We have a duty. It's the first time I've had one in my adult life. I'll not go down without a fight."

He's so beautiful, so good. My heart is full as I press my lips to his and wrap my arms around his neck. He strokes his tongue inside my mouth, and my knees get weak.

Pushing his coat from his shoulders, I can't get to his skin fast enough. I mutter a quick spell that leaves us both naked and our clothes in a heap near the tent flap.

"I really must learn that spell." Adam chuckles. "I do know a good one though." He flicks his wrist, and at our feet, a basin of water appears with a cloth resting on the side.

"That was impressive. Is the water warm?" I like the teasing. It makes me think, at least for a moment, that all is well in the world.

He crouches, swirls his finger around the basin, and steam lifts from the water into the cooler air. Dipping the cloth, he meets my gaze. "You're the most beautiful woman I've ever known, Beth. Inside and out, you fill my heart with joy. Whatever happens tomorrow, know that I love you and always will. Nothing and no one will ever change that."

Starting at my feet, he washes my legs, thighs, and hips.

The warm water and his hands spark desire between my legs. It takes all my will not to squeeze my thighs together for some relief.

Grinning up at me, he dips the cloth again and washes my stomach, arms and neck, kissing every inch of me until I can hardly stand on my own feet.

I grip his shoulders to keep from melting into a puddle as he slides his tongue along my neck to the back of my ear. Holding me in the circle of his arms, he washes down my back and over the swell of my ass.

"Everyplace but where I need you most." My voice is rough.

He kisses my cheek then captures my lips for a long, slow kiss. "I promise the teasing will all be worth it. Will you lie down?"

In a relatively short time, I've come to realize, I can deny him nothing. Lying on the pallet of blankets from my room in Windsor, I watch as he washes himself from head to toe. I can hardly breathe as he rubs the cloth along his hard shaft and lingers there with a soft groan.

Adam mutters a spell, and fresh water appears in the basin along with a clean cloth, which he wets before kneeling at my feet.

Leaning on my elbows, I watch as he bends my knees and presses them wide. My center pulses with need and a long sigh escapes my lips before he's touched me anywhere intimate.

He cleans me with such slow determination, it's as if I'm a religious icon and he the priest charged with its care.

If he takes much longer, my orgasm will come before he's made an effort in that direction. With the next caress of the cloth, I lift my hips, needing more.

Growling, he tosses the cloth in the basin. He lies between my legs with his head on my abdomen. "I want this night to be special. I want to give you everything I have, even if that is meager."

Thinking of the length and width of his manhood, I can't help but giggle. "There is nothing meager about you, Adam."

Tickling my ribs, he kisses my belly. "That's not what I meant."

"I know, but you're being far too serious. Make love with me and hold me in your arms tonight. That will be more than I ever expected from my life." I thread my fingers through his hair and revel in the scruff of his beard against my skin.

His arms wrap around my hips as he kisses his way down my abdomen. His hair tickles my inner thigh, and I sigh. My skin is so sensitive, I long to drag him up the length of my body and beg him to take me fast and hard.

"Not yet," he says, reading my thoughts. He plants tiny kisses over my center while he cups my bottom. His tongue splits me.

I scream and arch off the pallet.

Adam backs away and mutters a spell to keep our lovemaking noises from reaching outside the tent. "I don't want anyone thinking I'm killing you with anything but kindness, sweetheart."

Panting, I ask, "Can you kill me faster?"

A wide smile spreads across his face. "In a hurry? We have all night."

"Adam," I scold.

Adjusting his shoulders to press me wider, he wraps his arms around my thighs. With his fingers and mouth hovering so close that I feel the heat along my slit, he says, "As you command, my love."

When his fingers spread me wide, he blows a puff of air

that caresses my bud. So sensitive with arousal, I scream again. I lift my hips when he finally lowers his mouth and sucks hard.

Bouncing against his face, I'm calling out words that make no sense. I grip my nipples, looking for more. My body is on fire, and my core aches to be filled with Adam.

He slows his attention, licking a gentle path around my pearl. Unwrapping one arm from my thigh, he eases his fingers between my legs and presses two deep inside me. He rubs inside me while sucking harder and harder.

Gasping for air, I scream as my pleasure explodes. I shake with the intensity of the rapturous crescendo, which rolls over me so long, I'm struggling to catch my breath. "Adam."

Crawling along my body, he kisses my abdomen and between my breasts. "I could watch that for a thousand years." He pulls my nipple into his mouth and nips.

The pain is so good it sends a shiver through me. I wrap my legs around his hips. "I need you inside me."

"It's the only place I want to be." He notches his shaft between my netherlips, and I'm so wet, the head presses in without effort. Covering my mouth with his, he presses his tongue inside while burying his cock deep.

I cry out against his lips while he growls. Every inch of my flesh is heightened in sensitivity, and the base of his shaft rubs my pearl with every thrust. I'm on fire with the growing of a second orgasm. "Adam, I'm—oh, Goddess."

Pleasure shatters through me even harder than the first.

Adam stills his hips, but holding himself up on his forearms, he presses light kisses on my eyelids, cheeks, and forehead. "I love you, Beth. I have loved you for lifetimes and will love you until the end of time. If that time comes tomorrow, I will love you beyond this existence."

His oath is as erotic as his shaft still buried within me. I raise my hips, drawing him deeper. His rod presses a spot that renews my need for pleasure. "Oh!" I lift again.

Wrapping his arms around me, he rolls us so I'm on top. The new position brings him deeper. My body tightens around the delightful invasion, and I ride as if we're back on the road. On my knees, I press my hand to his chest. My nails create red marks, but I can't control the tightening of my muscles.

Thrusting his hips up every time I plunge down, Adam presses his thumb between my folds, rubbing my wetness in a tiny circle that brings me to the edge of euphoria.

We crash together, grunting and crying out as our releases collide.

Breathing as if I've run ten miles, I collapse on his chest.

He holds the back of my head, kisses my hair. With his other arm, he bands my back as if I might fly away.

"I love you too, Adam. I will love you for all lifetimes and in any world." After rolling off him, I let him clean me with newly warmed water. My mind is hazy as he snuggles in behind me and covers us with a blanket.

Considering how much is on my mind, I'm shocked I fell asleep, but after the travel and experiencing every possible emotion, I slept hard and deep.

Still, the sun is not yet up, and I'm awake. All the worries flood back to me as I find I'm the only person in the bedroll. Sitting up, I blink the dark tent into focus. Empty.

Drawing the blanket around me, I call for light and a ball of white light bobbles beside my head, confirming the tent is empty. Barefooted, I step outside.

June is feeding the fire, and a hint of gray light tells me the sun will arrive soon. She tosses a log in and waves at me. "Good morning."

My cheeks heat, and I have no idea why I should be embarrassed. "Hello, June. Did you see Adam?"

Wide-eyed, she shakes her head. "No. No one has stirred in the thirty minutes or so I've been awake."

I scan the sea of tents, and only a few people are beginning to step outside to tend their own fires. Looking farther out than the encampment, I see no one.

Stepping back inside, I hold in my tears as I pull on clothes fit for the battlefield.

He's gone.

At the bottom of my pile of clothes, the black wand Goddess gave Adam rests on the cloth floor.

CHAPTER
TWENTY-TWO

ADAM

The hardest thing I've ever done is leave Sara Beth sleeping in the predawn hours. She looked like an angel, while I tugged on clothes and left like a thief. I suppose I am worse than a criminal for stealing her love while knowing I had to go.

Just as Goddess foretold, I walk across the plain toward where I sense my brother and sister waiting. I've walked nearly five miles by the time I see them sitting quietly by a small campfire at the edge of the woods.

"I don't need you anymore, brother," Ariana says. Her voice is soft and vicious.

Kaden doesn't even look up from his mesmerized staring at the fire.

"Why have you bespelled Kaden?" I step around my brother and avoid looking directly at Trina's body lying face down in the grass. Facing Ariana, I see deep lines have formed around her eyes and mouth. Whatever she's bringing into herself is harming her.

"He had a moment of doubt, and I can't have that happen today." She chuckles. "All these years, we've planned and plotted for this day, and he never struggled until recently."

I sit on a stump just at the edge of the heat from the fire. "Didn't he know the consequences of what you plan? Did you explain to him that you would destroy this world and others and bring darkness?"

Meeting my gaze for the first time, she smiles, and it's like she's a young, carefree girl again. "You always were the smarter one. Too bad you have a morbid attachment to this place." She gestures to everything then wraps her brown cloak around her shoulders. "Why have you come? I told you I have no need of you now." She points at Trina. "That one will suffice."

My gut twists, but at least Trina is still breathing. "You and I both know the magic will be tainted if you use another's blood. Our blood is special. Isn't it, sister?"

"She will do," she says too fast.

"I will help you with opening the gate, if you release her back to the Windsor coven. I swear it." My heart is pounding so hard that it's a miracle she can't hear it.

"You swear it on your Goddess?" She spits out the last word.

It may not be possible to save this world, but I'm determined that Trina will not die in my place. "I swear, by Goddess, I'll help you open the gate. I'll add my blood to yours so you can complete the spell, but only if you guarantee her safety back to her witches."

"They will all be destroyed when darkness falls. Why should you care?" She rolls her eyes.

She can never understand. Still, I answer, "I may not be

able to control that, but I can save her so she's with those who care for her at the end."

"Tell me where you've been these last weeks?" She narrows her eyes. "How did you evade me after the scene by the church?"

If I lie, she'll know. Telling her the full truth would lose the light it's advantage. "Sara Beth Ware and I intended to stay away until after this day had passed."

"Then why are you and your pretty little witch back? Couldn't resist seeing my magnificence?" Her grin is as hideous as her black heart.

"Not exactly. Goddess told us you would use another." I tilt my head toward Trina.

Frowning, Ariana studies me. "I accept your offer to take that one's place."

When she makes no move to reverse her spell on Trina, I warn, "Let her go, or there is no deal, Ariana."

She flicks her wrist with another roll of her eyes. "I don't know why you love them when I am your family. I am great, and they are weak. You could be great too, Adam. Why do you choose weakness?"

When Trina rises to her knees, I kneel next to her. "Go back to the camp at the stones as fast as you can. Don't look back. Don't ask questions."

Terror alive in her eyes, Trina stands and looks at Ariana before rushing from the circle of light around the fire. She doesn't look back.

I return to my seat and look at my sister. "You wouldn't understand."

She shrugs. "What do you see in the witch you're bedding? Is it the sex? I quite enjoy that, but not enough to spend so much time with a man. Kaden refuses me."

"He's your brother." I speak before thinking, and my gut twists.

"He is my servant. He should do as I command. I have considered forcing him with magic, but discovered long ago, men are not as fun to lie with when they are bespelled." She examines her fingernails in the rising sun.

"Take the spell from Kaden now, please." I need to know if he's truly had a change of heart. It's possible Ariana just enjoys controlling him.

"Why? He's not harmed. I'd never harm him. He is my brother, after all." She throws her cape from her shoulders with more drama than is necessary.

"I too am your brother, and it would please me if you would release him from this spell. Do you worry he will leave you?" I'm treading dangerously, but I already know my life is forfeit. I have told my love how I feel, and I saved Trina, at least for the moment. It's more than I could have hoped for.

She mutters a spell, and I feel her dark magic push toward me.

Lifting my hands, I push the magic back, and it dissipates in front of me like a dark haze catching the breeze. "I'll not be forced to do your will, Ariana. I have given my word, and that will have to be enough for you."

Standing, she stomps her foot. "You are always so difficult. Never have you understood me or taken my side."

"You killed our parents. What did you expect?" It takes all my will to remain seated. I'm glad to know I can thwart her magic when I know it's coming. In the park, weeks ago, she caught me off guard. That will never happen again.

Snapping her fingers, she says, "Wake."

Kaden blinks, spots me, and stands, ready to cast.

I hold up my hands for peace. "I'm not a threat, brother."

Still disoriented, he looks at Ariana. "What is this?"

"Adam has joined us." Ariana says it as if she'd always expected it. She looks at me. "Those people were going to have me bound. Did you know that? They were so upset that I had been forced to deal with those monsters at the Order that they were going to allow the coven to bind my magic forever."

Looking confused, Kaden runs his fingers through his hair and backs away so he's not standing between us.

So much sorrow that might have been avoided if Ariana had been bound eight years ago. "They told you they would bind you?"

"Pfft. As if they would be honest with me."

Staring at the ground, Kaden stands with his spine straight and his shoulders rigid. "They told me."

It's all coming clearer. Mother and father would have been devastated upon hearing what Ariana had done at the Order. Kaden had done the wrong thing by helping Ariana escape. They likely scolded him and told him the coven would come and bind her for killing. Kaden loved our sister. It's hard to judge him harshly for trying to protect her. I doubt he thought she would kill our parents so heartlessly. "I see."

Kaden meets my gaze and nods, as if thanking me for not condemning him.

Ariana looks from me to Kaden. The smile that spreads across her face twists my stomach. "It's good to be together again."

A bright-blue tent appears next to a pair of trees to our east. Ariana giggles at my surprise and shades her face against the rising sun. "I need my rest. We move at dusk. Kaden, Adam has sworn to help me. I think him a witch of his word, but do not let him leave."

Kaden lowers his head.

"I'll not break my word."

Ariana disappears inside the tent.

Stuffing his hands in his pockets, and void of all his normal arrogance, Kaden asks, "Why did you come here?"

"To save the young witch you kidnapped," I say flatly. I'm full of questions and emotions, but I don't know if I can trust Kaden. I assume he still follows the dark, even if Ariana has abused his devotion.

"What was she to you?" Shoulders hunched, he kicks the ground.

"An innocent who didn't deserve to die in my place."

Kaden's head snaps up, and his eyes are full of shock.

I stretch my feet out in front of me and cross my ankles. "You don't think we're going to survive this, do you? Ariana doesn't care if we live or die, Kaden. She serves the darkness. I'm certain my heart is not black enough to live without the light. I cannot speak for your heart."

"I have not walked in full light in a long time. Goddess does not want me. Perhaps I'll live when the gates of hell open and darkness reigns." Facing the fire, he collapses with his legs crossed. "I'd hoped you would stay away. Even as I searched for you all these years, Adam, I was glad you stayed so far ahead of us. Perhaps my soul is lost, but knowing yours was safe with Goddess gave me peace."

Part of me wants to tell him my heart is still safe, but there's little point. Perhaps thinking he needs to save me will change the course of events. Drawing a long breath, I sigh. "I'd give anything to go back and start again with those frogs we set upon the high priest, brother."

He gives a joyless laugh. "No one gets a second chance."

Time to change the subject. "I missed my breakfast. Can we find something to eat before the world comes to an end?"

"Call a rabbit, and I will cook it." He smiles wickedly.

"You know I'll not use my gift that way, but we can track one or a nice pheasant." I like the idea of going into the woods and finding food with my brother the way we did when we were young. Nothing is the same, but perhaps he'll remember as I do.

Shaking his head, he sighs. "Why must it always be the hard way with you, Adam?"

Mimicking his action and sigh, I respond, "Why do you always choose the easy path, Kaden?"

An easy smile that also reminds me of simpler times spreads across his face. He stands. "Stay here. I will find something. You never could trap anything with much success. You'll only slow me down." When he reaches the edge of the woods, he looks from me to the tent then back at me. "You'll not run away?"

"I gave my word." It would be easy to escape, but Ariana would find another innocent witch to use in my place.

With a nod, Kaden walks into the woods.

I miss having Sara Beth in my head. I sealed away my mind while she slept so that she wouldn't hear me. She would have tried to stop me. Perhaps I could have convinced her that Trina deserved a chance to live, but we'd have argued. I prefer that we had a peaceful and loving night together. If she hates me for leaving, perhaps Trina's arrival at the camp will soften her anger.

It's so strange to want her to hear my thoughts. When Goddess first gave the gift, I wanted nothing to do with another person in my mind. Now I'm lonely without the sense of Sara Beth.

"Thinking of that high priestess?" Kaden walks toward the fire with a rabbit in his hand.

"I was, yes." There's no reason to lie about this. He probably knew I was in love with her before I was ready to admit it.

He pulls a bowl from a sack, then guts and skins the rabbit.

He puts the organs and head in the bowl and leaves it near the tent opening.

I assume they're for Ariana, but I'd rather not know if she eats the raw guts of animals or uses them for some unsavory magic. Instead, I focus on how deftly Kaden skewers the meat before sitting by the fire and burying the other end of the stick in the dirt. The meat rests close enough to the heat to cook but not burn.

He wipes his bloody hands on the grass.

Calling water from the air, I cause a small shower over his hands.

"Those magics were handy." He rubs the stains from his hands then dries them on his trousers.

"You could have called water for yourself."

He shrugs. "Ariana doesn't like for me to use your Goddess's magic. She says her master is stronger."

"I see."

He watches the meat cook. "You think of this witch when you freely chose to leave her. Why?"

"Why do I think of her?" It seems so obvious, but perhaps not to Kaden. "I have grown used to her company and her touch." A half-truth.

"I saw the way you looked at her. She has your heart. It must be quite a burden." He turns the stick.

Ariana's hand snakes from the tent flap and pulls the bowl inside.

My stomach churns. What has she become that she sleeps all day and eats raw remains? Trying to concentrate on Kaden, I say, "Why would it be a burden to be cared for?"

He glances briefly at the tent. "I have found relationships and love to weigh heavy."

In silence, we sit and watch the meat cook. I'm not sure how to respond, and perhaps it would be better to keep my own counsel. I suppose the duty to another's welfare can be a responsibility.

Kaden pulls a leg from the rabbit and gives it to me, then takes the other for himself while the rest of the animal continues to roast.

The leg is succulent and perfectly cooked. My stomach growls joyously at replacing my missed meal. I've grown soft since going to Windsor. Before finding a new family, I'd spent years not knowing where my next meal might come from. "Thank you."

He grunts and devours the meal.

The sun crosses the sky and creates odd shadows within the tent. What's inside hardly looks like a woman. Perhaps it's a trick of the light.

"Kaden."

His gaze meets mine.

"When the relationship is equal, the burden is shared and not so draining."

The mention makes his shoulders slump and the rings under his eyes darken. "An intriguing idea, but no matter what you say, brother, I can't leave her. She owns me."

I want to argue, but what can I say? It's possible his vow to Ariana or whatever master she serves will not permit him to alter his path any more than my promise can be broken. "I suppose we must see this through to the end."

He looks at the sun as it climbs higher. "Only a matter of hours now. All these years of planning and for you, running, and it is finally as she always knew it would be."

"Is it?" I look toward the encampment, but it's too far away for me to see the witches. In my mind, I see Sara Beth formulating a plan to destroy my siblings and me. I hold no grudge. She must win, or all will be lost. It's only that I mourn what I will never have again.

"Even when she was still a child, she said you would join us, and on that glorious day, we would claim all worlds as our birthright. Gods and goddesses will kneel before us and die in a moment of rage. She never wavered from the knowing." He pulls the remaining meat from the fire and offers me half.

Appetite waning, I'm unwilling to lose this moment of conversation over a meal with my twin brother. Besides, I'll need my strength for the evening. "I'm not sure her use of *we* was accurate. I think it likely you and I are as expendable as Trina was. Still, she was accurate about the three of us being together at this moment in time."

He grins as though he finds the idea of dying amusing. "At least it will be over soon."

The only emotion I can find for him is pity.

A feminine growl rumbles inside the tent.

"What has she become?"

He shrugs. "She is the future."

CHAPTER
TWENTY-THREE

SARA BETH

As the sun reaches the horizon, I push aside my sorrow. Despite Goddess saying that Adam would stand with his sister, I still pictured us going into battle together.

Sending Trina back to us was a good thing, but once he'd freed her, why didn't he return. I watched the west all day waiting for him. I long to believe he wouldn't betray us.

I let anger replace my tears and stand with my sister and brother witches in a circle fifty deep within and around the standing stones.

As the sun dips lower, mutterings begin in the west edge of witches.

His mind is closed, but I feel Adam approaching. I don't know how they intend to get through so many witches in the light. My knuckles are white around the shield staff, while the other items Adam and I collected sit heavy in my pocket.

Adam must not have wanted the wand to fall into his sister's hands, and that gives me hope.

As the last light of day falls, clouds roll in from the east. Laura lights the fire at the center of the stones. The wood catches, and the flames shoot twenty feet high. Rain drizzles down.

June stands at the great mother's side, and Trina directly behind her. Prudence squeezes my hand. "The rain is a good sign. Good for water magic."

Of course, she's right, but the thought of having to drown Adam with water magic makes my gut ache. I brush it aside. "Goddess strength and light!" I yell over the din.

"Goddess strength and light," the crowd calls back.

"We stand against the darkness on this, the third day, of the third month, in the third year." I draw a breath and hope for courage. "It is our duty and our honor to fight for the light and keep out that which does not belong."

"For Goddess and the light," they call back.

The sky crackles with lightning and thunder, blinding me for a second.

"Pretty words," Ariana purrs beside the fire. It's hard to imagine such a petite woman could be so dangerous. "They will not save you."

Kaden and Adam stand behind her like sentinels.

Holding a shiny golden bowl in his hands, Kaden looks dazed.

When Adam searches my face, I turn my gaze to his sister. "We will fight whatever you bring to this circle."

Ariana brushes her long red hair over her shoulder. "I'll admit, you've amassed more of an army than I would have expected, but you haven't any chance of winning this. Why not bow to me now, and I'll spare you? You can serve the dark and live." She speaks louder. "You can all serve the dark and live."

Even knowing she would not turn any of these witches, I hold my breath. If one good witch turned, it would be terrible.

The fire shoots higher until it looks as if it might touch the clouds. She scans the crowd, but there are no takers. "I'll not make this offer again."

Still, no one moves to join the dark.

My heart pounds, and I find my relief palpable.

"So be it." Ariana reaches toward Kaden, and he puts the bowl in her palm. As she drinks the contents, two streams of red ooze down her chin.

My stomach churns.

"She drinks the blood of her blood," Prudence says.

Offended that the bowl contains Adam's blood, I lift my hand and throw a spear of water at her.

Kaden steps in front of her and bats it away, and his forearm bleeds where it struck him.

"Fool!" Bowl discarded, Ariana lifts both her hands and screams words I don't understand, but they make me queasy.

Evil upsets the balance of all things.

Her eyes turn full black, and she bares her teeth in a terrifying smile.

The sky above us swirls in a black funnel. Energy rushes into the vortex, and it shakes with thunder. The funnel flattens twenty feet above Ariana's head. Rather than the cloudy sky of England, within the funnel is darkness so black and ugly it hurts my head to look within.

Despite my determination to let go of my attachment to Adam in case he really has turned, I have to look at him. My heart sinks at the graying of his skin.

Kaden too is pale, and his shoulders slump.

She's draining her own brothers for the power to open the gate.

I long to save Adam, but if I give him energy, it feeds

Ariana.

Gripping my arm, Prudence says, "Use the staff to shield him."

Swallowing my fear, I point the blue crystal at Adam and ask Goddess for his protection.

A beam shoots out, then forms a bubble around him. His cheeks pinken. Wide-eyed, he stares at me.

Over the thrashing wind of her gate to hell, Ariana screams, "You broke your vow." She claws at his face, but her hand bounces off the shield.

Collapsing to the ground, both twins look at their sister with the same horrified expression.

The head of a beast with horns, red eyes, and black skin pokes through the gate and gives a wild screech.

Laura calls upon water and wind energy to push the monster back where he belongs.

Another demon, small and with six legs, jumps to the ground. A stinger, wet with venom, tops his crooked tail. He charges the south side of the circle.

Three witches shoot magic at him until he splatters like a bug under carriage wheels.

More demons fight their way into our world.

Witches shoot into the vortex to keep them away, while the ones that get through are also dealt with.

I keep my head clear and hold the shield around Adam. Remorse for Kaden may very well be coming from Adam, but either way, I extend the shield to keep Kaden safe as well.

Ariana laughs as she waves her arms in a circle, widening the gate. Then, as if just remembering Adam's transgression, she spins and stalks toward him. "You swore on your Goddess to help me."

"Only to help you open your gate. I gave my blood. You opened the gates of hell. I have fulfilled my vow." He pushes to his feet and stands between Kaden and Ariana, as if he might save his brother. He wavers slightly, but he holds firm.

Ariana shoots sickly green lightning at him.

The shield holds, but Adam pushes his wind magic toward her. It escapes the shield and forces Ariana back a few steps.

Sylvia leans in. "We have to get Adam out of there."

Demons are coming through faster than we can beat them back.

William grabs a slimy beast by the horns protruding from the top of its head and wrestles it to the ground before it can escape the circle.

Esme shoots a magical arrow through its eye.

The demon slumps as black blood soaks the ground. Then it lies still.

Jonah says, "Sylvia's right. We can pull him out of the center. He's exposed and vulnerable with little energy left to fight back."

"No." I'll not risk them to save Adam. "We'll have to find another way." In this moment, I realize I trust Adam. He left to save Trina, and to do so had to make a promise to help Ariana. He's no longer helping her. He gave her what she needed to open the gate, but now he's fighting back with the little power he has left after being drained.

Ariana shoots more black magic at him. The shield is wavering, and the staff shakes in my hand. It's harder to hold as magic forces itself through the birch in a rush to meet the countering magic.

At the west edge of the gate, a demon as wide as the height of two men flies in. Warm air whooshes across my face from the batting of its leathery wings. Two legs hang from its dark-gray body, and witches duck from its huge, deadly talons.

With a wide human mouth, it shows a jagged row of teeth, dripping with thick slime. It circles to make another pass.

At the outer ring, a fire witch with long brown hair is hoisted to the top of a stone. I think she's from the Kent coven. She draws fire from the pyre at the center and hurls balls of flame at the flying monster.

It bats two away as if they're a child's toy. The third lights its left wing. The next crashes against its chest and sends it barreling to the ground, where it screams and burns.

Sussex earth witches band together and shoot magic arrows into the gate.

I have no idea how many demons are trying to come through, but the arrows slow them.

Adam collapses but keeps his magic shooting toward Ariana. His skin is so pale I worry he won't last much longer.

When I woke, and he was gone, I never thought anything could hurt worse than knowing he'd left me. Even with good cause, it struck like the tip of a whip. This is far worse. I feel as if I'll explode with the pain building inside me. The helplessness is pure torment.

Kaden, skin as gray as death itself, grips Adam's leg.

I lift my hand to lash out, but color creeps back into Adam's cheeks. Kaden is feeding Adam the last of his energy.

Adam shakes him off and says something I can't make out over the growing battle.

With a head as wide as one of the standing stones, a snake looks out the gate, its forked tongue slipping from its thin mouth. Its black eyes shift from side to side as it drops between Ariana and Adam, stopping their battle. It breaks the magic from both directions. Coiling its body, it lifts its head and hisses at Adam.

Ariana laughs and lifts her hands back to the gate. Green lightning cracks from her as she mutters another spell.

The words are unnatural, and my ears thrum as my

stomach knots as though I've eaten something not meant for human consumption.

In a slow flash of light and magic, a second gate opens. Not with the crashing of the first, but as if someone thrust their hands in a tiny hole in the sky, and gripping both sides, forced the opening wider. Within, it glows mossy green.

Screeching as if amused by the new opportunity, demons fly out of the first gate and into the second.

Both sides of the battle for Earth stop fighting to watch the second gate. It's as if time has stopped.

A moment later, bloody pieces of demon bodies drop back to Earth like refuse.

From above, the fae king's voice booms. "You dare attack me." Nothing remains of the amusement Midhir displayed when we took shelter in his woods. Terrifying and powerful, he shoots blue fire from the second gate.

Witches run from the center as their demon combatants burst into flames so hot, some melt into puddles and others explode.

Ariana screams and calls something into the demon gate.

While she's distracted, I grip the shield staff tighter and rush toward Adam. I take his hand and drag him along the ground. As if the gates are holding him, a sucking wind whips up, trying to swallow us. Gripping tighter, I dig my heels into the ground. Still the wind pulls at me. I don't know if it wants us both or just Adam, but I hold tight and meet his gaze. "I'll not lose you like this."

"I can't let them take you. They think I belong to them because they've tasted my blood." Adam opens his hand.

"No!" My grip is firm around his wrist. I can't let him go. Breath short and muscles aching, I'm ready to drop the damned staff to use both hands to hold Adam. "I don't care what they think. You belong to me, and I to you, Adam MacNab."

A hand wraps around mine on the staff. Sylvia's grip is relentless as she pulls with all her might.

Henry Dove grabs Sylvia around the waist, and determination strains his face as his arms bulge.

William and Esme hold on to Henry in a chain of love and family. A family unwilling to let any member go is stronger than any demon magic.

They all pull, and we inch away from the center, toward Windsor coven, who are battling a new group of demons.

Adam clasps Kaden's arm and drags him away from Ariana. At the edge of the inner circle, with little cover, Kaden lies unconscious in the mud and blood of the battlefield.

Weak and pale, Adam stares at me. "You're mad. You know that?" He wipes mud from his smiling face.

"It took me too many years to find the man meant for me. I'll not have that creature take you away without a fight."

A serpent as black as the mucky ground slithers past my feet. It rears back, eyes on Adam.

I stab the staff down as hard as I can. When I feel it's skull crack, I'm filled with nauseating satisfaction. The thing's scream is loud and high pitched, nothing like any snake of this world.

Minerva rushes over, kneels beside Adam, and cups his cheeks.

"My brother." He tries to pull away, but she holds tight.

"I'll do what I can for him, Adam, but Sara Beth will need you to help her. We all need you."

Adam allows the healing. His skin blooms pink and healthy. "Thank you."

She helps him to his feet and moves to see to Kaden.

Esme rushes to her side and lends her healing gifts as well.

Adam says, "Thank you for trusting me."

My heart clenches. I should have never doubted him. I let my sorrow and broken heart speak when my head and soul knew the truth. An apology will have to wait.

Demons drop from the gate by the hundreds. Small, large, winged, two and four legged, they rain into our world.

A man-size demon with slimy dark-green skin and glowing red eyes lifts a sword and rushes toward us.

Adam pulls fire from the center, forms a blade, and lets it soar into the demon's chest. "I'm feeling much better. It's good to be on this side of the battle line, dear one."

In the midst of the worst hell I've ever seen, joy blooms in my chest. "It's good to have you beside me."

Two more similar demons rush toward us. I thrust energy from the shield staff toward them, lift them off their feet, and throw them backward into the fire.

Water witches form a line, draw water from the clouds and create a wave that sends the demons back up into the hell gate.

As the water witches duck out of the way, earth witches shoot arrows at anything that escapes the wave.

The ground shakes with the thundering footsteps of a demon taller than the largest of the monoliths. It swings its arms and sends two witches flying. A deep growl rumbles from it.

Avoiding its stomping feet slamming the ground with the power of giant anvils, three Derbyshire fire witches, along with Laura, Lydia, and Isaac, rush in to beat it back with shooting flames.

Heart in my throat, I'm about to jump in when they set the beast aflame then use air magic to blow it back through the gate.

Ariana lifts her hands, mutters a third incantation, and a third gate opens.

Blue light pours from the newest gate, and Goddess's magic flows down.

Ariana curses and shoots her magic into the opening. The magic crashes up, and Ariana's body stretches long and thin in a grotesque distortion. Her pale skin darkens to an inky, unnatural black, and her eyes glisten with red light. Soft strands of hair morph into cords that swirl like dozens of snakes.

The creature that stands shooting dark magic into Goddess's realm has nothing left of the woman that was. This is pure evil. Despite the horribly haggish Ariana's assault into the gate, nothing happens in return.

Blue light continues to pour through the opening.

Stomping a foot with a banshee scream, Ariana doubles her magical assault.

More demons enter. Some crawl into the elfin world, and some to the Goddess's world. Most stay here and fight the witches.

A demon as tall as a tree thrusts his spiked arms through two witches' chests. They fall in puddles of blood.

More witches fall, and the ground runs red.

It's unbearable to watch so many witches die at the hands of evil. Fueled by desperation, I point the wand at the creature and pour water magic into it. "With water first I call for ice to cut and bend and slice. If right our Goddess sees, as I will, so mote it be."

The wand vibrates with magic and buries shards of ice in a demon. Once it falls, I shoot the ice daggers at a dozen more demons. One by one, they die, until I'm drained from the effort and have to stop.

Still more demons drop from the gate. There seems no end to them. How can we defeat an enemy who has an endless resource and cares nothing for life?

It's impossible.

Prudence places her hand on my shoulder. "Do not lose hope, child. You can win for all of us."

Energy surges within me, and my magic restores, but not my hope. Even as I force a smile for the great mother, my heart is sick.

CHAPTER
TWENTY-FOUR

ADAM

Pointing at the wand in Sara Beth's hand, Ariana laughs. "You come at me with trifles and expect to win. What a pitiful creature you are."

Even with my tainted blood, I feel no connection to the evil creature before me. Ariana is not my family. I have hope for Kaden, but Ariana was never of the light. The witches who fight and die, they are my family. They risked everything to save me when they could have left me to die in the center of the circle. I'm sure Ariana would have drained both Kaden and me dry if she'd had more time. We are nothing but resources to her, power and blood she needs to destroy worlds.

I want to keep my thoughts in the light, but anger fills me.

Demons fall from the other worlds. The ones that plummet from the world of fae or Goddess lay lifeless on the soiled earth. Those that drop from the demon's world seem to be recently born. Born of evil, they destroy as their first act.

My stomach roils, and my anger flares anew. I shoot water and fire at any demon I see.

Prudence kneels by Kaden with her hands on his head, while Jonah stands guard over both. A bear of a man, he holds an axe in one hand and a sword in the other. He could pass for a Highland warrior of old. It's odd to see the gentle giant looking so ferocious, but this is his family he's protecting. A man will do anything to protect the people he loves. Whether he protects Prudence, Kaden, or both, I feel akin to him, as I do to all of the witches of Windsor.

Still unconscious, Kaden breathes stronger and steadier.

I grip Sara Beth's arm. "We can win this. We have too much to lose to fail."

Our eyes meet, and she says, "I'm sorry I doubted you."

Shaking my had. "There's no need to feel sorry. We always knew I had to go to Ariana. Goddess said as much."

A tear slips down her cheek, making a clean path through the grime. "I should have trusted you.

It doesn't make a difference. I would have doubted too. I hold out my hand. "Trust me now."

A tight smile tugs at her lips. She hands me the wand.

It feels right in my hand. As well as it worked for Sara Beth, it was meant for me. Meant for this. "Use the staff to shield the gate."

Sara Beth lifts the staff toward the demon gate. A golden glow spreads from the crystal at the top, spreads like a bubble, and caps the demon gate. It bulges and undulates under the pressure of warriors of darkness, but it holds. Creatures stop coming through.

A mile in every direction, witches fight demons with the magic of Goddess, Hecate. Light fights against dark. Good against evil.

Demons fall to the ground, as do witches.

I shoot water and fire through the wand to kill as many demons as I can.

Like thunder, something pounds against the other side of the shield.

The golden glow dims but holds under the warping pressure of whatever is trying to get through.

Sara Beth cringes at the weight of it.

Ariana laughs, though in her current form, the sound is grating and hurts my ears. "He is come, and you will be the first to die."

She shoots her filthy magic toward Sara Beth.

I throw magic in the path of my sister's evil.

Sylvia rushes forward and beats back the dark magic with her light.

Frowning, Ariana tries again to get Sara Beth to lower the shield staff and let through whatever is pounding against the magic.

Sylvia holds her ground, and I realize she's gotten in the way of my magic. Perhaps so I can save my energy for whatever is coming next.

Henry Dove pulls back his arm and throws a knife toward what Ariana has become. It strikes, but she only stares at the metal in her chest.

I am elated. It's terrible to wish my sister dead, but she has no place in this world.

Then she pulls it free and tosses it aside. "I am a god. Nothing of this world can destroy me!"

Dread hits me like a hammer. Is it possible we cannot kill her? If we cannot defeat Ariana, then whatever is pushing against the shield will surely destroy us.

Sara Beth takes my free hand and whispers, "We have tools not of this world."

Two yards away, Laura takes the head off a demon with a

sword she's crafted out of fire. She looks from me to Sara Beth and winks before charging into another battle with a six-legged demon that lunges at her with claws and fangs.

Goddess's voice permeates the crash of death and blood. "Not one demon can be left in any world not their own. Fight with what they cannot understand. Fight with what makes your world special."

"Small task." I don't even try to keep the sarcasm out of my tone. I'll still never love the idea of a deity manipulating my life, but at least I understand a bit more now.

The pounding grows stronger. "I can't hold it back much longer."

Fight with what they can't understand.

I'm so stupid. Why didn't I realize this earlier. "Beth, I love you in this life and in all that came before. I shall love you in all the lives to come. Love is the emotion they—" I point at the gate. "Can't understand or relate to in any way."

She grips the shaking staff with both hands, barely holding on to the magic flowing through a god's tool. "How does that help us?"

The shield staff cracks. Pain streaks across her face as she's forced to drop the shattered pieces.

Something that can only be described as the devil drops to its feet next to Ariana, who again looks like a woman, though her eyes show no white or color other than black.

The devil is twice the height of a man and covered in brown fur. Two curved horns protrude from above his temples, and his eyes are black like Ariana's. Evil pours from him like pus from a wound. In a bass voice, he speaks. "You will all bow to me, or I will kill everything in this world. Save yourselves. Your pitiful goddess will die today. That miserable fae will perish as well. I've waited through millennia of worlds crashing into nothing and new ones being born for this day. Do you really think you can defeat me with your silly magics?"

Sara Beth crouches and picks up the crystal that once topped the staff. She places it in her palm with the piece of the sacred hart's antler.

I put the wand in her hand and clasp my palm over hers.

Magic of three kinds swirls between us.

The devil's eyes widen, and he points at us. "Stop. I command you to stop this foul magic."

Ariana runs toward us, hands raised like claws.

Trina pushes her back with a wave of air magic.

Stunned, Ariana screams for the other demons to attack.

Pointing the wand held in both our hands with the other items clenched together, I pray to Goddess for strength and that we're doing the right thing. "I love you, Beth."

"I love you, Adam."

Our magic flows through our hearts, down our arms, and shoots out of the end of the wand. Bright and pure white, it bursts like an endless cannonball at Ariana. She's pushed backward into her devil. Other demons are thrust backward.

Jonah touches my shoulder.

Sylvia touches his.

Prudence touches Sara Beth's shoulder, and Trina touches hers.

On and on, the train continues until every witch still alive feeds the love and magic of the three items clasped in our hands.

The devil screams, and the sounds shakes the earth.

It's hard to keep our feet, but somehow, we stand together, an unbreakable chain of magic and love.

Maybe that's the point, magic is love or love is magic.

Either way, the devil is losing his war with this world. He

grows smaller until he's the same size as Ariana, who clutches him like a lover.

Terrified demons run back into their world.

Prudence calls out, "Send them all back."

"To hell and never to return," Sara Beth begins.

I take up the spell, "Witches of the light stand firm."

"Our world. Our magic. Our love is free."

The entire company of witches calls out as one, "As we will, so mote it be."

Ariana's eyes show her shock as she realizes she's going to be sent to hell with her devil. She pushes on his chest, but it's too late. As one, they are sucked into the world of darkness.

Magic forces our hands open.

The hart's antler turns to a fine white dust that swirls up and creates a seal over the demon gate. Hecate's wheel with two opposing moons shines bright before it and the gate fade, as if it had never been there.

The fae king's low laugh echoes and then he stands before us.

At the center of the circle, the fire sputters out.

Goddess, in her diaphanous gown blowing in a wind that no one else feels, floats into view and stands beside Midhir.

They bow to each other before Midhir steps forward and bows to Sara Beth and me. "I am in your debt, witches. Should you have need of me, I shall repay what is owed."

Sara Beth's smile makes butterflies go wild in my gut.

This woman is everything.

She says, "I accept your thanks, Fae King. I cannot imagine a time where I would ask for your help, and you have already done your part by bringing the hart's magic to seal the gate."

Mischief lurks in his eyes, and he chortles as he fades from sight. "You never know when a fair witch may be in need of a handsome fae."

It would be funny if I wasn't a jealous man. As it is, I'm glad he's gone and will likely forget about us in a moment.

All the witches kneel as Hecate approaches. She's so beautiful it's hard to look at her, and even harder to look away.

I bow my head, take Sara Beth's hand, and pull her back to her feet.

Hecate smiles. "You have done well, children. Though, I knew you would. Love is your greatest gift." She looks at me. "Even your brother who was lost came back to you because of love."

To my right, Prudence sits with Kaden, who is still lying on the ground, unconscious.

"Will he live?" My heart aches at the idea of losing him again after getting him back for just a moment.

"Life and death are up to him." She smiles as if she knows I despise her frequently cryptic answers.

"What now, Goddess?" Sara Beth asks.

Her sigh sounds like a calm breeze. "Now you go on, child. You have done as I asked. You can live as you like. This world is safe for now. I cannot promise darkness will not try again to take your light, but I think it will need time to recover from this day."

"And you? Will I see you again?" Desperation and hope ring in Sara Beth's question.

Goddess fades. "I am always with you, as I'm with all witches in the light."

We stand staring at the killing field a long time. No one speaks as the sun breaks on a new day. We fought all night, and now the light of day illuminates the carnage left behind.

A light rain still falls as witches search for wounded among the dead and tend to both. The dead are carried to the center of the ring. A group including Minerva and Laura purify and sanctify the ground to get it ready for the funeral.

Sara Beth consoles each coven over their loss. Windsor also lost two witches. Mable Bale, a water witch, and Jennifer Maynard, an earth witch, were both killed in battle. Trina and Winnie cry softly as they clean their bodies to ready them for the pyre.

Sara Beth leaves the Kent coven's gathering to console Windsor's witches. She takes no time to mourn.

I hardly knew Mable or Jennifer, but I mourn their loss as I sit for the first time. It feels like years since I've relaxed, and even now, Kaden lies inside the tent fighting for his life. Prudence and Esme are with him and sent me out for some air. Feeling I should be doing more, I close my eyes and let my sorrow come.

Cold hands fold over mine. "You've done plenty," Sara Beth whispers. "Your brother is ill, and you've lost your sister. You stood with the light and fought for our world."

"I should have died in place of Mable or Jennifer." My face is wet with tears for them. None for Ariana. She made her choice, and I wept for the girl she was long ago.

Sara Beth wraps her arms around me. "No. Some things are not our business, and the time of our death is one of those. It is not for us to decide when we go to Goddess." Looking in my eyes, she cups my cheeks and tears roll down her face unchecked. "Besides, I need you to grow old with me."

It's hard to imagine any joy existing in the world when rain still falls on the battlefield, but the idea of spending my life with this magnificent woman spreads happiness inside me. "Does that mean you'll marry me, Sara Beth Ware?"

One side of her mouth tips up in half a smile. "Perhaps, when you ask me properly."

Looking over her shoulder, miles of carnage and sorrow are all I can see. I pull my attention back to her. "I'll do just that, when this part is over. First, we'll mourn our friends."

She smiles wide while tears track down her soft cheeks.

After a full day of rain rinses away most of the blood, the moon rises over Stonehenge. Demon bodies were carted to a field in the afternoon and burned without ceremony. When they were gone, the ground was salted and blessed.

Memories of the battle of dark and light will be with us for our lifetimes, but for now, we'll do right by our fallen brothers and sisters. Cleaned and wrapped in burial shrouds, fifty-six bodies lay at the center of the standing stones. Fifty-six souls gave their lives for the light.

Laura Pinkerton and Sara Beth stand hand in hand at the south end of the circle.

Sara Beth begins. "Mother Goddess, release these souls from this place and let them walk in blessed gardens of summer."

Laura continues. "As they enter dreams and are reborn, thank you for our time. Let their light shine down and give us peace."

Candles are placed at the north, south, east, and west. Sara Beth flicks her wrist to light them. "We light these candles to remember those who left us and shine a light for their journeys. With fire, and wind. With earth, and water."

Bowing her head, Laura says, "In the light of sun and moon, we know in peace we shall meet again."

Taking Laura's hand again, Sara Beth says, "Blessed be."

The congregation repeats, "Blessed be."

Fire streams from the two high priestesses' hands and ignites the pyre under the bodies. Smoke pours upward to heaven.

In silence, we all watch as so many rise to Goddess as one.

Witches hug and kiss each other as the fire burns. Unlike the superheated fire we burned the demons with, this fire will be allowed to burn naturally. While it does, everyone will speak of the dead and each one's life.

Making my way to Kaden's tent, I avoid the crowd. It's cowardly, but I feel some responsibility for the deaths. I can think of no way I could have acted differently, but it was my sister who instigated the killing.

Prudence waits on a stool by the tent flap. The fire dances in her watery eyes. "You know, it was that devil who invaded the heart of that young girl before she was old enough to fight back. Why he chose Ariana, I can't say, but it was not your fault any more than it was hers. She was a tool badly misused. Kaden was seduced because of his love for her."

"Your heart is too kind, Great Mother." I kneel in front of her.

She pats my head. "It is not kindness, child. It is a sad truth that you and your family were dragged into this darkness. Your parents suffered, and now you suffer. If Kaden lives, he will suffer as well."

"A fine picture you paint." I get up and move toward the tent.

Prudence takes my hand with more strength than I would have thought possible for one her age. "Suffer now, and tomorrow, find light. Celebrate life and love. You have a lot to be joyous about, have you not?"

"I have family," I admit. "I never would have believed I'd be accepted anywhere, yet these witches risked their lives to pull me out of Ariana's grasp. They used their power to heal me, and even heal my misguided brother."

Her grin is as hopeful as a young girl's. "Tomorrow, start

fresh in the light, Adam. Make your pact, and let the coven celebrate life and love."

Hope blossoms in my chest. Laughter surrounds the funeral pyre as witches pass bottles of wine and talk about their lost members with joy. They will stay awake until the last of the fire burns out.

Sara Beth stands scanning the crowd then sees me by the tent and watches.

She says something to Laura before leaving the circle and making her way in my direction.

CHAPTER
TWENTY-FIVE

SARA BETH

As we did all night, Adam and I sit outside Kaden's sick tent. We were vigilant, keeping our eyes on Kaden and the fire burning down to embers.

Esme and Minerva took turns caring for Kaden after Prudence was convinced to go to sleep.

Hand in hand, we watch the sun rise in the east as it always does, as if the world had not nearly been lost in a pit of hell. "There is something hopeful in a new day."

He squeezes my hand. "Indeed." After a long pause, he says, "Prudence told me I should leave my regret behind me today and bring cause for joy to the coven."

"Funerals are meant for remembering and mourning. Now we must find a way to go on and live in the light."

Witches start packing up their tents and camps. The fire has burned all the way down, and only a few wisps of smoke remain. A few gather ashes to keep in memorial urns.

"I know we both are tired, and I'm in need of a long bath. I know I have less to offer you than you have on your own." He stares down at our linked fingers.

"You are more than enough." My voice is tight and full of all the emotions I'm holding in check.

Adam kneels in the mud in front of me. I'm already low since the stool has sunk three inches into the muddy ground. He takes both my hands. "I know I'm not nearly worthy of you, but I hope to be, one day, Beth. Even knowing it, I have to ask. Will you marry me? Will you be mine in this life and all those that follow?"

Emotions overflow, and tears wet my cheeks, blurring my view. His face is covered in grime, yet he's still the most handsome man I've ever seen. No proposal could ever be more beautiful. "I will marry you, Adam MacNab. I will marry you in a hundred lifetimes. You are the other half of me, and I waited all my life for you to come down from your Highlands and find me."

Dashing away a tear of his own, Adam presses a hard kiss to my lips. "I apologize for keeping you waiting, my love. It would seem there were many things that had to happen before you and I were ready to accept each other."

"It would seem so." I grasp his face in both hands and kiss him until I'm out of breath.

"What's this then, right out in the light of day?" Sylvia asks.

Henry Dove stands at her left side, his face bright with amusement. "It looks like a good idea to me."

Before he can lean in, she slaps him on the arm and keeps her attention on us.

Pulling himself out of the mud, Adam stands and brings me up with him. "Sara Beth has agreed to marry me."

"Thank Goddess." Sylvia pulls Sara Beth into a hug. "I worried you'd be stubborn and make him wait months more."

With a hearty laugh that turns heads, Sara Beth hugs her friend. "Not about this. Some things are meant, and it's silly to be stubborn about them." She nudges Sylvia toward Henry as she lets her go.

Sylvia frowns, but Henry laughs and hugs Sylvia around the waist. "I wish you both much happiness. When will you marry?"

In my head, Adam says, *"Today would not be soon enough."*

Minerva steps out of the tent. "He's doing better, but he'll not be ready to move for at least a few days."

Sylvia, still in Henry's arms, says, "Sara Beth and Adam are going to marry."

Even exhausted, Minerva smiles brightly as she pulls me into a tight hug. "I'm so happy for you." She hugs Adam. "You've brought joy to my oldest and dearest friend, and now you will be my brother."

Adam's mind runs with emotions and thoughts of a real family. "We'll marry when Kaden is well enough, if that is all right with you, Beth?"

My cheeks heat at the nickname in front of so many people. "You can all return to Windsor as soon as you can pack our things. Adam and I will stay with Kaden until he's ready to travel."

From the next tent, Esme and William emerge. Esme shakes her head. "I'll not leave you here alone. We shall stay with you and return together in a few days."

Sylvia props her hand on her hip. "I agree with Esme. I shall not leave you. What if you need help?"

As touched as I am, I know everyone is tired and could do with a hot bath and a good meal. "We survived several weeks on our own, and then we were traipsing around the countryside. I'm sure we can manage just caring for Kaden here."

Minerva's gaze is distant, and a moment later Jonah arrives.

Jonah embraces me in a giant brotherly hug. Shaking Adam's hand in his beefy one, he grins. "I'm happy for you both." He frowns. "If you think I guarded your brother all through the battle just to leave him and you behind, and lay awake worrying in my soft bed, you've lost your senses. Minerva and I will stay at Stonehenge until we can travel home together."

It's futile to argue with them about something I don't really want. As much I look forward to a future with Adam, I never want that future to exclude our coven, our family. "I give up. I thought you'd all like a decent meal and bath, but clearly you prefer the rain and chill of tent living."

On the second day after the funeral, I walk around the standing stones. Hard rains have washed away most of the grime of battle.

Laura approaches. "High priestess, I've come to bid you farewell."

I take her hands. "There's no need for titles between us."

"You were kind to give me part in the funeral, but I saw your power, and that of your mate. You could rule this isle if that were your will." She squeezes my hands.

I shake my head. "That magic was borrowed from gods, Goddess, and kings. I'm just a witch."

She laughs, and the sound is musical. "You can think that if you like, Sara Beth Ware, but you are far more. You slew a devil and sent him and all his minions back to hell. You saved this world and two others. The nonmagical people of this place may never know what you did for them, but I'll not forget. Witches will tell tales of you and Adam MacNab for generations to come. Soulmates who used love to let light conquer darkness. There will be songs."

Oh dear, I hope she's wrong. "I'll miss you, Laura. You've been a good friend to me and my coven."

"And you to me and all the Derbyshire witches. We shall meet again, and until then, I will write to you if you permit it." She gives me a small curtsy.

Flattered by her deference, I don't know how to take it. My cheeks heat. "I would be thrilled to correspond, dear friend."

She hugs me. "Be well, happy, and live in the light of Goddess."

"Safe travels. You will always be welcome in Windsor. Should you have need of me, you may ask it at any time." I release her and my throat tightens as she walks to the carriage waiting nearby.

Lynda and Isaac wave from the bench.

I return the wave and dash away an errant tear. Finishing my trip around the stones, I press a hand to one and let the deep magic flow through me. The ancients who cut these stones and dragged them to this place knew it would be a circle of power, but could they have known it would host a battle for good?

Adam's hand covers mine. "I doubt they saw the future, but perhaps they knew we would need this place to gather and show evil that love will always prevail."

I lean on the stone, and Adam presses a hand on the rough surface on either side of my head. He presses his lips to mine. A low hum rumbles deep in his chest. "Will I ever feel unruffled by kissing you?"

"I certainly hope not." I let my hands rest on his waist. "If I were the only one on fire every time we touch, it would be a sad day."

With only the Windsor coven left at the circle, I lean forward and kiss him. His tongue slides against mine, and I wish there were privacy and a hot bath handy.

Grinding the hard ridge of his shaft against me, he growls. "Your thoughts will drive me insane, Beth."

Breathing hard, I slip under his arm and put some distance between us before I'm tempted to hike up my skirt and let him take me against the stones of the sacred circle. "Were you looking for me for some other reason than mutual frustration?"

He shakes his head, and with one hand still on the stone, takes several long breaths. Finally turning to face me with his desire under control, he smiles. "Kaden has woken. He's sitting up and holding conversation."

I throw my arms around him. "That's great news."

"He's asked to speak to you and me together." He takes my hand, and we walk together to Kaden's tent.

The weather is warmer, and the rain has finally stopped, though the clouds linger. The tent flap is tied back to allow fresh air inside. I duck inside and sit beside the bed.

Kaden is still too pale, but his eyes are full of life. "Thank you for coming, high priestess."

"I'm happy to see you looking so much better." Relief floods me. He's never made a good impression and has often been frightening. However, his death would have hurt Adam, so I'm pleased he will live.

"You are too kind." He sighs and stares at his hands, lying against the brown blanket covering him to the chest. "I don't deserve your kindness, nor do I deserve the healing I've been given."

"Adam is our family, and you are his. We helped you for his sake, though we'd not have let you suffer, regardless." I don't mention that if not for Adam's love, he'd likely have been killed by Ariana.

He shifts on the cot. When his eyes meet mine, they are full of remorse. "I loved my sister, and when this began, I didn't know how ruined she was. By the time I did know, I didn't see a way to leave her. I'd used up any love my brother might have had for me."

Adam is silent but, in my mind, I hear his sorrow.

"It would seem that was never the case. He saved you when he might have left you to Ariana's whims." There's no point being cagey.

His eyes shift to Adam standing near the exit. Gratitude and so much more shine in Kaden's eyes. "I'm grateful, and I know everyone is waiting for me to be healthy enough to travel. I overheard two witches talking early this morning." He fiddles with a frayed bit of blanket.

"You don't wish to return to Windsor with us? You are not a hostage, Kaden. You may go where you please." We aren't jailers, and the idea worries me.

"It's not that. You are all too kind." His hesitation is accompanied by shifting his eyes from his brother, to the blanket, and back to me. "I'm not fit to live with witches in the light." He holds up a hand so Adam doesn't dispute the fact.

I send Adam a silent word asking for his patience and trust. "Go on."

"The last eight years of my life have been a dark fall from grace. While I see the path was wrong and dangerous, I feel that darkness pushing at me from the inside. I should not be allowed to live with those in the light at this time." He hangs his head.

Everything arrogant and proud that Kaden was when he first came to Windsor is gone. He's contrite and remorseful. He's honest, which is maybe more of a surprise.

254

"What do you want to do?" I lay my hand on his arm and let calm flow through me.

His shoulders straighten, but his expression relaxes. "I don't know if they will take me, but perhaps the Order can help me find the path of light again."

The Sacred Order of high witches have a long memory. They may not wish to take on such a burden after he helped Ariana escape years ago. They may deny him entry or demand he be bound.

"I don't know what they will say, but I will write to them if that is what you wish. It's possible they will ease your path, for I think you made choices during the battle that show you have chosen light."

Adam pulls a second stool over to the bed and sits. He grasps his brother's arm. "They might bind your magic."

Kaden's lips tighten, but he lets out a long breath and meets Adam's gaze. "Yes. They might, and that may be for the best. Since I don't trust myself, brother, I have to put my faith in others. I'm sorry."

Torn between his love for Kaden and what is right, Adam's mind is at war.

"I will send a message today. It will be a while before we hear back." It's time to be high priestess. Standing, I fold my arms over my chest. "Your brother and I are to be married. You will come with us back to Windsor." I hold up a hand to stop Kaden's denial. "I will have William keep your magic held. It's not a binding, but it will stop the use of magic should your darker side push forth. You will attend our wedding if you wish. Then if the Order will have you, we will see you to Glasgow."

"Thank you, high priestess," Kaden says softly and reverently.

I'm about to leave, but there's more to say. "You know,

Kaden, we all of us have darkness within. No one lives perfectly in the light. Without the dark, there would be no light, or at least the contrast would be foreign to us. Try not to dwell on the evil. Focus on good. We are to be family."

His lips tip in a brief smile. "You and Adam will be happy. I'm sure of it, high priestess."

"Thank you. You and I will be brother and sister. You might call me Sara Beth." The mood needs lightening.

Adam's heart lifts, which does wonders for mine.

"Sara Beth," Kaden says. "Thank you."

I step into the damp grass and a shard of sunlight pushes through the clouds. It's the first in days.

Minerva meets me a few yards from the tent. "He should be well enough to travel tomorrow, if you're ready to go home."

"More than ready." I give her a quick hug. "I'll tell everyone to start packing. We'll leave at first light."

No sight has ever been as glorious as the city of Windsor with the castle and Eton still there to greet us two days later.

A long week later, we're dancing at my wedding.

Holding me close, Adam asks, "No complaints from your mother today?"

When I woke this morning, I wondered if Mother would protest in some way, but she's been quiet. I shake my head. "Not a word or a grumble. No laughter in your head, I assume."

Squeezing me tight, he whispers, "I'll admit June laughed this morning in the common room, and I had a moment of panic until I rushed out and saw that she and Trina were gossiping."

I note the tightness around his eyes. "Are you worried about our trip?"

"I'll save that worry for tomorrow. Tonight, I want to celebrate the miracle of Sara Beth Ware becoming my wife."

Joy floods my heart. "When Prudence said the words to bind us, I felt I heard them many times, Adam. This is not the first time we've pledged our hearts and souls to one another."

"Nor will it be the last." He kisses my cheek.

"You can do better than that!" Jonah calls over the music and merrymaking.

My cheeks heat.

Pulling me tight, Adam kisses me hard on the lips for longer than is normal in company.

The guests cheer and clap.

Heart pounding a beat that tells me I wish they would all leave and let us go to our bed for the night, I push him back with a light slap meant for show. Though, I'll admit, in a fine black suit and blue waistcoat made for the wedding, my husband would turn any lady's head.

He grins, reading my thoughts. "You are far more a sight than me, my love."

I skim my hand over the lavender lace that covers the bodice of my gown. Prudence gifted me the clothes, bringing us both to tears when she told me I was like her own daughter, and she wished me joy.

"I thought the great mother and I would cry ourselves a small pond before we restored enough order to try the dress on." I laugh, rather than let the emotions overtake me again.

The music turns to a reel, and Adam guides us to where Sylvia, Henry, and Minerva are enjoying wine. They procure two more glasses and pour for Adam and me.

My stomach twists at the first sip. Pushing the wine aside, I feel magic growing inside me.

Adam studies me.

Before he can ask, Henry says, "You'll leave for Scotland tomorrow?"

Adam's smile is forced. "We're taking Kaden to Glasgow, and then I'm going to show Sara Beth Inverness, where I was born."

"How long do you think you'll be gone?" Minerva studies my face and then looks at my hand covering my stomach.

"Just a few months." I give her a wink and hope she'll keep my secret at least until I can tell Adam he's going to be a father.

"Best to be home before it gets cold." Minerva smiles.

Sylvia nudges my shoulder. "No one would blame the two of you if you sneaked up the steps and away for the night. It's nearly two, Prudence has gone to bed, and the neighbors are starting to make their way home."

"Do you think so?" Excitement builds in Adam, as if it were the first time we'd be making love.

Laughing, Sylvia says, "Go!"

The dancing is in full stomp when we make our way upstairs and into my room. Adam's things now share the space. It's strange to find a man's boot left out, but I like having him part of my life. It feels right.

As soon as the door closes, Adam creates a privacy spell to keep any noise from inside the room silenced to the rest of the house. "What happened when you drank the wine?"

"Will you untie this dress?" I'm teasing, but I can't help myself.

His heat warms me from behind as he stands closer than necessary to untie the dress stays, and then the light corset beneath. Soon I'm in nothing but my chemise, stockings and shoes.

Adam wraps his arms around me from behind. His hand

splays over my abdomen and the witch growing inside whirls as if she knows her father is there.

With a gasp, he backs away.

Unable to read if his surprise is full of joy or worry, I turn. Perhaps it's both.

Once I'm facing him, he drops to his knees, and cradles my stomach. "Is it a girl?"

"I think so." I run my fingers through his hair. "How did you know?"

"She feels like a girl," he says.

"She does. Please tell me you're happy, Adam." My heart is pounding as if I ran a few miles.

Eyes glistening, he looks up at me. "This is the happiest day of my life. To have shared our marriage with our family would have been enough. This..." He caresses where our baby grows. "This is beyond any joy I thought possible." He presses a kiss to the baby.

"I'm relieved. I didn't know how you'd react to a child after all we've been through with your sister." It feels as if a load has been taken from my shoulders.

"Nothing evil could come from you, Beth. Besides, we'll be careful in making certain none of our children ever become targets."

"What took your sister will need decades to heal, maybe more. We may be long dead before the demon world is strong enough to make another attempt at conquering this land." I drop to the floor with him. "But we'll tell the tales so that ours, and those who come after, will remember and be ready."

He nods. "More than just a cryptic children's story, mind you. We won't want it to be thought of as fable rather than history."

"Time will decide how the tale is interpreted." I sigh at his stern expression. "We'll do our best to make the warning strong for generations to come."

Brushing his fingers through my hair sends pins tinkling to the floor. "Let me take you to bed now. Unless you're too tired."

Still on the floor, I straddle his lap. The move pushes my chemise to my hips. "I hope to never be too tired for passion, husband."

He grinds up, and his hard shaft rubs between my thighs.

On a moan, I reach down and tug the fall of his trousers. Then I settle myself on his thick, long shaft with one plunge.

I scream with pleasure, drowning out his moan.

Gripping my hips, he moves below me, thrusting deep.

Pleasure rolls over me each time he fills me. I rise on my knees.

Adam thrusts harder and faster. He slides his thumb against my sensitive pearl.

I throw my head back as ecstasy crashes over me. My body shakes.

Coming with a long, low groan, Adam pulls me down in a warm embrace. "Beth, you're amazing." He's breathing hard while he presses kisses to my shoulder and neck. "Let me take you to bed for the rest of our wedding night."

He thickens again inside me but retreats as he pulls us both to our feet. He picks me up, cradles me, and carries me to the bed.

"That sounds like an excellent idea."

Snuggled under the covers, he holds me and kisses my forehead. "I love you, Beth."

The words, the kiss, his arms, this is all I'll ever need. "I love you too, Adam."

Thank you for reading Pure Magic. I hope you loved Sara Beth and Adam's story as much as I enjoyed writing it. I'm thrilled to bring you my brand of history mixed with fantasy and romance.

If you missed any of the Witches of Windsor books, you can find them all on my website: http://asfenichel.com/books/witches-of-windsor/

Check out **Dragon of My Dreams** if you want something fantastic and modern.

DIEGO

Being a dragon in a town filled with monsters isn't so bad. A bunch of scales and wings isn't the worst affliction to hit this town's residents. However, I don't like being alone or having people run away when they see me. And with more humans moving to town, that happens more and more. Most of the time, I keep to myself or with a select group of good friends who are also monsters. I sell my jewelry and rent space in my art gallery. It's a dreary but acceptable way to live.

The moment Scarlett walks into my jewelry shop, she changes everything. Becomes my everything. I can tell that she's hiding something, and I'm almost certain someone in her past hurt her. As a man and a dragon, that's not something I can live with. Now that she's entered my dragon's lair, I'll do anything to protect her.

SCARLETT

I stumbled upon Screamer Woods by accident. The unique residents make it the perfect place to hide out from my ex. He may find me anyway—he has before—but this place is so far off the beaten path, it may take a while. In the meantime, I can sell some artwork and refill my coffers before I have to run again.

Seeing a vampire or a fairy doesn't scare me. I know what a *real* monster is and does. Meeting Diego is an unexpected bonus. Too bad I'll have to bolt soon. I could get used to the way Diego looks at me. The way he makes me feel. If only the monster in my past would stay away and let me live happily ever after with the dragon of my dreams.

ALSO BY A.S. FENICHEL

HISTORICAL PARANORMAL ROMANCE

Witches of Windsor Series

Magic Touch

Magic Word

Pure Magic

The Demon Hunters Series

Ascension

Deception

Betrayal

Defiance

Vengeance

HISTORICAL ROMANCE

The Wallflowers of West Lane Series

The Earl Not Taken

Misleading A Duke

Capturing the Earl

Not Even For A Duke

The Everton Domestic Society Series

A Lady's Honor

A Lady's Escape

A Lady's Virtue

A Lady's Doubt

A Lady's Past

The Forever Brides Series

Tainted Bride

Foolish Bride

Desperate Bride

Single Title Books

Wishing Game

Christmas Bliss

Christmas Chase

CONTEMPORARY PARANORMAL EROTIC ROMANCE

The Psychic Mates Series

Kane's Bounty

Joshua's Mistake

Training Rain

The End of Days Series

Mayan Afterglow

Mayan Craving

Mayan Inferno

End of Days Trilogy

CONTEMPORARY EROTIC ROMANCE

Single Title Books

Alaskan Exposure

Revving Up the Holidays

SHORT CONTEMPORARY ROMANCE

WRITING AS ANDIE FENICHEL

Dad Bod Handyman (Lane Family)

Carnival Lane (Lane Family)

Lane to Fame (Lane Family)

Changing Lanes (Lane Family)

Heavy Petting (Lane Family)

Summer Lane (Lane Family)

Hero's Lane (Lane Family)

Icing It (Lane Family)

Mountain Lane (Lane Family)

Christmas Lane (Lane Family)

Texas Lane (Lane Family)

Dragon of My Dreams

Turnabout is Fairy Play

Visit Andie's website for the most up to date list.

www.andiefenichel.com

Visit A.S. Fenichel's website for a complete and up-to-date list of her books.

www.asfenichel.com

ABOUT THE AUTHOR

 A.S. Fenichel (Andie Fenichel) gave up a successful IT career in New York City to follow her husband to Texas and pursue her lifelong dream of being a professional writer. She's never looked back.

Andie adores writing stories filled with love, passion, desire, magic and maybe a little mayhem tossed in for good measure. Books have always been her perfect escape and she still relishes diving into one and staying up all night to finish a good story.

Originally from New York, she grew up in New Jersey, and now lives in Missouri with her real-life hero, her wonderful husband. When not reading or writing she enjoys cooking, travel, history, and puttering in her garden. On the side, she is a master cat wrangler and her fur babies keep her very busy.

Connect with A.S. Fenichel
www.asfenichel.com

Subscribe to A.S. Fenichel's newsletter:
www.asfenichel.com/newsletter